BEYOND PARADISE

BARBARA NOLAN

Ann
great meeting you
B. Nolan

SOUL MATE PUBLISHING
New York

BEYOND PARADISE

BARBARA NOLAN

Cover Design by Syneca Featherstone

This book is a work of fiction. The names, characters, places, and incidents are the products of the author's imagination or are used fictitiously. Any resemblance to actual events, business establishments, locales, or persons, living or dead, is entirely coincidental.

Published in the United States of America by

Soul Mate Publishing

P.O. Box 24

Macedon, New York, 14502

ISBN: 978-1-68291-813-5

ebook ISBN: 978-1-68291-790-9

www.SoulMatePublishing.com

To my mom

who always said hard work

makes all things possible.

Acknowledgments

I'd like to thank Cheryl Yeko for her interest in my work and to Syneca Featherstone for my fabulous cover and all the staff at Soul Mate Publishing. A special thanks to Bonnie Hearn Hill who believed in my work all those years ago and gave me the confidence to move forward with my dream. Plus the editors along the way who have enriched my education of the writing process, and the wonderful critiques I have received on TNBW site. I would also like to thank my family for their patience and constant support.

Chapter 1

Cheryl Benson loved drunks. They made her job so easy. Approach the target, capture their attention, and make the grab. But *grab* was such a harsh word. To her, it came second nature, like brushing her teeth or combing her hair. A choreographed routine she performed nightly at the Oasis, a dive bar wedged between decaying, abandoned warehouses and tumbledown tenements at the end of a Brooklyn pier.

At twenty-three, her level of expertise assured the mark never realized their valuables were missing. The thrill of the theft was her addiction, but lately, she'd been restless. The conscience she thought deserted her returned at the most unexpected times.

She wound her way through the maze of tables that choked the smoke-filled room. Even the state of New York didn't care if these people puffed their brains out.

"Here you go, gentlemen." Cheryl laid their change down and leaned in to make sure her blond hair teased her best assets straining against her flimsy tank top.

Her gaze lingered on each of the three eager faces, but she'd already selected her target.

"Hey, she called us gentlemen," the guy with the biggest beer gut hollered over the din of rowdy customers and hard rock music. "She sure don't know us very good." That made them all guffaw and slap each other on the back.

"It was my pleasure to serve you tonight." She lingered at the side of the quietest one of the group.

"I'll give you something to service." Big Mouth leered, making a repulsive hand gesture.

She bent just enough to make the strip of material she called a skirt rise to an almost indecent height. “Maybe next time, handsome.”

Be attentive to the loudest one in the group while fleecing the other two. Guys like them were easy, although the usual adrenaline rush left her nauseous. She walked toward Nicky, slumped at his usual perch at the far end of the bar. His only concern was whether or not the results would pay off the long list of bookies he held at bay, but he wasn’t to blame. Her life of crime began way before Nicky.

“How’d we do?” Nicky asked.

He used the word *we* without hesitation, yet she assumed all the risks. Such a shame, because Nicky had been fast, sharp and quite charismatic when he’d swept her off the streets four years ago.

Freedom.

She forfeited that for a warm room, regular meals, and the option to keep her clothes on. She’d readily given up stripping in some of Brooklyn’s seediest clubs to run cons with him, but what started off as a way to survive morphed into a bad habit she desperately wanted to break.

She unzipped the secret pocket at the waist of her pleather skirt and handed the money over to him, then tugged on her micro mini.

“*We* did good.” She shifted to relieve the pressure of the five-inch stilettos holding her feet prisoner.

“Not as much as usual.” He fanned through the money, then tapped her cheek with the wad of bills. “Especially after Sal gets his cut.”

She always kicked back some for herself first, which she hid in a tampon box under the bathroom sink of their apartment over the bar. Let Nicky worry about Sal, the chain-smoking owner of the Oasis. He sounded three breaths away from having a heart attack anyway.

"Slow night." She took a half step back so the tension in her body wouldn't give away the backpack she'd packed earlier and stashed in the rear of their closet. Tonight, she'd make her escape out of the life, and take her brother, Dylan with her. Getting him off the Brooklyn streets became her main focus, because the little boy who once adored her grew and found new heroes on the street who offered swag and power.

"Hey, I know this place is a few steps down from what we're used to, but I'm working on a big score." He caged her in as his hand grazed her cheek.

A few steps down? A year ago they'd rented suites in uptown hotels, ordered room service, and lounged at VIP tables in the hottest clubs. But it was more than that. Her heart just wasn't in it anymore.

"I don't want much, Nicky."

"What's with you?" Nicky leaned in to kiss her, and she pulled away. "Are you still thinking about that guy last night?"

"He had his kids' pictures in his wallet." Her stomach clenched with the latest waves of regret. "Maybe he needed the money for them."

"He would've drank it all away." Nicky shrugged off her concern. "We did him a favor. Instead of stumbling home drunk off his ass, he probably went home early."

She'd once believed Nicky's every word. His smoldering good looks, schemes, and promises had captivated her. Made her feel like she mattered. Now, he was just another raggedy-jeaned hood who sniffed and twitched from too much coke.

"I suppose."

But tonight, her dream of a life without Nicky could come true. A life where she didn't go to bed at three in the morning and wake up after noon. A nine-to-five life. A straight life. A life with more daylight.

"Fuck." Nicky stared over her shoulder.

She followed his gaze to a guy who could've rocked a *GQ* cover. She tried unsuccessfully not to gawk, snared by six-plus feet of yummy male wrapped in a black designer button-down shirt and slacks that could probably pay the rent on her room upstairs. Long, lean muscles rolled with every deliberate step. Dark hair cut to perfection and even darker eyes squinted against the smoke-filled room.

"Hey, Jonny," Nicky said. "Can I get you a drink?" He snapped his fingers for the bartender, but Jonny remained serious, a grim twist to his lips.

She shivered anticipating the danger that swirled around him. His quick once-over cut through her and her muscles tensed with all kinds of red flags.

"You know why I'm here." His voice sounded bored, but its rough rumble sent a jolt straight to her toes.

"Doesn't mean we can't have a drink first." Nicky slapped the bar top and shouted for the bartender.

"Maybe you'd rather do this in private." Jonny's gaze shifted to her again.

His eyes were black. Deep, haunting, and soulful, lingering just long enough to make her wonder what he was thinking.

"I got no secrets from her," Nicky said.

"Fine." Jonny shrugged. "You owe ten grand. I want it. Tonight."

"Tonight?" Nicky's leg twitched as he gulped at the cheap whiskey the bartender placed in front of him.

Nicky had gambling debts, but owing a guy who could star in *The Godfather, Next Generation?* Not smart.

"You have it or not?" Jonny's eyes narrowed, but his tone remained even. His smooth, low rasp intimidated more than if he'd yelled the question.

"I got five hundred," Nicky offered.

Jonny pursed his lips. She sensed he didn't like his job either.

She'd given Nicky way more than five hundred dollars this week. Were the drugs screwing with his brain and telling him he could outsmart this guy?

"This isn't gonna end well." Jonny's cool, calm voice raised the little hairs on the back of her neck, and old loyalties to Nicky nagged at her. True, she wanted to get far away from him and his drama, but she didn't want him floating face down in the East River.

"He can give you more than that." Her voice surprised her. Like her thoughts tumbled out of her mouth without her permission.

"Shut the fuck up." Nicky squeezed her arm, then yanked her to his side.

Jonny stepped into their space and glared at Nicky until he released his grip. Jonny's commanding presence gave him an air of authority. This wasn't some tough guy act, this was real, raw and . . . *Sexy as hell.*

"Seems like she's got more sense than you." Jonny jerked his chin in her direction.

"I don't know about sense." Nicky switched gears. "But she does have some *very* interesting talents." The amount of sleaze in his voice made her regret her moment of sympathy.

She shook her head in disgust. Then Jonny did the same thing.

"The money. Either you have it, or you don't."

"All right." Nicky dug into his jeans pocket and pulled out a wad of cash. "Here's three grand."

Jonny's gaze skimmed over them. A quick twitch of his lips, like he had some great idea, then he snatched the banded money from Nicky's hand and waved it in front of his face. "Your girlfriend bought you another week." He pocketed the money.

Nicky huffed out a long-held breath. "Now we should have that drink of the good stuff."

When Nicky walked around the bar to retrieve a bottle of bourbon, Jonny turned those pitch-black eyes on her. Her pulse pounded under his scrutiny as she tugged at her too-short skirt, then wrapped her arms around her bare midriff.

"I have a feeling your boyfriend isn't always so nice." His voice lost its edge and became as smooth as honeyed whiskey.

He leaned in close enough for her to get a whiff of his cologne, an exotic mix that sent a bolt of heat to her spine. She held on to the bar to steady herself. His hard eyes softened, as he scribbled a number on the back of a business card, then handed it to her.

Jonny Vallone, Owner. Paradise Lounge.

"You ever need anything, come see me." Jonny leaned in and murmured against her ear. "'Cause you don't belong here."

She opened her mouth to respond, but Nicky returned with the bourbon, poured two glasses, and slid one toward Jonny.

Jonny stepped back and pinned Nicky with a stony glare. "Next week, the usual drop-off." He glanced around the seedy room. "Don't make me come down to this shithole again."

When he spun back to her, he winked so quickly she almost missed it. Then without another word, he wove his way through the crowd, and she sighed with a strange sense of loss.

"That fuckin' guy, coming in here talking to me like that." Nicky shot one bourbon, then the other. "Who the fuck does he think he is?"

She twirled the card in her fingers. "Apparently, the owner of the Paradise Lounge."

"He must've pissed somebody off if he's down here making collections." Nicky grabbed her wrist and ripped the card from her hand. "He gave you this?"

"Yeah."

He read it and smirked. "If you plan on doin' him, make sure he takes it off my tab, 'cause thanks to you I'm out three grand."

She snatched back the card and rolled her eyes at Nicky's crude remark but couldn't suppress the fantasy as her mind replaced Nicky with Jonny, her knight in black Brioni.

The loud rock music, clinking glasses, and rough laughter would fade away. Jonny would hold her close, not able to wait, both of them breathless. He'd nuzzle her neck, and she'd feel the scratch of his stubbled jaw. Hot, sweet and slow. His hands roaming, then palming her ass and lifting her until she could feel his . . .

"You listening to me?" Nicky shouted.

Her fantasy zapped like a cartoon cloud. What was wrong with her? The last thing she needed was another bad boy in her life.

"Yes." She switched gears as Nicky jostled her away from the bar and into the back hallway.

"I'm working on a new deal that's gonna put us over the top."

"Great."

At one in the morning with the anticipation of freedom on her mind, having to listen to another one of Nicky's get-rich-quick plans made her ears bleed.

"This time I got us a sure thing."

"Really?" Even she heard the sarcastic edge in her voice.

"C'mon baby, don't be like that." Nicky slid his hands down her back. "I can still picture you on those expensive European sheets while I fuck . . ."

"It's Egyptian cotton sheets."

"European, Egyptian, who the hell cares. The point is, it's a sure thing."

Another sure thing? Like his producer friend in L.A. who hustled them to a seedy garage in Burbank for porn flicks.

When she refused to join in, Nicky ranted and screamed insults at her for about ten seconds before he slapped her hard enough to leave a welt under her left eye.

She should've left him then but going back to her mother and her latest druggie boyfriend wasn't safe either, and in some crazy way, she feared being alone. When they returned to Brooklyn, Nicky became more erratic. The drugs and the liquor were the symptoms, but failed dreams and lost hope was the disease.

She wasn't waiting until he lashed out again, and with her take from tonight and the other money she'd socked away, she had enough for two one-way tickets for her and her brother far from New York.

"All right, let's hear it." She controlled her breathing and feigned interest in Nicky's next scheme.

"Hey, Nicky." One of his thug friends waved him over to the bar.

"Stay here." He pointed his finger at her face. "I'll be right back."

Perfect. Now she could call her brother. She moved further down the hallway where it was quieter.

"Hey," Dylan answered on the third ring.

"You all set for tonight?"

"Yeah, can't wait to get out of this shit city," Dylan shouted over people arguing in the background on his end, and her maternal alarm kicked up. "Why, what's wrong?"

"Nothing."

Not likely where Dylan was concerned. Driving cars that didn't belong to him, missed meetings with his parole officer, scoring drugs for his stripper girlfriend from whacked-out dealers. The list went on and on, but tonight she didn't have time to decode his latest drama. Because if everything went as planned, maybe she could save both of them.

She raised her voice to ensure he could hear her. "Just make sure you're at the corner of 86th and 4th."

"Yeah, I got it."

"All right. I'll see you in an hour. Don't be late. We have to leave tonight."

Silence and then the phone disconnected. She prayed that for once Dylan would act responsibly and do as she instructed because there was too much at stake to screw up.

She swiped her phone, sucked in a deep breath, turned and stared into Nicky's narrowed, accusing eyes.

Chapter 2

Jonny brushed the invisible dirt off his shirt as he stood outside the Oasis. Just being inside the place made him want to take a shower, then run to his dry cleaner.

He sucked in a deep breath hoping for some fresh air, but the smell of rotten fish and stagnant water surrounded him. A stench that clung to everything. Including the decaying tenement two blocks away that he'd spent most of his twenty-nine years trying to forget. One whiff and it all flooded in, but he didn't need any reminders. His memory was crystal clear.

Running wild in the streets, doing anything to make a buck. It'd been rough, but he'd worked his way up. Frank Barnett knew talent when he saw it and made him the frontman for the Paradise Lounge, the man's legitimate money washing machine. Jonny made the Paradise a hit and raked in stacks of legal cash, but Frank still liked to drag him back to his past and keep him in line with side jobs like tonight.

Freedom.

He'd surrendered that years ago in exchange for money and power.

Jonny needed a drink. Not the cheap bourbon out of a dirty glass that Nicky offered. A high-end scotch, or a smooth tequila from his private stock. That would wash away the bad memories. Make him forget nights like this, the Oasis, Frank, Nicky. But not the blonde.

Fuck. He didn't even know her name. He liked to put a name to his fantasies, and he had a strong suspicion she'd be a headliner, at least for the next few days. Silky, straight, platinum blond hair that reached the middle of her back and brushed the swell of her breasts. She wore the slutty clothes like a fashion model. All long legs, curvy hips, and a tiny waist that belonged on a runway, not hanging out with Nicky Falcone in a dump like the Oasis.

He'd expected her to be all over him, trying to seduce him into giving Nicky a pass, but, the way she'd wrapped her arms around herself covering her sexy shape said shy and almost embarrassed. Wash off the heavy makeup, and you had a girl next door not a small-time hustler.

Her gaze followed him, anticipating the worst, on point and ready to bolt. Not that he would've blamed her. Hooking up with Nicky and working at the Oasis were two of her worst life decisions.

Either way, they hadn't exchanged more than four sentences, but a reckless desire to save her overwhelmed him. But pulling out his business card? It didn't make sense. The club cards were for vendors and sales reps, and him handing it to her had nothing to do with business. It had to do with making good on failing another woman in his life. Evening the score and maybe chasing away the guilt. When she flashed those pleading green eyes at him, he felt the connection. He hadn't said a word, but she knew. Yeah, she felt it, too.

The wad of cash weighed heavy in his pocket and reminded him of bigger problems than the fate of a hot blonde, like the phone call he had to make. Frank in a good mood unnerved him, but not getting all his money from a lowlife like Nicky would make Frank unbearable.

He swiped his contact list and prepared for the worst.

"Yeah," Frank answered before the first ring ended.

"I got three grand." Frank liked bad news fast.

"Should've been ten."

"Better than five hundred."

"Five hundred?" Frank stretched out the two words.

"Yeah, that's what he first offered."

"You do anything about it?"

"Figured he's more useful in one piece."

Some payment was better than none, and a thief with mangled fingers or broken arms couldn't work. "Stupid fucker even tried to pawn off his girlfriend."

Silence. Never a good sign.

"Girlfriend, huh?" Frank's voice was tight. "You taking the rest of my money out in trade?"

Jonny frowned. "Fuck no."

But that jacked up the first fantasy. *Rescuing her and getting her away from Nicky, and out of that dump. It would get crazy fast. Hot, wet kisses. Sweet and dirty up against a wall, a door, or any flat surface where he could wrap those incredible legs around his hips, and sink into her so deep that . . .*

"Did you hear what I said?" Frank shouted into the phone, shattering the best part of his night.

"Yeah . . . No. What?"

"I said," Frank slowed his voice as if talking to a child, "I'll be by later."

Code for he'd be bringing a duffle bag of money that Jonny would finesse through the club's account. Fuckin' wonderful. Bad enough Frank degraded him again into collecting tonight, but now he'd have to entertain him, too.

On impulse, he spun around and pushed through the splintered wooden door of the Oasis again. He fixed on the spot at the end of the bar where he'd seen her last, then scanned the room. No sign of her or Nicky. He didn't want to think about where they were or what they were doing, so he left.

He hoped the walk back to the Paradise would straighten him out. Maybe it would smooth out his nerves, and he could finish his fantasy about a woman he planned on investigating until he knew all her secrets.

Chapter 3

"Who were you talking to?" Nicky pinned Cheryl with a hard, cold glare then caged her in until her back hit the wall.

"Dylan."

Maybe he hadn't heard all of the conversation.

"And where the fuck are you going?"

"Nowhere." Deny, deny, deny. Maybe if she said it long and loud, he'd believe her.

"Don't lie to me. I heard you."

"Let's go upstairs and talk." She'd lure him toward the back stairs, placate him, then she'd sneak away after he passed out.

"No!" He jerked away from her and paced the small, cramped hallway. "You're not leaving me." He stopped dead in front of her and pounded his fist against the wall inches from her head. "Cause I taught you everything I know."

She flinched but refused to cower. "Everything about being a petty thief."

"I didn't hear you complaining when you were sucking down champagne in those uptown clubs." Scowling, he loomed over her. "Now all of a sudden you're some kinda goddamn princess."

The whiskey on his breath made her dizzy, and the coke in his system made her wary. She slipped around him, gambling that putting some distance between them would settle him down. At the end of the hallway, the crowd shifted and she saw him. Jonny Vallone. Standing by the entrance, neck craned, eyes searching. A frantic impulse urged her toward him. Then Nicky swooped up from behind, hustled her back down the hall and out the side door into the alley.

The steamy night air wrapped around her bare legs, and her spike heels caught on the uneven cobblestones as Nicky half dragged, half lifted her around the broken beer bottles, mangled shopping carts, and overflowing dumpsters. Midway down the narrow passage, he stopped and caged her in against the crumbling brick wall. She tasted the sweet stink of discarded liquor and day-old garbage in the back of her throat, while a neon sign cast an eerie greenish shadow across Nicky's face.

"What kind fuckin' game are you playing?"

"What do you mean?" She forced her voice into coy innocence.

"You're never gonna leave me." He held her jaw then raised his massive forearm and wedged it against her throat.

Her hands grappled with his arm. "All right, stop."

He eased up the pressure, and she forced down the bile in the back of her throat as a primal warning shot through her nerve endings. She'd come so close to getting away. She couldn't wait another minute, she had to act now.

"I knew you'd come around." His calloused fingers scratched the raw skin of her neck.

"Sure, baby." She ran her hands up his chest, parted her lips, and when he moved in to kiss her she pushed him hard.

"Bitch!" He staggered, and she darted around him.

"It's over Nicky!" Her words bounced off the bricks of the alley walls.

"We're not over until I say we're over." He lunged at her, and she sidestepped away from him, then reached into her bra and pulled out the knife he'd given her long ago for protection. She hit the tiny button on the side, and a long, menacing blade appeared.

"What the fuck are you doin' now?" Nicky mocked.

She glanced over her shoulder. The side door was so close. Her brain scrambled to stay calm but the adrenaline surging through her hot-wired her nerves.

"Give me that blade." He swayed, and she used the opportunity to run.

The heavy thud of his boots against the concrete closed in behind her, and then his thick hand clamped onto her shoulder. She jerked to a stop, every muscle taut. Her gaze darting right and left, seeking an escape route.

"Where you goin', huh?" He spun her around, fisted her tank top and raised his other hand. A wave of dizziness rocked her. Drunk and high, yet he still overpowered her.

She jerked away from him, and the silvery metal of the knife flashed, as she sliced it through the air between them. The heavy thump of her heart drowned out all sound.

He dove for her and stumbled. His stoned eyes flickered. He swayed and then pitched forward. She squeezed the knife tighter, and the pressure of his body drove the blade deep. Nicky clutched at his gut, and she jerked away still gripping the knife. Seconds later, a gurgling erupted from the back of his throat and their eyes locked, his frozen in disbelief. He doubled over and collapsed. He twitched a few times, as a steady stream of blood seeped over the bricks and under some busted crates.

She concentrated on her breathing as it sawed in and out of her lungs. Her stomach churned and she wrapped her arms around herself, desperate to force down the sickening nausea. She kneeled beside him, slowly stretching out her arm until her fingers pressed against his neck. Nothing. She pushed harder and felt a pulse. Weak but there.

Relief flowed through her and she struggled to focus. Call 9-1-1? Be arrested for stabbing her coked-up boyfriend outside a dive bar? Depend on a system that failed her and her brother for years?

Freedom.

She'd come so close.

The slap of leather-soled shoes against the uneven stones broke the silence. She searched the shadows, but silence surrounded her again.

She backed away from the pooling blood, turned and ran toward the street. Incredibly fast considering the stupid stilettos she balanced on rubber legs. Lungs burning, feet aching she stopped to catch her breath and guilt consumed her.

She couldn't just leave Nicky there bleeding out. Sure, he turned out to be an asshole in the end, but they'd had some good times in the beginning. Going to the beach and eating hot dogs at Coney Island. Plus, in the confusion she realized she dropped the knife. The bloody knife with her finger prints. She'd retrieve the knife, call 9-1-1 and stay with him until she heard the sirens. Guilt was one thing, but she didn't plan on sticking around for the questions. And there were bound to be a shit ton of questions.

Her feet protested the whole way down the alley. Shadows and distorted shapes from the ancient security lights played tricks with Nicky's body making it seem like someone was crouching next to him. She moved closer and froze. A man with his back to her hunched over Nicky. He must've come from the club's side door. He felt for a pulse, paused, then picked up the bloody knife. The blade flashed as he sliced the knife across Nicky's neck.

She flinched and shoved her fist in her mouth to choke back the scream. A thin line of blood seeped from Nicky's neck and she knew he was dead. In less than five minutes, she'd stabbed someone and then witnessed a murder. Totally fucked up, even for her screwed-up life.

A manic desire to laugh bubbled up inside her. The ground tilted, and she grabbed onto a stack of discarded wooden crates. The top one teetered and she reached out to steady it a second too late. It crashed to the cobblestones and echoed against the narrow passage. She slammed her back against the brick wall using the remaining crates for cover. Holding her breath and making herself small and invisible while squeezing her eyes shut. If she couldn't see him, he couldn't see her, right? Yeah, that theory stopped working in kindergarten.

Slowly, she opened her eyes and peered through the broken slats. Her theory must've worked because the guy ignored the falling crate and was now ransacking Nicky's pockets and cursing. Then he stood, turned toward the light and she gasped again.

Frank Barnett. Brooklyn thug, controller of the Bensonhurst streets from 86th to the docks, suspected money launderer, extortionist, and murderer. Great. The famed criminal was much shorter than she imagined.

He whipped out his phone and mumbled into it. Probably arranging the disposal of Nicky's body. She used this distraction to crouch down low and make her escape. With only one way out of the alley he'd have to pass her, and she would be exposed any second. Her brain said run fast and run hard, but her heart couldn't resist one last glance.

Frank stopped and stared at her. There was at least twenty feet between them, but she could feel the darkness of his cold gaze. Predatory and lawless. Daring her, and when his feet shifted in her direction her instincts kicked in.

She ran out of the alley and then weaved her way down another narrow passageway. Staying off the street was easy. The burnt-out buildings and abandoned warehouses created a tangled maze. A labyrinth she'd been familiar with since childhood. When her feet were numb, and her breathing seared her lungs, she stopped, braced her hands on her knees and sucked in sweet oxygen until she could breathe without gasping. She peeked over her shoulder, relieved to see no one except the homeless who took up camp around the vacant buildings.

For a brief second she sent up a prayer of thanks, but relief quickly evaporated as she reviewed the highlights of her night.

She'd witnessed a murder by a key crime figure. A dangerous man who would end her with one phone call. He'd seen her, and although the lighting was shitty his criminal super powers probably gave him night vision. And scariest of all, he hadn't chased after her. Why would he? With his army of goons, finding her would be easier than slicing Nicky's throat.

Oh yeah, she was fucked.

Chapter 4

Luckily, Cheryl had her phone and enough money to jump into the first cab she saw and escape ten blocks to Brooklyn Heights. She'd called Dylan, and when he hadn't picked up, she left a message. By now he must've figured she wasn't showing up. Their plan would have to wait until she could get back to the apartment and retrieve the cash she'd stashed, but right now going back to the scene of the crime and facing Frank Barnett made her knees weak.

Nicky's lifeless body flashed through her brain. She'd never wanted it to end this way. Where had the time gone? Where had her life gone?

"Whatever happens I need to make some big changes," she said into the muggy night air. "Just not tonight."

She stared at the neon Paradise Lounge sign, then at Jonny's card, as a light mist clung to her skin. Sad that her only refuge was a guy she didn't really know, but everything about him screamed money and power. All she needed was a place to stay until she could retrieve her money. She'd tried to call him, but his phone went straight to voicemail. He'd said to come see him if she needed anything, although he probably wasn't expecting her outside his club two hours later.

The club beckoned to her. A safe haven, an oasis. She sucked in more damp humidity, smoothed her hand over her clothes, threw back her shoulders and prepared for her biggest con ever. Convincing a guy she hardly knew to help her.

Crossing the street, she ignored the ridiculous line winding around the club and went straight to the entrance.

The muscle-bound doorman stepped forward and blocked her way. She beamed at him with more confidence than she felt as his gaze ran over her micro mini and tight tank top. Men, so predictable.

"I know the owner, Jonny Vallone." His frown told her he'd heard that line a million times. "It's important I find him." She flipped out the business card and showed him the hand-written cell number on the back.

He examined the writing, then stepped to the side and spoke into his headset. She shifted her feet as others went in with a wave of a hand. She considered rushing the line, when he turned to her.

He's up in the offices." He gave a quick nod like a facial tic. "Take the elevator in the back to the second floor."

"Thanks." She moved past him, afraid any eye contact would make him change his mind.

It felt good to be out of the dampness, lost and invisible in the throbbing club scene. Protected by the throng of strangers that flowed and meshed around her to form one out-of-control party. House music pounded from the DJ booth as Victoria Secret look-a-likes danced on raised pedestals in skimpy outfits.

On another night, at another time, she would've enjoyed the slight buzz after having one extra drink that made the world seem bright and shiny. Dressed to attract, working the room and scoping out the plethora of designer watches, gold chains, and wallets jutting out of back pockets. She and Nicky would've . . .

Her heart kicked up, and her palms began to sweat. Loud conversation collided with pulsing music, while musky cologne and the sweet scents of perfume surrounded her. She felt like a snowball on a tropical island. Out of place and melting fast.

One level up, she stepped off the elevator and surveyed

the space. To her left was a smaller, more intimate area which appeared to be for VIP clients, and to her right was a hallway. Two doors on one side were marked as restrooms, with two closed, unmarked doors further apart. She stopped by the first door and knocked. When she didn't get an answer, she knocked louder. Still no response, so she tried the doorknob. It turned beneath her hand, so she pushed the door open, stepped inside, and froze.

A guy leaned against a massive desk tucking himself in while a topless redhead got off her knees.

She hadn't expected to interrupt her own personal porn show, and the little squeak she made caused him to stare right at her. Wow. *Jonny Vallone, Owner. Paradise Lounge.* No wonder his phone went straight to voicemail.

"Shit." He jerked to a standing position.

"Who the hell is she?" the redhead shrieked, stood, wiped her mouth with the back of her hand, then retrieved a cheap satin robe off the floor and dragged it around her.

His opened shirt hung off his shoulders, revealing long, lean, muscular arms, and taut abs exactly as she'd envisioned them at the Oasis. Her gaze traveled to that sexy as hell V where his abs met his hips and fine hairs that traveled south to his . . .

"What the fuck?" His voice deep and rough like he'd spent the night—getting a blow job. His eyes, like hard pieces of black coal, bore into her and demanded answers.

So much for Prince Charming coming to her aid, although the sight of his smooth bronze skin as he righted his shirt and pants rendered her speechless. Was the stubble along his jawline intended or the result of too many nights like this one?

Cheryl cleared her throat as heat traveled to her cheeks. All her conning skills vanished and were replaced with ridiculous mental banter.

Sorry for interrupting your blowjob, but I'm the girl from the Oasis. The one with the loser boyfriend, who by the way will never pay his gambling debt 'cause he's dead.

"Do you always barge in without knocking?" he asked.

"Do you always get blowjobs in your office?" she countered.

His lips curved, and she didn't know if he was amused or thinking of ways to kill her. Either way, after stabbing Nicky and then witnessing his murder, she wasn't in a position to judge what he did in his private office. Although, he really should consider locking the door.

"Cheryl?"

She spun around, and her mouth fell open for the second time that night.

"Eddie?"

She couldn't believe it. Eddie Morgan leaning against the doorframe.

"What are you doing here?" they said in unison.

"Jonny and I own this place."

Eddie must've made thousands a night, but his shaggy blond hair, worn, frayed jeans, vintage concert T-shirt, and scuffed engineer boots made him look like he should be straddling a Harley, not owning one of the hottest clubs in Brooklyn. It didn't matter how much time slipped by, he still made her feel safe.

"You know her?" Jonny asked in disbelief.

"Jonny, this is Cheryl." Eddie waved his hand between them.

"Yeah, we've met," Jonny said with the uncivilized attitude of a wolf.

An awkward silence followed until she said to Eddie. "Can we talk somewhere in private?"

~ ~ ~

After riding the elevator to the third floor, Cheryl followed Eddie through a foyer and into the living room of a very spacious apartment.

Cheryl spun around. “This space is great.”

Exposed brick walls, hung with modern tapestries, softened the decor of glass, chrome, and black leather. A built-in, granite-topped bar covered one wall, adorned with crystal tumblers and stocked to overflowing with an assortment of liquors and wines of every variety. A flat-screen TV, worthy of a small theater, dominated the other wall. Manhattan chic in Brooklyn.

Eddie motioned to the couch as he sat in the opposite chair. Growing up, her and Eddie were inseparable, but he didn’t approve of Nicky and their friendship deteriorated to random texts and phone calls.

“Jonny and I worked crazy hours in the beginning, and it made more sense to live over the club. Now, we each have a penthouse on the Upper East Side.” Eddie lit up a cigarette. “We use this if we don’t feel like driving to Manhattan.”

“I had no idea you were involved in this club.”

Finally, her nightmare made sense. Fate brought her here. Not for Jonny’s help, but Eddie’s. She’d confide in him just like the old days. Confess her part and tell her biggest secret about Frank Barnett. Eddie could be trusted, and he’d know what to do.

“Jonny and I have been running it for about six months. The guy who backed us wants to keep a low profile.”

“Jonny seemed a little intense.” Especially when those jet-black eyes ran over her.

“He comes on strong. You just have to get to know him.”

She’d pass on that. She had enough drama in her life. “A club in Brooklyn, a penthouse on the Upper East Side. It sounds like you have it all.”

“A long way from that crappy apartment building where we grew up.” He blew out a long stream of smoke and frowned. "Sometimes, though, I lay in bed at night and know something's gonna fuck it all up."

She plucked the cigarette from his fingers and dragged deep. "This reminds me of sitting on the fire escape in the old days, trying to catch a breeze while you listened to all my problems."

"Why don't you stop stalling and tell me what's going on?" Eddie rose and in two steps moved next to her on the couch, snatched back the cigarette, and crushed it into the ashtray. "Your last text was from LA. Nicky had some movie connections out there?" His tone belied his doubt. "Knowing him, you're lucky it wasn't some skin flick."

"Funny you should say that."

"Please tell me you didn't . . ."

"No." A flush circled her neck as she remembered her brief encounter with porn.

"I'm glad you came to me, but why now?"

No need to tell him she'd really come to see Jonny. Her gaze flitted around the trendy apartment and an uncomfortable guilt crept over her. She couldn't lay this burden on him. He had too much to lose. Dragging him into her mess would be the ultimate act of selfishness, and she refused to be the one to *fuck it all up.*

"It's complicated." Lying to Eddie would be the supreme test of her conning skills. Bad choices tormented her and coming here tonight topped the list.

"Start at the beginning."

She drew in a deep breath. "Nicky and I had a fight. A bad fight." Truth.

"Did he hit you?" Eddie searched her face looking for evidence.

"Just pushed me around, but I'm tired of his schemes and lies." Another truth.

"I told you way back he was no good. Shoving coke up

his nose. Losing big at the track, he owed everybody. It's a miracle he's still alive."

"Yeah, a miracle." Her voice caught on the last word.

"So, you broke up with him?"

Was that the proper term for leaving your dead boyfriend bleeding out in an alley? Even Hallmark hadn't come up with a card for that one.

"Are you all right?" Eddie asked.

"Just a little thing I get sometimes." Her heart thumped in her throat. She fought off what had become an unwelcome reaction whenever Nicky's image popped up. Each breath like sucking air through a straw. "It's nothing." Her mind screamed for control, but her nerves refused to listen. Her insides jolted like an electrical current with a bad switch and no off button.

"Just like that, you're leaving him." His crystal blue eyes demanded the truth.

"Everything you said about him was right." Focus. Concentrate on his voice. Her heart slowed, and her breathing became easier.

Eddie nailed her with a knowing look. "I hope you mean it this time."

"I do."

"You can stay here as long as you want."

"I was thinking about leaving Brooklyn."

"Going to Manhattan?"

"More like Mexico."

"Are you sure you're not in some kind of trouble?"

"Nothing I can't handle."

She refused to entangle him in a murder with a known criminal like Frank Barnett. No one would win, and it would jeopardize everything he'd worked for. She'd stay here tonight. Then tomorrow she'd get her money from the apartment and leave Brooklyn behind.

Chapter 5

Jonny dismissed Bambi, the redhead with the skills of a Hoover, then vented his frustration on the office door as he slammed it behind him.

Cheryl. His blonde fantasy girl had a name. She was the last damn person he'd expected to see again tonight, and that brought on a shit load of other questions. Like why Eddie never mentioned her and what was she doing here? Yeah, he gave her his card, and yeah, he'd said come see him—but two hours later?

A heat flashed through him, and he wrapped his hands around the cool brass railing and concentrated on the action below. He hoped that the bouncers communicating on their headsets, and the bartenders and waitresses who kept the party going, would make him forget how Cheryl's voice jacked up his heartbeat and made him harder than Bambi's blowjob.

Angela appeared at his side. "I've been looking for you all night."

The vision of Cheryl vanished. "We're slammed tonight. I got a lot going on."

Club manager and part-time girlfriend, Angela was all pouty lips, dangerous curves, and constant demands. Although she ignored it when he strayed every once in a while, she kept a running tally in jewelry and designer clothes.

"I'm needed downstairs." She waved a hand at the crowded club. "One of the girls has a costume malfunction, and as usual, I'm the only one who can fix things."

He watched her walk away. Every guy in the place eyeballed her, but for him, the thrill was gone.

His phone buzzed, and he fished it out of his pocket.

"Yeah," Jonny grunted.

"You really ought to improve your phone etiquette," Frank said.

He rolled his eyes.

"I have to tie up a loose end tonight, so I won't be coming by the club."

"Thank fuck," he mumbled into the dead phone. One less headache.

An hour later he found himself in his office unlocking the bottom drawer of his desk. There, under a false bottom, lay his vice, his one guilty pleasure. He carefully removed the cellophane package, laid it on his desk, and inhaled. Good stuff.

Even after all these years, Yodels still returned him to his childhood. Money was non-existent, thanks to his jailbird father but somehow his mother, a Cuban immigrant with limited English, managed to keep the family together and have this special treat for him and his little sister.

He'd just wiped his mouth and threw the napkin in the trash when Eddie sauntered into his office.

"How do you know Cheryl?" he asked before Eddie was halfway into the room. "And where you been hiding her all these years?"

"She's a friend from the old neighborhood." Eddie pulled out a cigarette and lit up.

"And all this time you haven't seen her?"

"Just random texts, and a few phone calls." Eddie frowned. "We lost touch after I gave her shit about hookin' up with Nicky Falcone."

"Yeah, I saw that loser tonight. Still hasn't paid up. Frank wasn't happy."

"Supposedly, she broke up with him." Eddie settled on the leather couch across from Jonny's desk.

"She looked like she was ready to bolt at the Oasis."

"I hope so."

"You don't believe her?"

"Something's off." Eddie blew out a stream of smoke. "I told her she could stay in the apartment upstairs tonight. I'll ask her more tomorrow."

Yeah. He had some questions of his own. Like why would she be with that loser in the first place?

Eddie leaned in and flicked the tip of his cigarette into the crystal ashtray on the coffee table. "And what the hell were you doin' with Bambi? I mean, she's here less than two weeks, and she's already screwed everybody from the bouncers to the DJ."

"Geez, you're kidding, and here I was gonna ask her to marry me and have my kids," Jonny drawled, then uncapped a water bottle.

"You're lucky Angela didn't catch you."

"It was just a blowjob."

"It's my experience most women don't see the difference," Eddie warned. "Angela knows a lot of what goes on here. I don't think you want her pissed off and vengeful."

"First of all, she doesn't know that much, and second, I'm not gonna get caught."

"If you keep getting sucked off in your office with the door unlocked, I'd say the odds are not in your favor."

"Angela and I have an understanding." He drained half the water bottle. "I do what I want, and Angela's very understanding."

Eddie rolled his eyes, and Jonny's mind spun back to Cheryl. Her obvious surprise at seeing Eddie told him she didn't know he was part of the club. So, if she didn't come to see Eddie, she must've come to see him.

Interesting.

"And forget about Cheryl," Eddie warned.

Fuckin' Eddie could read his mind. Like he hadn't wanted to forget her.

Wasn't working.

~ ~ ~

Later that night, Jonny pushed through the large metal doors, exited the club, and inhaled the damp, night air. He found his limo and Max—his driver and longtime friend—waiting by the curb. At six-foot-three, two hundred and fifty pounds, Max's duties went beyond driving, and made anyone think twice about giving him a hard time.

Max glanced in the rearview mirror. "You look tired, boss."

"Long night." He sunk into the leather seat and closed his eyes. His mind wandered as the limo moved away from the curb and headed for his Manhattan penthouse.

Twenty-five minutes later, the mirrored doors of his private elevator parted with a whoosh. Happy to be off the confines of the elevator, he admired the view of the East River from the wall of glass wrapped around the corner living room. He'd lived here for a year, yet it still amazed him. A big jump from the dump he and Eddie shared down by the docks, furnished with Salvation Army furniture and cockroaches that outnumbered them one hundred to one.

"How're you doin', Killer?" he asked as his black and white striped cat curled around his ankles and through his legs. She purred and pushed until he scooped her up and nuzzled the stub that used to be an ear.

He'd rescued her one night on the pier when some punks were using her as a science experiment. They'd already cut off one of her ears, poked out one of her eyes, and were in the process of dousing her with gasoline when he'd intervened and threatened to do the same to them. Skinny, dirty, and full of fleas, he'd named her Killer to boost her confidence.

After a visit to the vet and a few weeks of regular feedings, she'd gained weight and thrived. Now, she strutted around his penthouse like the queen of the palace. He hugged her, then let her jump out of his arms, thinking they'd both done pretty good for themselves.

He walked into the bedroom, flipped on the light, and flinched.

"You're awful tense." Angela rose from the chair and went to the bar in the corner of the room. "Who were you expecting?" The accusation in her voice was unmistakable.

"No one. I'm just surprised." She poured Johnny Walker Blue into two tumblers. Her perfect figure filled the La Perla Black Label negligée he'd given her the last time she caught him screwing around.

"It's Friday, and we spend the weekend together, right?" She crossed the room and handed him the intricately cut glass.

"Why were you sitting in the dark?"

"I was enjoying the view." She motioned to the floor to ceiling windows featuring another view of the East River. "That cat of yours hissed at me when I moved her off the bed."

"Jealous?" he joked.

"Me or the cat?" Angela quipped.

"You're a lot alike." He sipped the smoky liquor, enjoying the hot burn in his throat as he headed toward the bathroom.

She stepped in his path. "You remember when we first met?" Her manicured hand clung to his arm.

"Taking a shitload of Frank's money to the Caymans, and you were scared of flying. You had me in a death grip until I got a couple of shots of tequila in you."

She arched her back. "I did not."

"Yeah, you did," he teased.

"We were young then." Her finger traced the front of his shirt.

"We were never young."

Angela's trip down memory lane was her way of dragging him backward, so they could move forward.

She undid his belt buckle, and he watched her, rigid and tense with arousal, but instead of Angela's brown eyes he saw Cheryl's green ones. She slid her hand inside his pants and stroked him. His hips twitched, but he didn't know if it was from Angela's hand or visions of Cheryl.

"Sometimes I miss the old days and that hot, wild, tough guy who was so wound out."

"Things change." He hadn't meant to say it. He should've given her the answer she wanted. Eddie was right. Keeping Angela happy was good for business, but lately . . .

"Someone saw Bambi go up to the offices tonight."

"Maybe she didn't feel good and had to lie down."

"As long as she wasn't lying under you." Her grip on him tightened.

He gently removed her hand. "We said a long time ago we weren't gonna ask each other those kinda questions." He stepped back, refastening his belt.

"What if I did? What would you say?" She lifted the tumbler to her lips but didn't drink.

"I'd say we don't ask each other those kinda questions." Game over.

She lowered the glass, her eyes sharp as she stared at him.

"We had a good run but—"

"A good run?" She slammed the tumbler onto the granite bar top. "What am I a goddamn horse?"

"It's just not working for me anymore." He swallowed a big gulp. Why the fuck did he start this at two in the morning?

"You're breaking up with me?"

His casual shrug lit a fire under her. She slammed herself into the bathroom and returned a few minutes later fully dressed.

"You can spend the rest of the night with that damn cat. I'm out." Then she flung the negligee at him. "And you can give that to your latest whore."

She huffed out of the bedroom slamming that door too, and Jonny released a sigh of relief.

He refilled the tumbler and sipped deeply. Whatever they'd had died a long time ago. Their relationship centered around making the club a winner, and they'd competed for every ounce of success. Sure, she had a bangin' body, and in the beginning it worked, but Angela's first love was money, and they'd both used each other to get what they wanted. Now, it was just business with benefits, nothing more.

It did surprise him she left so easy, but revenge was more Angela's style.

He stepped over the negligee and gazed out into the dark night, rolling the tension out of his shoulders. Time to move on, time to—Cheryl popped into his brain again. The gutsy way she barged into his office and threw his shit back at him. A savvy, in-your-face confidence, with none of Angela's manipulation. Yeah, if Cheryl stabbed you, she'd show you the blade first.

Chapter 6

The persistent buzzing of Jonny's cell phone, and the bright sunshine streaming through the windows doomed his morning before it even began. Squinting at the glare, he checked the caller ID. Everybody knew he didn't open his eyes before noon.

Annoyed, he swiped the screen. "Yeah, Frank?"

"I need to see you in my office."

"At eight o'clock on a Saturday morning?"

"I needed you at seven, but I let you sleep till eight. What's the matter? You getting soft from too much fuckin' around?"

"No, what's the problem?" He stretched and rotated his tight neck muscles.

"The problem is your attitude. Now get your ass down here."

He didn't appreciate being summoned like an errand boy. Trudging into the bathroom, Jonny showered, dressed, called Max for the car, and thirty minutes later he stood in the elevator.

The traffic from Manhattan to Brooklyn was light. Apparently, he wasn't the only one who slept in on Saturday mornings.

When Max eased up to the rear of the warehouse on Pier 59, Jonny stared at the Barnett Coffee Importing sign painted in white over the cracked brick. Frank's way of fooling everybody into thinking he was legit.

"What the hell is that?" Max pointed to what looked like a dog's tail as they walked toward the metal stairs of the warehouse. Frank had three German Shepherds who roamed the docks for security purposes, but they were so skinny, he doubted Frank ever fed them. He guessed if they ever bit anybody, it would be more from hunger than defense.

"What the fuck?" The dog lay on its side with a bullet hole square between its eyes. Jonny followed Max up the metal stairs, stopped on the landing, and looked at the animal. He swallowed hard as he fingered the dog biscuits he always stuffed in his pocket when he went to the docks.

Max stayed behind to talk to some of the guys in the warehouse while he trudged down the hall to Frank's office. He knocked and opened the door.

"You finally got your ass out of bed." Frank motioned to the wooden chair opposite his desk.

Frank's compact, stocky frame housed an ego the size of the Empire State Building. In his mid-forties, he dressed like he'd just left the golf course in every color of polo shirt and pleated chinos in the Ralph Lauren collection. And even though he paired them with matching pullover sweaters, he still looked like a Brooklyn hood.

Twice divorced, with a teenage daughter in college abroad, he never talked about his personal life, stayed away from social media and never talked to the press. Keeping a low profile was a characteristic his associates admired.

"I pull late nights at the club." Jonny stifled a yawn. "Ain't getting home till after three a.m."

"*Aren't* getting home till three a.m.," Frank corrected.

Just what he needed, another goddamn English lesson.

"You didn't get me down here to rag on the way I talk."

"The way you *speak.* No, I didn't, although more attention to your grammar would prove useful."

His back stiffened against the hard wooden chair. Frank and his subtle ways of getting his point across. Even his office was subtle. No flashy decorating, only the basics. Wooden desk, computer, printer, and fax machine. Even crime had gone high-tech.

Off in the corner, a small, free-standing bar was stocked with Jack Daniels. Frank's favorite. He wasn't a man who was into pleasing others.

"What's with the dead dog outside?" Jonny asked.

"Damn thing wouldn't stop barking." Frank shrugged. "It was annoying."

His heart pounded hard against his ribs. *Fucking psycho.*

"There's word Carl at Local 1126 is talking strike." The dog forgotten, Frank moved on to business. "Empty trucks don't make money."

"So what does that have to do with me?" He stretched his legs out in front of him.

"I want you and Eddie to set up a meet with Carl on the docks. Reinstate the reasons why a strike is not advantageous at this time."

Frank sounded like a college graduate even though he'd never made it past the tenth grade, and Carl was nothing but a thug who'd muscled his way up the teamsters' union. He liked to take kickbacks for getting his men jobs, then extorted the bosses with strike threats. And Jonny wanted nothing to do with any of it.

"C'mon Frank, Eddie and I don't do that kind of work anymore." He shifted forward. "I think it would be better . . ."

"I don't pay you to think," Frank interrupted. "I pay you to do as you're told." He kept his voice silky smooth, but his meaning was clear. "Just 'cause you're walking around in a designer suit and screwin' every high-class piece of ass in the club doesn't make you a celebrity. When you came to me, you were nothing but a punk kid from Bensonhurst in need of a big favor."

Frank used Jonny's past like a noose around his neck. The more he resisted, the tighter Frank pulled. Lately, he was starting to choke.

"You haven't forgotten, have you?"

Even if Frank wasn't shoving it down his throat on a regular basis, he would never forget. How could he? That day changed his whole life.

A hot, steamy July night in Brooklyn. Like walking through water, and unless you were from there, you couldn't know it. On nights like this everybody hung out on the front stoop because their tiny, airless apartments were stifling.

Jonny climbed the stone steps, and the animated crowd became silent. They stared and whispered behind their hands, and he knew that something terrible happened. Arms held him back, but he broke free and followed the trail of yellow crime scene tape to his mother—dead on the kitchen floor.

His heart shattered into pieces. The cops were saying something. Domestic fight, yelling, screaming. Did he know anything about it? He knew too much about it. It was his life for all of his seventeen years. His mother's bloodied face and broken body weren't a surprise.

Guilt propelled him out of the room, then out of the apartment. The cops called to him, wanting to question him. He hit the street running.

By the time he barged into Frank's office, he wanted revenge. His mother's death wrecked him. He wanted his father to pay for what he did.

"No, I haven't." The familiar tic in his left eye kept a beat with the pulse in his neck.

"Good, good." Frank stood, moved around his desk, and placed his hand on Jonny's shoulder. "Oh and . . . We don't have to worry about Nicky anymore."

Jonny furrowed his brow.

"He's paid in full."

~ ~ ~

Not able to reach Eddie on his cell phone, and knowing he wasn't at the penthouse, Jonny told Max to take him to the apartment above the club.

His mood ran somewhere between frustrated and pissed off. Frank didn't push his buttons he stomped on them. Sending him and Eddie down to the docks? What kinda shit was that? Just another way for him to control them and keep them down.

And what was that crack about Nicky? No way that deadbeat came up with the money. Thoughts of Nicky brought thoughts of Cheryl and a whole new level of frustration.

Finding Eddie's bedroom locked, he yelled through the door. "Eddie, you in there?" Not getting an immediate response, he pounded harder and shouted louder. "C'mon Eddie, unlock the fuckin' door."

A few seconds later, Cheryl flung open the door in Eddie's T-shirt and boxers, her hands planted on her hips.

He looked past her to the empty rumpled bed, and his mind scrambled. He envisioned sliding her between the sheets and running his hands up her smooth, toned legs until he wrapped her around him while his mouth sucked on those beautiful . . .

Then his fantasy exploded in his face. What if those rumpled sheets were the result of her and Eddie? He gave serious consideration to killing his best friend.

"Where's Eddie?"

"He left."

"Was he here last night?" He already knew the answer, and it made him wanna put his fist through the wall. Fuckin' ridiculous.

"Yes, but I can't see where that's any of your business."

The same attitude from last night seeped from her every pore, and it all became clear and ugly.

"Mmmm, I bet." He caught the way Eddie's T-shirt fell low enough to catch plenty of cleavage. Frank said Nicky paid up, and now he knew how.

"What's that supposed to mean?"

"Nicky sent you here to con Eddie into giving you the money he owes, right?" He glared at the unmade bed, then at her. "And what better way to do it than on your back."

Her eyes widened. "Seriously?"

Wow, she was good. Giving him the big eyes and playing the defenseless girlfriend at the Oasis. Nicky taught her well.

"Eddie's my friend, but when it comes to women, he doesn't make the best choices." He shoved his fists into his pockets to prevent him from yanking out every tousled blond hair on her beautiful head.

"You don't know what you're talking about."

Jonny leaned on the doorjamb, getting in her space. "He tends to go for the ones in trouble, the ones who want money, the users. So why don't you be a good little girl, get yourself dressed, take whatever money he threw at you, and slither on back to Nicky."

She squeaked out an exasperated yelp, then slammed the door in his face. Yeah, she was good, and he'd fallen for it. Hard.

Chapter 7

Had Jonny just called her a hooker? Slamming the door in his smug face was too good for him. How had she ever envisioned him as a good guy? Obviously, she'd been wrong. He'd probably only given her his card so she could become another one of his harem women.

No, thanks.

Cheryl yanked on a pair of sweatpants she found in the dresser drawer, rolled the waistband a few times, and smoothed her hair in the mirror. The nerve of that arrogant ass. Daring her into a fight, in his designer clothes and impressive body. The same one she'd admired up close and personal last night. And his voice. A threatening rasp that made her think of sex, or how he would sound whispering in her ear while he . . . What on earth was the matter with her?

Restless and irritated, she cracked the bedroom door to make sure he'd gone, and then she stomped around the empty apartment. Her natural curiosity coaxed her into peeking in the bedroom at the end of the hall. By the designer clothes in the closet, she guessed it belonged to Jonny.

The double framed photos on his dresser intrigued her. One showed a girl circa 1960 in her teens, with palm trees in the background. The other, a recent picture of a girl in a parochial school uniform, both with a remarkable resemblance to Jonny. They appeared so pure and innocent. Somehow she expected someone like him to have naked women plastered over the walls.

Back in the living room, the sun streamed through the floor to ceiling windows giving the whole space a bright open appearance. A long way from her dumpy apartment over the Oasis. She'd contemplated going there and getting the money herself, but that could be risky. What if someone asked about Nicky or saw her coming out of the alley last night? Or worse, she ran into Frank Barnett.

When she retrieved her phone from the bedroom, she noticed the battery was almost dead. She'd need to ask Eddie for a charger. She punched in her brother's number and prayed that he'd answer. As much as she loved him, she couldn't depend on him. At twenty he was as street smart and savvy as a forty-year-old, yet as immature and reckless as a fourteen-year-old. But she loved him with the intensity of a mother and the critical edge of a sister.

By the fourth ring, she anticipated the automated recording when he picked up.

"Dylan?"

"Cheryl?"

"I need your help." Sheets shifted, and a female voice whined in the background. "Are you with someone?"

"Yeah, we were partying kinda hard last night," Dylan mumbled. "Can I call you back?"

"No," she yelped. "Listen to me. I want you to go to the Oasis and get my money. It's in a tampon box under the sink. Then bring it to the Paradise Lounge."

"Why there?"

"My phone is going to die soon, so just listen. Come in the back door of the club and take the elevator to the third floor. I'm in the apartment over the—"

She pulled the dead phone away from her ear and mumbled a curse. At least she'd gotten through to him, and hopefully, he would pull it together and do as she asked. Following orders and going by the rules were not Dylan's style. Number one reason he'd been in and out of juvie since he was thirteen and even her warnings of real jail time now that he was twenty fell on deaf ears.

Granted the kid had a rocky start with a mother more interested in drugs and men, sometimes one more than the other, instead of her own children. And although Cheryl protected him when he was younger, she'd hardly been a shining example. An argument Dylan threw in her face whenever she came down too hard on him. Yet, underneath all his swagger and false bravado, she saw the scared little boy who cowered against her in his bed when the yelling got too loud, or the party got too wild.

She occupied herself with a few trade magazines on the coffee table, flipping through the pages, and checking the wall clock every three minutes until finally there was a knock on the door.

She opened the door, they hugged, then separated as Dylan checked out the apartment.

"Nice place." He stepped around her. "Fuckin' huge."

He towered over her at six-feet-four, and his muscular built, shoulder length dark brown hair and the scruff outlining his jaw made him appear much older than his twenty years.

Her backpack slung over his shoulder filled her with relief.

"What happened last night?" he asked.

"Long story." She would not involve him in her mess.

"Something to do with the douchebag?"

Dylan didn't like Nicky either.

"It's complicated."

Dylan eyeballed her for a second then strolled around the spacious living room. "This place rocks. How'd you end up here?"

"Eddie Morgan from the old neighborhood owns it with another guy." *Who is annoying, arrogant and ridiculously hot.* "They also have penthouses on the Upper East Side."

"Not bad." He picked up one of the crystal glasses off the bar. "What happened to Nicky?"

"What do you mean?"

"He usually has you on a short leash. Where is he?"

By now, probably at the bottom of the East River.

"We broke up."

Short and simple. Truth and lies intricately twisted.

"No, shit?" He had the same disbelief in his voice as Eddie.

When had she become that submissive and predictable? "We're over."

"About time." Dylan stepped behind the bar distracted by the different liquors showcased on glass shelves. "You gonna be staying here for a while?"

"No. Now that you have my stuff we'll go ahead with the original plan. You got the money, right?"

"Yeah, about that?"

Oh, she didn't like the sound of that at all.

"Please tell me you got the money."

"When I got there Sal already tossed all your stuff out. Bitching how you and Nicky ran off and ditched him for three months' rent." He held out the backpack. "I was lucky to get this."

"The money was under the sink." A steady pulse pounded in her ears. "In the tampon box."

He screwed up his face. "I told you, everything was gone."

"Shit. Now, what are we going to do?"

Dylan picked up an ornate shaped bottle from behind the bar. "We could always try some of this fine Bourbon."

"First of all, you're underage."

His raised eyebrows confirmed the absurdity of the comment.

Dylan's first taste of whiskey came at the tender age of twelve when one of mama's boyfriends thought it would be fun to get the kid drunk. And sadly, at twenty, she didn't have any delusions about Dylan's experimentations.

"And secondly, we don't take things that aren't ours."

Dylan shouted with laughter at that one. The irony of her being a pickpocket and him being able to hot-wire anything with an engine was not lost on either of them.

She huffed out a breath. Being parental exhausted her especially when she was so bad at it.

She slumped onto the couch. "Three thousand dollars. Gone."

"Stay here for a while." Dylan flung his arm around the room. "You said they got some other penthouses. They probably won't even notice you're here."

"What about you?"

"I still got that room by the body shop over on State Street."

"And you're going there to work every day, meeting with your PO? Staying out of trouble?"

"Yeah, yeah. I'm like a boy scout." He held up the wrong two fingers of the boy scout salute.

Right. A tatted-up boy scout in low slung, faded jeans, a hoodie, lace-up motorcycle boots, and a small silver hoop in his ear. One look at him and a scout master would have a heart attack. Then he made a goofy face and smiled. A smile that probably made the girls drop at his feet seconds before they dropped their panties.

She envied him. No matter how bad or how bleak the situation, his upbeat attitude was contagious if a little Peter Pan-ish. He'd had the same shitty upbringing as her, and yet he still had hope. Still thought he was living the dream.

He sat next to her and slung his arm around her shoulders. "Don't worry, Sissy, you'll think of something."

His heavily muscled arm made her feel protected, and his infectious grin and pet name for her gave her hope. If she could just shake the sensation that her life was about to unravel.

Chapter 8

Jonny sat across from Eddie at their regular table at Vincent's on 86th Street. Their early Saturday night dinners were usually the calm before a crazy night at the club, but not tonight. "Where were you all morning and afternoon?"

"I slept in with some rich chick at the Towers." Eddie pushed a basket of garlic knots toward him. "Her husband's a lousy lay, always away on business. You know, the usual." Eddie smiled with satisfaction. "Anyway, her bedroom had a great view of the Hudson."

"How many women were you with last night?"

"What?" Eddie furrowed his brow.

Jonny leaned in. "Are you screwin' Cheryl?"

"Fuck, no."

She said you were there last night." It pissed him off that he cared.

"Yeah, and we talked, that's all."

"Did she hit you up for the money Nicky owes Frank?"

"Nah, said she broke up with Nicky and wants to get outta Brooklyn."

Huh. Could he have been wrong about her? "She has a real attitude though."

"Funny, she said the same about you."

She must've talked about him to Eddie. Great. Now she had him thinking like a teenager in heat.

Eddie watched as Jonny rearranged the silverware for the hundredth time. "What the hell is wrong with you?"

"Nothing, I was just . . ." Then it pissed him off that Eddie noticed.

"I don't get you. You got Angela all over your dick. You got the dancers giving you head, and yet you're thinking about a girl you don't even know."

"Fucked up, right?"

"Yeah. Be smart for once and leave it alone. Let me handle her."

Jonny tore into another garlic knot and mashed the dough between his fingers. "While you were enjoying the view at the Towers, Frank hauled me out of bed at eight this morning."

The hovering waiter clinking ice against the glasses didn't help Jonny's nerves.

The waiter left, and Jonny leaned in. "He wants us to set up a meet with Carl on the docks."

"What the fuck?" Eddie's voice vibrated with anger. "We don't do that kinda work anymore."

"Lower your voice." He jerked his chin over his shoulder. "We don't need the whole damn place knowing our business."

The waiter returned to recite the specials. Sensing Jonny's mood, Eddie ordered veal parmigiana for both of them, a Chianti for Jonny, and a beer for himself.

"According to him, we're still a couple of dumb thugs from Bensonhurst," Jonny continued when the waiter left. "He started on all this loyalty shit, and how he hopes he still has our respect."

"Fuck him and his respect," Eddie growled out. "He still treats us like we're running numbers over on 86th Street."

"Consider it our last job for Frank 'cause everything went down today. Contracts signed, money exchanged. Looks like that midtown space is ours." When the waiter returned with the wine, Jonny drank a generous amount while Eddie sipped his beer.

"Nice," Eddie said.

"Already started the renovations we talked about." He

sighed. "I'm thinking four to six weeks, and we're open."

Their dream of having a club in midtown and breaking away from Frank finally materialized. He had the money, and the space, but he also had Frank breathing down his neck and dogging his every move.

"Have you said anything to him about it?" Eddie asked.

"I've told him, but he blows it off because it's not what he wants to hear."

When the food came, Eddie dove in, but Jonny picked at it with his fork, then pushed it aside, and sipped at the wine.

Over coffee, Eddie continued to rage about Frank being an asshole, but he only half listened. His brain stalled on Cheryl. Nicky was a fuck up, and he sure wouldn't let his meal ticket go that easy. Plus, she looked like she ran out in the middle of the night.

His gut told him something didn't add up. And his gut was seldom wrong.

As they waited for the check to come, Jonny's cell phone buzzed. He fished it out of his pocket, checked the caller ID, and showed the screen to Eddie.

They exchanged a look before he put the phone to his ear.

"Yeah."

"Is the meet with Carl all set for tonight?" Frank didn't waste words.

"Yeah," Jonny answered.

"Make sure everything goes our way."

"Don't I always," he said into a dead phone.

His ears hummed, and his heart rate shot up. Amazing what a thirty-second conversation with Frank could do.

~ ~ ~

Later that night, the foggy mist over the harbor hovered around Jonny like a sweaty hand. It coated his throat and filled his lungs as murky water lapped against the pilings.

He used to love coming down to the docks as a kid. Even shivering with the icy wind howling off the East River, he would dream about living in one of those luxury Manhattan penthouses. He'd watch the comings and goings outside of Frank's office. The guys wearing custom suits and zipping around in flashy cars.

Now he wore the designer clothes and drove a luxury SUV. But taking Frank's shit and meeting with a crooked union boss on a misty waterside dock fucked with the dream. Like a rat trapped in a burning building with hot flames licking at his back while he ran higher and higher until the only way to go was down.

The full moon and the warehouse security lights cast eerie shadows over the men as they assembled. He would've rather had a root canal without Novocain than stand on this splintered pier. They eyed each other while Eddie and Max stood to the side. Jonny faced off with Carl, the union negotiator, and another guy who twitched and rocked on the balls of his feet.

What a joke. Carl was just another guy on the take who didn't give a shit about his men or the union as long as his BMW and Hampton's beach house were paid up. And thanks to Frank, he had to do business on a deserted pier with this hothead and a tweaker.

"Hey, Jonny, haven't seen you down here in a while," Carl goaded. "Taking time off from your cushy job at the Paradise?"

"It's real simple." Jonny ignored his sarcasm. "We don't want a strike, and that means everybody stays on the job tomorrow."

"And what do we get in return?"

"Nothing."

"You know the rules, Jonny." Carl waved his arms around. "You gotta give us something."

"I don't gotta give you anything."

"You think you can come here and tell us what to do, and we're gonna roll over without any incentive?"

"Your incentive will be walking away from here tonight." Jonny moved close enough to smell whatever garlic laced food Carl ate for dinner.

"You're a crazy motherfucker," Carl spit out.

"I know." Jonny sensed Eddie and Max closing in behind him.

"Are you gonna let this pretty boy club owner tell us what to do?" Carl's edgy companion challenged.

"You better tell your boy to calm down," Jonny warned.

"Who the fuck is he calling a boy?" The tweaker yelled seconds before silver flashed in the dim lighting. The knife slashed through Jonny's shirt and across his bicep so quick and sharp he didn't feel it until he saw blood seep through the material.

A second later, Max spun around, grunted, and smashed his fist into the slasher's nose. His hands flew to the pulpy, bloody mess, sending the knife skidding across the cement pilings. Max swung again, and the guy staggered to the side before he hit the pier with a thud. Fisting his bloody shirt, Max hovered over him with his arm cocked.

"He's not worth it," Jonny spat out.

Max released him and straightened, but Jonny saw the tic in Max's jaw. The slasher slumped to a relaxed position, and Max drove his size fourteen shoe into the guy's balls. The ear-splitting scream pierced the desolate pier.

Eddie glared at him. "Stupid fucker."

Jonny turned to Carl. "You were told weeks ago no strike, and now you come here and start shit with people you can't control."

"But, Jonny." He held his hands up and backed away. "Listen . . ."

"We're done listening." Eddie turned to Max. "Take him

into the warehouse, and make sure he knows how fuckin' pissed off we are."

Max pulled a roll of duct tape from his pocket, flipped it in the air and caught it with a smirk. Carl's cries of protest mixed with his partner's moaning, as Max pulled him up the pier.

The wooden planks creaked under their feet as Jonny and Eddie approached the SUV. Eddie motioned to his bloody sleeve. "You better get that looked at."

Jonny mumbled a curse at the amount of blood already staining his shirt. "Just take me to the club."

Inside the SUV, he released the glove compartment and grabbed a handful of napkins. The Pizza Hut logo was immediately saturated with his blood. So much for Eddie's advice on eating healthy. Pizza Hut kept him from bleeding out all over the interior of the Escalade. Fifteen minutes later, they eased into the lot behind the club. In that short time, his arm developed a heartbeat of its own, making every movement painful.

Eddie heaved open the heavy fire door. "Go upstairs and clean up. I'll take care of everything down here."

He contemplated walking the fifty feet to the elevator or taking the stairs right in front of him. Not wanting to run into anyone, he opted for the stairs. At the third-floor landing, he regretted his decision. Wrestling with the metal stairwell door, he arrived in the small hall leading to the apartment. He unlocked the door and saw one light was on in the living room. Then he remembered he wasn't alone.

Chapter 9

Cheryl washed the few dishes she'd used and scrambled to come up with another plan. All those months of squirreling away that money and now it was gone. At least she had a place to stay and some of her clothes from the back pack.

She startled when the door open. Expecting Eddie, she did a mental eye roll when she saw Jonny. The light from the room cast a shadow over him as he stood at an odd angle, cradling his left arm. His expression was tense, or maybe pained.

"Are you all right?" She moved closer, zeroing in on the deep red stain on the sleeve of his shirt.

"I ran into a little trouble tonight."

"Looks like more than a little." The slice in his shirt definitely came from a knife.

"It's just a cut." He swayed and grimaced.

It was way more than a cut but arguing with someone as stubborn as him was a waste of time. "You better sit down before you fall down."

He looked skeptical, probably surprised she wasn't freaked out by all the blood.

"Do you at least have a first aid kit?" She couldn't let the guy bleed all over his polished hardwood floors.

"There's one under the bathroom sink." He jerked his thumb in the direction of the hall, then headed for the couch.

She returned to the living room with the first aid kit, a towel from the bathroom, and stopped.

He'd removed the torn, bloody shirt, and rested against the couch with his eyes closed. His bare, broad chest was taut with lean muscles cut across the impressive abs she'd admired the night before. A tattoo of barbwire encircled the muscled bicep of his good arm, and the light from the lamp cast a silvery shadow over another tattoo covering the left side of his ribs, a heart inside a cross inked over a jagged scar. She moved closer, but his eyes fluttered open, and she glanced away. The edges of his lips curved up, but it wasn't taunting like the other night.

Moving behind the bar, she assessed the selection, returned with a bottle of tequila, and answered his questioning expression. "This should dull the pain a little." She carefully peeled away the blood-soaked napkins from his inflamed bicep.

He slugged a few healthy gulps straight from the bottle and handed it back to her. "Eddie said you're from Brooklyn, too."

Interesting. They talked about me.

She focused on his wound, being careful not to hurt him, but when she placed the towel under his arm, she couldn't help noticing the way his muscle contracted beneath his smooth, bronze skin.

"This is going to sting," she warned, then poured the alcohol over the wound.

"Shit!" He clenched his jaw. "What a waste of a two-hundred-dollar bottle of tequila."

"You're pretty casual about a six-inch gash and losing a boatload of blood." She dabbed at the wound with the sterile pad, cleaned it, then wrapped the gauze around his arm a few times before she taped it into place.

"I've had worse," he mumbled.

Like the scar he almost camouflaged on his chest. Maybe she wasn't the only one with secrets.

He looked at the bandage job. "Not bad." The slow, lazy grin caught her by surprise.

“I’ve had some practice patching people up.” Her heart flip-flopped at the memory of Dylan and all his smash-ups. “That could get infected.” She busied herself putting the first aid kit back together. “And I’m sure you need stitches.”

“It’ll be fine.”

An uncomfortable silence passed between them until he motioned for her to sit. “Eddie says you’re staying here for a few days.”

She nodded and perched on the edge of the leather cushion. Life taught her revealing too much could be deadly.

“He also said you’re not with Nicky anymore.”

“Right, again.”

“Good move, the guy’s a loser.” He scrubbed his hand over his jaw. “I shouldn’t have made that crack about the money.”

“No, you shouldn’t have.” Wow, was that an apology? “Did he really owe you ten thousand dollars?”

“Not me directly.”

His eyes locked with hers. She swallowed hard and tempered her expression.

She glanced at his arm. “Does that *cut* have something to do with collecting money too?”

His jaw tightened, and she braced for a scathing comeback, but he reached for the tequila with his good arm instead. “Why don’t you get some glasses so we can enjoy this the right way?”

The slight tremor in his hand when he pointed to the bar told her she’d hit a nerve. Retrieving two glasses, she placed them in front of them and he poured the silvery liquid. Jonny downed his immediately.

His fingertips brushed against her arm. “Drink up.” He pointed to her untouched shot glass, then motioned to his arm. “You did good.”

For a split second, the sarcastic player disappeared, his black eyes melted a bit, and she saw some compassion. The same caring that intrigued her the other night at the Oasis. A soothing warmth flowed over her along with an instinct to run.

She pushed the shot glass aside and stood. “I told Eddie I’d meet him downstairs.”

His eyes tracked her as she moved around the coffee table, and when she turned toward the door she willed herself not to look back.

Another bad boy was not in her future plans.

Chapter 10

Cheryl rolled the tension out of her shoulders as she descended the concrete stairs of the stairwell leading to the club. Sitting so close to Jonny on the couch while his ebony eyes searched for answers had unnerved her and set off every alarm in her survival checklist. She pushed through the security doors, and the throbbing music surrounded her. The chaos of people kicked up her heart to a bubbling frenzy as she craned her neck in search of Eddie. She weaved her way deeper into the crowd until she came to a small clearing on the other side of the room.

"Hello, Cheryl." Frank's harsh whisper thundered over the house music. Her breathing slowed, but her heart hammered faster. "You looked shocked to see me."

Shocked, stunned and paralyzed with fear. Yeah, that explained it.

"Nothing surprising about the owner keeping an eye on things."

"But I thought—"

"Jonny and Eddie were the owners." He smiled. "Their names are on the lease, but it's my money that runs the place."

Jonny and Eddie worked for Frank Barnett? Disturbing on so many levels.

He leaned in. "Don't worry, I won't tell anyone what you did." She shuddered as his hot breath stung her ear.

"I didn't—"

"You lured Nicky out to that alley and stabbed him." He

smiled at her. "By the time I came along, you'd already slit his throat."

The strobe lights illuminated his face with pinpricks of color.

"You know it didn't happen that way." Her voice rose but no one noticed with the pounding music. "I was defending myself."

"It's just a matter of semantics." The smile turned into a sneer. "I wore gloves, so the only prints on that knife are yours. It's called evidence. Cops like that."

Cops or anything related to the system that had neglected her and Dylan sent a chill down her spine. And a thug like Frank Barnett would have a precinct filled with crooked cops on his payroll that would be more than happy to do whatever he wanted.

"And I'm thinking this hot ass of yours could be very useful." Frank squeezed her arm, then pulled her to his side. "As long as that knife and Nicky's body don't reappear."

People laughed and danced to the music around them completely unaware of her bizarre situation.

She yanked her arm away and twisted out of his grasp. "What do you want?"

Her street sense burst through her panic. A guy like Frank Barnett always had an angle and pinning Nicky's murder on her was only the beginning.

"Nothing." He smiled wider. "Yet."

Eddie came up alongside her. "Hey, I've been looking for you."

Frank's gaze burned into her. "We were just getting to know each other."

"Is everything all right?" Eddie looked from her to Frank.

"Of course." Frank spread his arms wide.

Frank and Eddie exchanged a quick glance that she didn't understand. "I think I'll go back upstairs."

Eddie nodded, and Frank grinned. "Nice meeting you."

She cut around the perimeter of the club to the elevators. The silver doors parted, and thankfully she was alone for the short ride to the third floor. She gripped the cool metal rail against the mirrored walls and sucked in a deep breath. Frank's calm, cool voice unnerved her, but the revelation that Jonny and Eddie worked for him blew her away. All the pieces fell together. Jonny was collecting for Frank at the Oasis, and when Frank didn't get his money, he came to finish the job.

Then the matter-of-fact way he'd pinned Nicky's murder on her. His flawless appearance and polished voice belied his twisted mind. Fact and illusion collided, and the deadly chill of his eyes said, psycho.

In her rush to leave Eddie's apartment, she forgot the key he'd given her, so she knocked. Jonny answered the door, still shirtless, and still rocking those great tats making her irregular heartbeat kick to overdrive. Her choices for the night ranged from a devious killer to an off limits, sexy as hell, bad boy. Both equally capable of sending her life straight to hell.

"What happened?" He opened the door wider and she entered the apartment.

She struggled to stifle a yawn as his gaze raked over her. She didn't have the energy to explain, or even to lie, so she remained silent.

"You've only been gone for twenty minutes, and you come back looking like you've seen a ghost."

"It's nothing." Every street-smart instinct blared out a warning. Frank was Jonny's boss, so who knew where his alliances lay.

He motioned to the red marks Frank left on her arms. "Was Nicky here?

"I told you, we broke up."

"You're running from something. I know the look."

She mashed her lips together to keep the truth from spilling out. How could a man she'd just met and didn't like very much find her weaknesses and make her feel so vulnerable?

"Please stop." Her voice quivered as the words choked her.

"Then tell me what you're really doing here."

She called upon every skill that kept her alive as a child and seen her through her teenage years.

"You helped me before." He motioned to his arm. "Maybe I can help you."

"I don't need your help."

"I never met anyone who needed help more."

Shit. His simple statement drove a wedge under her restraints, while his eyes examined her. Seeing her guilt, knowing her truths.

"I'm fine." A crazed laugh threatened to escape, but she squashed it.

"You're not, now tell me why."

His persistence sent adrenaline rocketing through her, and all her stifled emotions from the last two days bubbled to the surface like some frenzied volcano.

"Because I stabbed Nicky."

She hadn't wanted to say it, she hadn't planned on saying it, but once again her mouth took over before thinking.

~ ~ ~

Jonny blinked a few times. "You what?"

"You heard me." She averted her eyes.

He moved her to the couch, then poured a shot of tequila. "Drink this."

She gulped the clear liquid and squeezed her eyes shut for a minute.

"Explain."

"Nicky and I had a fight. A bad fight. He was hitting me, and I pulled a knife." The words rushed out, then she swallowed hard. "I didn't want to hurt him, but he fell into the knife and . . ."

Her voice faded off, and her face paled. He pried the shot glass from her hand and refilled it. "Drink."

She shot the tequila then rolled the glass between her hands.

"Was he alive?"

"Yes."

"And you left him in the alley?"

"Yes."

"Was anybody else there?"

"No."

Her rigid back and shrill voice sounded defensive, not distressed. Like his questions were annoying her. Her story had way too many holes, but why would anyone confess to a crime they didn't commit? Unless the truth was worse. Fucked up, but he'd play along for now.

"What you did was self-defense. Nobody deserves to be hit."

"Guys get mad; they hit. It's the way it is."

"I would never hit you."

And he meant it. No matter how crazy a woman behaved, he'd never resorted to violence. He'd never become a violent animal like his father.

"I just wanted to get away from here. Take my brother and start over."

"And you didn't tell Eddie any of this?"

"No. I couldn't . . . I didn't want to tell anyone."

Her gaze darted away from him, and it crushed his heart. His mother had that look. Fear with a lot of shame mixed in.

"But you told me?"

"I've been so scared." She set the glass on the coffee table.

After an endless silence, he traced the side of her jaw with the tip of his finger, and when he leaned in, she met him halfway.

"I've got you." He pushed a stray hair away from her face and kissed her, wanting to taste more of her, be part of her, sink into her sweetness and make all her fears go away.

His eager hands roamed up her back. A decent man would've paced himself, given her space, but he'd never been a decent man when desire overwhelmed him. He nipped his way down her slender neck, loving the feel of her skin against his lips. He knew what he wanted. He'd wanted it ever since he'd seen her at the Oasis.

He fumbled with the hem of her T-shirt, and she covered his hand with hers.

"You want me to stop?" His words caught between a sigh and a gasp.

She pushed his hands away, tugged her shirt over her head and flung it onto the couch.

"This isn't a game." He meant it as a warning, but the lust in his voice made it sound more like a challenge.

"I know." She gasped as he snaked his hands around her waist. "'Cause games have rules."

For one tantalizing second her eyes dared him with desires as overpowering and primal as his. Shit, he was fucked. So, so fucked. Standing, he snatched her hand and jerked her up, thankful for the numbing effects of the tequila on his arm. He pulled her toward the bedroom, nudged the door open with his foot, then kicked it closed.

She slipped off her shoes and wiggled out of her jeans until they pooled at her feet. A heat boiled in the pit of his stomach and shot through his veins, melting him from the inside out. One part of him wanted to take time and explore every inch of her, while the part that controlled him was as hard as steel and dying to find its way into her warm, wet body.

He tumbled her to the bed, crushed his mouth to hers and pushed his tongue inside until they were both gasping for breath. She arched her back, and he stripped away the thin scrap of lace covering her sex. Edging his hand between her thighs, he slipped one finger inside her heat, then two. Her soft sweetness quivered as he plundered her folds with a steady rhythm until she purred.

He increased the pressure, until she shuddered and moaned against him.

"Ohhh, don't stop," she whimpered.

"Don't worry, baby," he assured her. "I'm gonna make you come so hard, you won't be able to see straight."

Two heartbeats later, he captured her mouth in another demanding kiss, leaned toward the nightstand, yanked open the drawer, and rummaged around for a condom. Tearing it open, he sheathed himself, then spread her thighs wide. She arched her back to meet him seconds before he thrust inside her.

Her lips nuzzled his neck, and he wanted to go slow. Wanted to savor this, take his time, but his hips had other ideas. Holding his breath, he pumped into her hard, and when she wrapped those beautiful legs around his waist, he drove deeper. It was crazy and unbelievable, something he'd never experienced. Something he would only feel with her. And something that could bring his world down around his ears.

"See what you do to me?" He fisted the sheets and watched his body take her. And when she watched him too, it almost made him blow.

"C'mon baby," he growled in her ear. "Wanna hear you screaming my name when you come all over me."

Her spasms hit again, and she milked him, sucking him in deeper and deeper. "Ohhh, Jonny."

His name on her lips made him thrust into her harder, his fingers kneading her ass until he broke apart and came so hard that for a second everything snapped to black. They stayed locked together. Gasping. Her head still nestled in his shoulder. Her thigh still draped over his back. He shifted as the pain returned to his arm. Then reality hit like a pile of unpaid bills.

She stared at him either confused or embarrassed. He felt edgy too, so he stayed silent.

"Did we really just do that?" she asked around nervous laughter.

"If you gotta ask, I must've done something wrong."

"Oh no, believe me, you did everything right."

"Hey, Cheryl, are you up here?"

"Shit, it's Eddie." She clutched at the sheet.

He rummaged around on the floor for his pants, yanked them on, and slipped into the living room.

Eddie frowned and did a double take at him shirtless, zipping up his pants. "Is Cheryl here?"

"No . . . I mean, yeah."

"She seemed upset before." Eddie looked around the room. "Is she all right?"

"She's fine." He ran his hand threw his hair. "She, ahhh . . . wanted to lay down."

"Oh." Eddie zeroed in on her shirt flung over the couch.

"My arm is pounding like a bitch." He motioned toward his bandage. "I think I'll stay here for a while." Truth. He should've been paralyzed after the sex they'd had.

"Sure." Eddie looked back once and left.

When he entered the bedroom, Cheryl had the huge bed sheet draped around her as she gathered up her clothes. Guilt and confusion crowded his brain.

"Eddie must know I was in here." She flicked her hand at him, shirtless, barefoot, his pants half undone. "And you look like you just fell out of bed after rolling around with a fast fuck."

"It was more than a fast fuck," he mumbled.

He stepped in her path, bringing them face to face. "You were upset before, and I don't want you to think I was . . ." Again, the guilt consumed him.

She pressed her finger to his lips. "I appreciate what you're trying to do, but you can't help me."

He cupped her chin. "We're gonna figure this out."

"I'm in too deep."

She stepped back, and his hand dropped away. She bundled up her clothes and motioned toward the bathroom. "I'm going to get dressed."

"Sure."

Everything about this woman screamed trouble. Even though she confessed to a stabbing, he sensed something worse hiding in the shadows. Something that could unravel both of them and send his dream club straight to hell. He should give her up before things got messy, but he had a feeling opening up a million-dollar club in Manhattan would be easier than succumbing to the ache of letting her go.

He'd just looped his belt buckle and turned toward the door when Angela walked into the bedroom.

Chapter 11

"What are you doing up here?" Jonny heard the edge in his voice.

First Eddie, now her. Way too many goddamn people with a key.

"Eddie said you got hurt." She flicked her hand at his bandaged arm. "I wanted to see how you were."

"I'm fine." He didn't buy that for a minute. Angela didn't do compassion.

She scanned the room and zeroed in on the rumpled bed. "I didn't like the way we ended things the other night. I hoped we could talk."

"There's nothing to talk about."

She reached for his hand. "Fine, then we won't talk." Placing it on the plunging neckline of her skin-tight dress.

He fixed his gaze on her forehead, his expression blank.

"I'll bet I could make that arm feel better," she purred, all silky sweet and dripping with an innocence she didn't possess.

He pulled his hand away. "I don't think so." He waited for the pout and the hair flip, and when it came he easily resisted.

The pout changed to a sneer. "How do you think this makes me look, if you just drop me?" She tossed her tangle of ebony curls over her shoulders. This time in anger, not seduction.

Angela loved all her possessions. Designer clothes, purses, spa treatments, all the things his money could buy.

"So, you're just worried about your rep." He pulled his lips into a cool smile.

"I'm worried about you too."

That would be the day when Angela worried about anyone but herself.

"Frank isn't going to like this," she said.

He flicked a few quick glances toward the bathroom door, and she caught him.

"What's the matter with you?"

"My fuckin' arm is killing me." He closed the gap between them, clutched her arm and herded her out of the bedroom. "I told you the other night, we're done." At the entry door, he paused and collected himself.

She looked him over. "You're going to be sorry."

"Are you threatening me?"

Her cold gaze made good on the warning, two seconds before she strutted out.

He closed the door, leaned against it, and regrouped. Throwing Frank in his face, like she expected a reaction. Those days were over. In a few weeks he'd have his own club and he didn't have the energy for her or her drama. And he sure didn't need a scene with her and Cheryl, the woman he'd just had hot, crazy sex with.

Still basking in his reprieve, he entered the bedroom, sat on the bed, and ran his hand over the rumpled sheets. He'd had tough women, scheming women, broken women, and in a way, Cheryl was all three. But it was her vulnerable side that drew him in, the way she'd pleaded for help without saying a word. That was a side he couldn't, and didn't want to, ignore.

A few minutes later, she came out of the bathroom dressed. He moved fast, caging her in against the bathroom door, leaving no room for her to move or escape. Her kiss-swollen lips and tangled hair sucked the air out of his lungs and made him want her all over again.

"I need more of you." He laid his cheek against hers and groaned into her neck. "I wanna fall back into bed and fuck you till . . ." He pushed his hips against her, and a soft little moan escaped.

"We have to stop." Her palms rested on his chest, but instead of pushing him away, she ran them over his shoulders.

"I got a friend downtown who can hook us up with passports fast, and we're outta here." He kissed her, then mumbled against her lips. "You and me on the next plane to Cabo."

"And how would that work?"

"We leave and go where no one can find us." Even he couldn't believe he'd said it. He never imagined he'd sound like one of those sappy movies, but it didn't matter as long as they were together.

"You can't leave the club, and I won't leave my brother behind. From the day he was born, he's been mine." Her voice hitched. "I love him."

Her simple words squeezed his heart. So fuckin' plain and honest.

"I can't make any more stupid mistakes."

He furrowed his brow. "Stupid mistakes?"

"Not you, not us." She touched his cheek. "But don't feel because of what happened you have to . . ."

His brain zeroed in on the word *us.* He huffed out a breath. "You don't get it." He hoped his words would make sense. "I'm not the one who saves the girl, the one who does the right thing."

"I know, but . . ."

"You make me want to be better. And believe me, I'm not that guy."

"Well, that's true."

They whipped their heads to the voice behind them. Angela stood in the doorway assessing the situation.

"I knew it." Angela marched into the room. "You see a woman, and you just have to screw her?" She spewed her venom on Cheryl. "I hate to break it to you, honey, but Jonny can't keep his dick in his pants."

"Don't," Jonny warned.

"No, I think this poor girl should know about you." She got in Cheryl's face, but Cheryl didn't flinch. "We have about twenty dancers, and I'd say he's screwed at least half of them." Angela faced him. "Right, Jonny?"

"That's enough." Jonny pressed the tips of his fingers to his temple.

"Fine, tell her I'm wrong," Angela dared. "Tell her you haven't slept with half the women in this club, plus the rich and famous clientele who find you so irresistible."

Cheryl squared her shoulders and faced Angela. "If everything you say is true, it looks like you were the bigger fool for being with him."

His lips kicked up into a smirk. He'd seen Angela make the toughest dancers in the club cry over a ripped costume, yet Cheryl stood up to her. That took guts. He wanted to pull her into his arms just for that.

Angela opened her mouth to retaliate, but Cheryl had already stormed off.

"Cheryl, wait," He called after her as she ran from the room, slamming the door behind her.

They stared at the door, as Angela geared up for round two. "What was going on here?"

"I think that's pretty obvious, don't you?" The smell of sex still hung in the air, but he had no remorse, and Angela knew it.

"You broke up with me for her?" Angela sneered. "Nicky Falcone's leftovers?"

Angela went right for the jugular. Attack or be killed.

"It's time for you to go." He turned away from her and half expected something to whiz past his head. Angela had a crazy fucking temper, and more than once he found himself ducking some of his finest glassware.

"I'll go, but don't think you can shut me out because I'll make you pay." She stood her ground.

He spun around. "You won't make me do anything, and if you try, you'll be sorry." He kept his voice dangerously low. "Now get out."

Angela's tawny complexion became blotchy with rage. Her eyes flickered with a million deadly thoughts before she stomped into the living room. He followed her, and when she toppled a priceless vase to punctuate her dramatic exit, he wasn't surprised.

He stormed down the hall and found Eddie's bedroom door locked so he banged and kicked at it a few times, then gave up. Who could blame Cheryl for locking him out after that shit show. He returned to his bedroom, eased against the headboard, closed his eyes, and saw Cheryl's face. He had just had her, and all he could think about was having her again. Her scent was in the room. It surrounded him. It taunted him. It held him captive.

~ ~ ~

In less than a minute Cheryl fled Jonny's bedroom and locked herself into Eddie's. With her ear pressed against the door, she heard more shouting, something crash, a door slamming and then silence.

"Cheryl!" Jonny shouted.

She jumped away from the door as it rattled under his pounding.

"Open up!"

He banged, yelled and kicked at the door a few more times but she stayed quiet, and he finally gave up. Sucking in a deep breath, she swallowed past the lump in her throat. She would've loved to fling the door open and fall into his arms like a scene from some old movie, but that would be another colossally bad decision.

The grim facts mounted up fast. The first night she'd seen him with some bimbo on her knees in his office. Even his bitchy ex-girlfriend said he screwed everything that walked, and this was the man she picked to tell her darkest secret. It must've been some fucked up gene she inherited from her mother which made falling for the wrong men part of their DNA.

But something didn't fit because Jonny the uncaring player conflicted with the man who wanted to protect her. The man whose dark, sultry eyes melted when they made love. She usually hated the term, but tonight making love fit. A night so full of mysterious contradictions. His impatient fingers and the way he responded to her. The touch of his hand grazing her hip, and the way he filled her, made her come around him, pulsing and stretching her and spoiling her for any other man. She hugged herself with the possibility of wanting such a man. Or the possibility of such a man wanting her.

Tears gathered, but she refused to give in to them. She'd learned long ago crying never solved anything.

Chapter 12

The following night, Jonny stifled a yawn and wished he'd taken the coffee the bartender offered him earlier. After last night's shit storm, he'd gulped his way through the rest of the tequila and passed out. As Cheryl predicted, his arm got worse, but a trip to the doctor and getting thirteen stitches with a raging hangover was not a great way to spend the afternoon.

Now he sat in his office with his head and arm throbbing in unison, each competing to see which would make him hurl first. He popped another pain pill to dull the physical pain because nothing would dull the feel of Cheryl's touch. How her fingers worked him over until he saw double, or how she trembled when he lit her up and made her melt around him. Pain or not, his dick got hard just thinking about her.

Most women he'd been with were like a bad porn movie, screaming and gasping and saying things about his dick even he didn't believe. But with Cheryl, it was all soft murmurs and passionate sighs. An honesty that can't be faked.

He rolled his shoulders to relieve the tension in his neck seconds before Max and Eddie filed into his office and assumed their usual spots. Eddie slouched on the couch lighting a cigarette, and Max perched on the edge of his desk.

"I still can't believe it." Eddie blew the smoke toward the ceiling. "I knew she was keeping something from me, but stabbing Nicky? That is fucked up."

He'd filled them in earlier, and now he eyed Eddie, then Max.

"This shit's a mess," Max grunted.

"That fuckwad deserved it," Eddie said.

Jonny fought to focus past the pain pills. "If it's true."

Eddie and Max shot him a look.

"Why would she make it up?" Eddie asked. "Most people deny that shit not admit to it."

"Nicky was small time, but he did have a rep on the street." Jonny ran his hand over his jaw. "We would've heard something. She stabs him and he vanishes. Her story has too many fuckin' holes."

Max nodded, and Eddie cleared his throat. "She asked me about working here."

Jonny's chest tightened. Why hadn't she asked him about a job? *Not much time for talking when I had my tongue shoved halfway down her throat.*

"I put her at the main bar." Eddie's eyes bore through him waiting for a reaction. "She's got plenty of experience, and once she learns how the club works, we can move her up to the VIP."

Hell if he understood it. A week ago he hadn't even known Cheryl. Then she flung herself into his life, patched up his arm, fucked him into a coma, and spit out a confession that would make most men run for cover. Not the traditional beginning to a new relationship but —She was all he could think about.

"What happened with Angela?" Max asked.

Jonny glanced at Max. The man usually kept his thoughts to himself.

"She left me a very detailed text this morning explaining exactly what I could do with the club and her job," Jonny drawled. "I think it's physically impossible, but the bottom line is, she quit."

"So how much new barware do I have to order?" Eddie ground his cigarette into the ashtray.

“Took her anger out on the vase in the foyer.” Jonny shrugged. “Ain’t a good fight unless somebody breaks something, right?”

“Thank fuck, I hated that thing,” Eddie added.

“And of course she reminded me Cheryl was with Nicky first.”

“Jealous women do the best research,” Eddie observed.

“Better than the fuckin’ CIA,” Max agreed, then asked, “Did Angela mention Frank at all?”

“Why would she?”

“Frank was the one who put her here, and you and her . . .”

“What are you saying, she was fuckin’ me on Frank’s orders?”

“Nah . . . forget it.”

Max’s comment made the muscles in his chest contract again, especially since Angela insinuated the same thing.

“So just to be clear, you and Cheryl . . .” Eddie cocked his head.

“You got a problem with that?” Jonny snapped.

“Not the way you think.” Eddie waited a beat. “I just don’t wanna see her get hurt.”

“And you think I’m gonna hurt her?” Jonny stood and came around the desk.

“It’s me you’re talking to, remember?” Eddie blew out a sharp breath. “You can’t just fuck her and forget her like all the rest.”

“I don’t get it.” Max pushed off the desk and faced him. “Why her? Is she so good in the sack you’re willing to . . .”

Jonny stepped to Max. “Shut it.” Anger turned the two words ugly. Goddamn irrational, but again the impulse to protect Cheryl unraveled him and made reasonable thinking impossible.

Max could’ve easily taken him out. He had at least three inches and fifty pounds on him, but the larger man stepped off. “I didn’t mean nothing by it.”

An awkward silence filled the room until Eddie moved between them. "Why don't we all dial it down?" Eddie clapped his hand over Max's shoulder.

"I just don't want any trouble," Max mumbled, then slouched out of the office.

"You gotta ease off," Eddie warned when they were alone.

"I'm a little on edge."

"More like over the edge."

"It's just . . ." Even he didn't understand his compulsion to play the hero, but he couldn't ignore another woman in a hopeless situation. Maybe evening the score would end the guilt that gnawed at him like a toothache.

A sharp knock stalled their conversation, then they looked to the door as Frank swaggered into the office.

Jonny blew out an exasperated breath that should've contained fire.

"What's up?" Eddie said.

"Should be my dick, but it's my blood pressure." Sarcasm and Frank were not a good mix, so Jonny stayed silent.

"Why don't you go down and check in with the bouncers," Frank nodded to Eddie and then to the door.

Eddie stared down the shorter man, then flashed Jonny a look before he left the office.

"What's with him?" Frank asked.

"He doesn't like being talked to like shit." He hoped the twitch in his eye wasn't noticeable.

Frank roamed around the office. "Then maybe he should remember that twelve months ago he was just another punk running the streets."

"You come up here to bust balls, or you got something on your mind?" Jonny sat behind his desk. The need for some distance between them overwhelmed him.

Frank snatched two tickets off his desk. "Why're *you* going to the NY Bar and Nightclub dinner?"

"To thank all those city officials who pushed through the variances for my new club." Jonny pictured those documents locked up tight in his office safe.

"Sounds like you've forgotten your obligations." Frank kept his voice low, but a vein throbbed in his forehead.

"I didn't forget nothing." His gaze cut to Frank.

"So you're just going to leave?" Frank's voice raised enough for Jonny to hear the anger.

"I told you months ago I have people lined up to take my place."

He'd been grooming the beverage manager for weeks. He'd told him all this, but as usual, Frank only heard what he wanted to hear.

"And how do you see this playing out?" Frank stepped forward and rested his palms on the desk.

Jonny leaned in. "I can go wherever I want." They were close enough for him to get a whiff of Frank's heavy cologne. "I got my own money."

"What the fuck are you talking about?" Frank slammed his fist on Jonny's desk so hard it almost toppled a half-filled water bottle. "Your money is my money. You think you'd have those hot babes blowing on your dice if you were still some cheap hustler over on 86th Street."

Cheap hustler. Frank hurled the insult like a rusty spike.

"Yeah, I do," he spat. "Cause I would've made it, with or without you." His voice held more emotion than he'd intended.

Jonny's cell vibrated on his desk, and they both grabbed for it. Frank beat him to it, swiped the phone and canceled the call.

"What the fuck?" Jonny jumped from his chair.

"I don't like interruptions when I'm talking." Frank tossed the phone on the desk.

He contemplated snatching it up, but instead, he clenched his fists so hard he could feel his nails digging into his palms.

"Just remember you have some outstanding debts that can never be repaid."

Nobody had to refresh that memory. It would live in his subconscious forever.

Jonny barged into Frank's office that night breathless and sweaty. His mother's broken body wrecked him. He wanted revenge. He wanted his father to pay for what he did.

Frank listened in silence. Then he reached into his top drawer, pulled out a gun, and slid it across the desk. "Let's take care of your business."

"You know where to find him?" Frank asked when they hit the street.

Jonny knew. He'd spent plenty of nights dragging his father home from his sleazy hangout.

When they entered the bar, Jonny called him out to the alley where they faced each other, father and son.

"You finally did it," he said. "You finally killed her."

"She was nothing but a worthless tramp."

"Shut up." His hand shook as he pointed the gun at his father.

"You don't have the balls to pull the trigger," his father taunted, "'cause you're useless like that cunt mother of yours."

All the years of anger, fear, and frustration welled up in him. He held the gun with both hands to control the shaking.

His father spewed out a mean, harsh laugh. It was the last sound he ever made.

A second before his knees buckled, his eyes registered one emotion, shock.

Frank stepped to Jonny's side and slipped the gun from his limp hand. "I didn't think you'd be able to do it, kid."

Jonny stared at his father's limp body, then nudged him with his foot.

"Don't worry; he's dead. You don't take a shot like that and live."

Jonny scanned the alley, concerned about onlookers. "I thought you were still in the bar."

"I figured you might need some help." Frank curled his lip. "You were right. He was an annoying prick."

"I wanted to do it . . . I just couldn't."

"The first time is the hardest. After that, it gets easier."

"I guess." His voice sounded far off and dazed.

"Get outta here and let me take care of it." Frank holstered his gun and shoved the other one into the back of his pants.

Jonny felt washed clean. Free for the first time.

"And another thing," Frank's voice snapped him to the present. "I know you're banging that hot piece, Cheryl."

Angela probably spilled all the gory details, but the glint in Frank's eyes when he said Cheryl's name made his stomach clench.

"Screw all the chicks you want but forget about the Manhattan club, or you're gonna have more trouble than you can handle." Frank closed the gap between them. "You get my meaning?"

"I got it."

Chapter 13

Jonny banged out of his office, then kicked the door closed for good measure. He stormed behind the bar in the VIP Room, filled a glass with ice, and shot the seltzer gun over the cubes. He snatched a lime off the condiment tray.

"These lime slices are too thick," he yelled at the bartender, then held a glass up to the light. "And there's water spots on the glasses. Rewash them."

"The lights are low, half the people are wasted," the bartender said. "Nobody knows; nobody cares."

"I do." Jonny ran his hand over the black granite bar. "We didn't pay thousands of dollars for Italian stone to have my hand stick to it. Wipe it down."

He straightened the cocktail napkins, threw away the offensive limes, snatched his glass, and settled at the end of the bar.

He hated the way Frank's visit rattled him. It reminded him of the large part he played in his dangerous game. Back in the day, Frank came off as his savior. He convinced him of their friendship, influenced him with money, and persuaded him to ignore the duffle bags of small bills that materialized monthly. But there were times like this over the years when the truth crashed in on him, and even the power and money made it hard to deny what Frank was about.

No trust. No allegiance. He acted like he owned him. Another decoration in the club, like the plush suede booths or the strobe lighting. He'd misjudged his power, but he wouldn't abandon the chance to have something of his own, no matter what the cost.

Cheryl and him were trapped in a life they no longer wanted. A situation his gut told him was bad. Real bad.

"Did you forget about our meeting, Vallone?"

He started at the harsh voice behind him, then plastered a smarmy expression on his face. "Look who's here, Brooklyn's finest, making the streets safe for all the good citizens."

Captain Kevin Farrell was a stereotypical NYPD cop with his broad Irish features and ruddy complexion. Only in his early forties, but his sandy-colored hair was thinning, and his big, gut saw too many donuts.

"You're breaking the fire codes." He motioned to the half-lit cigar Farrell chomped on. "This is a non-smoking establishment."

"Call a cop." Farrell pulled at his ill-fitting suit jacket. "Now cut the bullshit, and let's get this done."

"That's why you can't get ahead in life, Farrell. You've got no manners."

"That's 'cause I gotta chase after lowlifes like you." Farrell shifted his feet.

The captain's anger had nothing to do with his high moral character. It was all about jealousy, because Farrell was stuck out in Queens in a small Cape Cod with a fat, frumpy wife and four screaming kids.

Jonny reached into his pants pocket and slapped a folded white envelope stuffed with hundreds on the bar. He hated the guy, but he loved to antagonize him, so he motioned to the beer gut hanging over his cheap suit. "You oughta take some of this money I throw at your precinct every week and buy yourself a decent suit. You're starting to look like a slob."

"You're lucky you're under Frank's protection."

"Are we done here?" Jonny pushed away from the bar. "'Cause you're starting to make my head hurt."

Farrell mumbled something as he huffed off, and Jonny ignored him. He had no problem paying off the cops. It was the price of doing business, but he hated the cocky sense of entitlement of every crooked cop on the take. Playing both sides and loyal to no one, which made them extremely dangerous.

What a fucked-up night. First Frank, then Farrell. Too restless to sit, he settled against the railing overlooking the lower level of the club. Watching the crowd ebb and flow into each other usually energized him and filled him with pride but not tonight. Scanning the crowd below him, he spotted Frank at one of the side bars. A few seconds later a woman joined him. Not a surprise. Frank had a flock of women on call, but the curves and the wild tangle of curls spilling halfway down her back were all too familiar.

He bent forward, pressing his thighs against the rail, straining for a better view. The woman leaned in, and Frank grabbed her closer for a kiss. He straightened, fished his phone out of his pocket, hit the number for the bartender, and waited. He was ninety-nine percent sure, but he wanted to be positive.

"Who's with Frank?" he demanded.

The bartender confirmed what he already knew.

Angela.

~ ~ ~

It hadn't taken Cheryl long to get back into the rhythmic routine of making drinks. And making drinks at the Paradise exceeded any of the dumps she'd ever worked. Earlier the head bartender showed her the POS system and where all the basics were kept, and after that, it all fell together. Concentrating on the customer's wants and needs at the busy main bar kept her mind free of all the static in her brain and made the time pass incredibly fast.

After last night's monumental fuck up with Jonny and his girlfriend, she welcomed some mindless work. She probably should have felt guilty getting caught by Angela. But a bitchy girlfriend interested in marking her territory sucked the guilt right out of her.

Thankfully, he gave up his assault on the bedroom door, and soon after the main door to the apartment slammed. She figured that either he decided sex with her had been a huge mistake, or he was off to hunt down Angela and drag her back to his Upper East Side penthouse for some make-up sex.

She'd spent the remainder of last night devising her latest plan, and thankfully Eddie agreed to hire her as a bartender. A job she'd always loved and a quick way to make cash. In two weeks she could put her getaway plan back on the front burner. She wouldn't have as much as before in that short time, but it would be enough for her and Dylan to get out of New York.

She'd artfully avoided Jonny all night. When he made his rounds earlier, she easily kept her attention on the blender mixing up a batch of margaritas, as she watched him out of the corner of her eye.

~ ~ ~

Eddie joined Jonny at the railing of the VIP, and they zoomed in on the same couple.

"He's hooking up with Angela to screw with me. He's a psychotic fuck and she's a vindictive bitch." Jonny shoved his hands into his pockets to prevent punching something.

"Just keep your head in the game," Eddie said.

"I'm going to my office." Jonny pushed off the railing and stopped, as Frank moved away from Angela and headed toward the main bar. He motioned to Cheryl, then waited.

~ ~ ~

Cheryl glanced toward Frank standing at the end of the service bar then back to her customer. She placed the perfectly poured Cosmo on the little cocktail napkin, replaced the vodka and cranberry juice and ran the credit card.

She couldn't stall any longer. Might as well suck it up and get it over with. Frank eyed her right up until she stopped three feet in front of him. Happy for the service bar between them, she stayed silent forcing him to speak first. Silly but it did give her a small sense of control.

"You look very professional." Frank smiled.

Scariest thing she'd ever seen.

"Thank you." He wanted professional, he'd get professional.

"I need a favor." Frank leaned in. "There're some documents in Jonny's office safe that would be better in my hands."

A favor in her book was bringing home milk or loaning someone five dollars, not breaking and entering.

"You have access to his office. Why don't—?"

"Because I'm asking you."

"No, I won't betray him and Eddie."

"Won't do as I ask, or don't want to go to jail for murder?"

Her heart banged against her ribs.

"Wednesday night Jonny will be at a dinner. I'll take care of Eddie, and with your skills it should be very easy."

Except that she wasn't a safecracker.

"I'll text you the combination. Don't screw up."

Frank turned and melted into the crowd. Her phone buzzed in her pocket a few seconds later and when she swiped the message a combination of four numbers appeared. Great. Now she could add burglary and betraying the two people who wanted to help her to her resume.

~ ~ ~

Jonny squinted against the dim lighting as Frank talked to Cheryl. He couldn't make out her expression, but her body language spoke volumes. Caution. Apprehension. Fear.

"Whaddya think that's about?" Jonny asked.

"Got no idea," Eddie said.

"Frank looks intense." He squinted against the strobe lights.

"Frank always looks intense, but she looks scared shitless."

"What could he be saying to her?" A chill shot up Jonny's spine. "You think he knows her?"

"Nah, Nicky and her pulled small time shit," Eddie said. "Way too under the radar to interest Frank."

When Jonny looked back to the main bar, Frank had left, and Cheryl was back making drinks like nothing happened.

Frank and Angela together could turn his life to shit without even breaking a sweat, but Frank and Cheryl together stirred up all kinds of unhealthy emotions. He massaged his temples to ease the ache over his left eye.

"Ease up. It'll all come together," Eddie said.

As long as it all didn't come crashing together on top of them.

Chapter 14

Money, guts, and a little luck created Beyond Paradise, and Jonny reveled in satisfaction as he sucked in a deep breath. The smell of fresh paint, shellac from the hardwood floors, and the rich, heady scent of Italian leather from the banquettes filled him with pride. The thirty-thousand-square-foot midtown space became his whole world. It meant a break from Frank and everything that kept him tethered to a world he no longer needed or wanted.

"We did it." He must've made his point, because he hadn't heard another word from Frank, and he wasn't a man who hid his opinions.

"Yeah," Eddie refilled their glasses with an aged Bourbon that would sell for eighty dollars a glass.

"Permits issued. Inspections waived. Simon Davis really came through."

They'd met earlier with the famous club promoter whom they intrigued with their ideas for fixing all the problems left by the former owner.

"The bouncers the security agency sent looked like a bunch of thugs," Eddie grumbled. "I want professionals, not guys who are gonna pop at the first sign of trouble."

"So call another agency. I want these guys vetted and trained well before we open." He checked his watch, already anticipating the formal dinner and the chance to promote his own club.

"Looks good, right?" He nudged Eddie as the construction crew raised the ornate mirror over the main bar. "Even Davis thinks we got a hit."

"Yeah, sure," Eddie mumbled.

"What the fuck is wrong with you? You're acting like somebody cut off your dick."

"We've never worked with a promotor before. Why now?"

"Maybe it's time."

Everybody in the business knew Simon Davis and the clubs he backed in Vegas, New York, and Miami.

"I just don't know why we're bringing someone else in on this."

Davis wants to invest in our concept and take it to LA, Chicago, Vegas." Jonny leaned in. "Do you know what that means?"

"Yeah, Frank will come down even harder."

"Frank was right. We were punks back then, but now we have powerful people behind us." He sipped the bourbon. "Don't you get it? Davis and his people don't want to deal with thugs like Frank. They want to deal with businessmen."

"You better tell Frank that 'cause he's a fuckin' psycho." Eddie gulped at the bourbon.

"Forget the shady deals and back alley arrangements." Jonny spread his arms wide. "We run our club like a corporation, with health insurance and pension plans, not like some after thought to wash Frank's money."

"And how do you see this going down?"

"I can't do the meetings on the docks and skimming money anymore." Jonny dragged his hand through his hair. "I wake up most nights in a fuckin' sweat, my heart pounding so hard I think I'm gonna die."

"You can't become a good guy overnight."

"Even Frank can't fight against big corporations and people with real power."

"Yeah sure, you're out popping champagne, and Frank's popping .45's."

"Why you gotta question everything?" He brushed Eddie off, not wanting to admit he'd had the same concern.

"Every time I come here, I expect to see it tossed." Eddie spit out the words as though he'd been holding them in way too long. "Frank's version of fuck you."

Eddie had an annoying knack for looking inside his brain and pissing on his dream. Still, Eddie's instincts saved his ass more than once, but this time he was wrong.

~ ~ ~

Later that night, Cheryl struggled to keep it together as she poured drinks, ran tabs, and blocked out everyone, but her nerves were as brittle as the swizzle sticks that decorated the drinks.

Frank called in his marker and made his request. Tonight, she'd do his bidding because disobeying Frank Barnett had serious consequences.

When Jonny stopped at the end of the service bar, she did a double take. His custom-made tux stole her breath.

"Hey." He leaned over the service side of the bar.

A hot flush heated her cheeks, and she busied herself with arranging the limes and lemons in the condiment tray.

His hand covered hers, then wrapped around her fingers.

After an awkward silence, she mumbled, "Hey."

Since their night together he'd invaded her dreams and her daily thoughts and now he stood in front of her looking like every woman's fantasy with just the right amount of quiet thoughtfulness to make her wonder. Was he feeling as anxious as her?

Still holding her hand, he guided her around the end of the bar until she stood in front of him.

"I didn't like the way things ended the other night." His eyes searching. "I can't get you out of my head."

Wow. Now he was reading her mind.

"I got an important dinner tonight, but after that, I'd like to see you."

Oh sure, right after I rob your safe. Guilt strangled the words right out of her.

"We need to talk," he said.

"Sure." While he went to his fancy dinner, she'd play a role that came way too easy.

Thief.

Chapter 15

The hotel lobby of the Marquis overflowed with tuxedos and evening gowns. Jonny already spotted the mayor, a senator, and a few A-list celebrities trying to avoid prying questions from the press. Security corralled the paparazzi outside, but they were elbowing each other to get a prime shot through the floor-to-ceiling, plate-glass windows of the entryway.

He hustled his way toward the elevators taking people to the rooftop ballroom, but it was slow going. Velvet ropes sectioned off the elevator banks, with valets counting off the exact amount of people that could fit in each elevator. They didn't want the cream of New York society crammed in like cattle shoulder to shoulder.

He maneuvered himself into one of the elevators alongside an elderly matron squeezed into a beaded dress at least two sizes too small and a skinny, hook-nosed woman who ogled him as though he were a hot fudge sundae. In less than a minute, the elevator ascended the thirty floors. The few seconds allowed him time to smooth the front of his tux and check his tie in the mirrored walls.

Exiting the elevator, he moved among more of New York's elite. Some he recognized as regulars of the Paradise, although most averted their eyes. Amazing how when they were guests at his club they jockeyed for his attention. He adjusted the knot of his tie again and wished the whole night was over. Crowds made him claustrophobic, even at the club, he always carved out a little space of his own.

The room shimmered with tiny lights of green, purple, and hot pink in what he guessed was a Mardi Gras theme. Centerpieces spilled over with tropical flowers in all colors, and uniformed men and women wore masquerade masks as they circulated with silver trays of champagne and hor-d'oeuvres. It amazed him the ways the rich found to waste their money. People were everywhere, either clustered in conversation or milling around trying to find their table.

"Jonny?"

He turned to the familiar voice.

"I'm sure I'm not who you were looking for."

"Angela." He twisted his lips. "Where's your boyfriend, Frank?"

"Don't sound so defensive." She fingered the diamond-encrusted necklace clasped around her neck. "He treats me good."

"What do you want?" The hard edge of his voice made her eyes narrow.

"Listen." She looked over her shoulder, then touched the sleeve of his tux. "Frank's talking about you and . . ."

"What kinda game are you playing now?"

"I won't deny I would've enjoyed you getting a good beat down, but he's gone way beyond—"

"And you're trying to help me?"

"Just be careful."

Angela's cryptic warning made him uneasy, as he threaded his way to his table, but he brushed it off as another attempt at the drama she loved so much. He stopped to survey the crowd, and the smell of sweet perfume made his stomach curl. The elaborate mirrored bar called to him, but he had too much at stake, and too much to accomplish tonight to let alcohol get in the way.

"Hey Jonny, over here." Frank waved him over to a table only a few feet away.

"Fuck," Jonny mumbled.

He let his gaze slide over the table. Frank sat next to some cheap hoods and women that were definitely paid for, except for Angela who nailed him with a steely glare. He marveled at the irony. The deadly and uncivilized masquerading as well-bred elite. Maybe this party theme wasn't so outrageous.

Frank stood, slapped him on the back, and pulled out a vacant chair next to him. "Have a seat, relax."

He wanted to tell Frank to fuck off, but he had to stay and fight for the one thing that mattered. His independence. Frank's firm hold forced him down. "Sit."

Feeling like a trained dog made his eye twitch.

"You think you don't need me anymore?" Frank sneered. "That you're too good for us?"

A few years ago he would've been thrilled to sit at this table with them, but now he knew them for what they were—a bunch of cheap thugs who hung out with pros. So yeah, he did think he was too good for them.

"I don't know what you're talking about."

"Buying that club was a big mistake." Frank pressed his forearm harder.

The other three goons were busy entertaining the hookers, but Angela just stared at him. Her jaw so tight he could almost hear her teeth grinding.

"But I'll give you one more chance to let me in on it." Frank smiled. "What do you say, partners?"

He leaned into Frank's ear and whispered, "Go fuck yourself."

Jonny yanked his arm free and stood. Frank stood with him and clamped his hand around his shoulder and squeezed. "Think you're a tough guy, huh?"

A flicker of a warning flashed through Jonny's brain. Frank usually played it cool, especially in a room full of people he wanted to impress.

"You think you're fooling everybody?" Frank shoved him, his voice laced with malice just loud enough for Jonny to hear. “Screwing that hot piece Cheryl.” Frank raised an eyebrow. “I understand she’s got a pussy that’s so juicy . . .”

Jonny slammed his fist into the side of Frank’s jaw then braced himself for a retaliation that never came. When Frank smiled full out and rubbed at his jaw, another warning bell rang in Jonny’s head. This night was about to go straight to hell.

He sensed other people around them mumbling comments, but he stayed focused on Frank until security guards broke through the circle of onlookers and flanked Jonny on each side. What a joke. The guards had guns that never left the holster strapped around their bulging guts.

“This man attacked me.” Frank addressed the guards, his beady eyes bright with superiority.

One of the guards grabbed his arm, and Jonny pivoted out of his hold. “Don’t fuckin’ touch me.”

“As you can see, he’s very violent.” Frank smirked.

“I don’t want any trouble sir, but you’ll have to leave,” one guard insisted as the other moved behind him.

Frank set him up. And he fell for it.

“You need to leave, sir.” The guard repeated.

His hands were balled into tight fists, and his insides were raw with frustration. “Fuck off. I’m going.”

He stormed out with the two guards close behind him. He picked the express elevator to the lobby, then vented his anger on the button. His heart pounded so hard he could feel it in his throat. He fought for control, but . . . fuck, he wanted to slam something hard. Anything to get rid of this ball of frustration burning the pit of his stomach.

The guards stayed at his back like he was an escaped convict until he entered the elevator. He pushed the lobby button and flipped them off seconds before the doors whooshed closed.

His phone buzzed, he checked the screen, and saw six missed calls from Max.

Swiping the screen, he barked into the phone. "What the hell do you want?"

"Eddie's been beat, bad."

His head spun. He reached for the elevator wall, and his balance returned.

"Get to the club," Max said. We brought him to the apartment, but he don't look good."

"Call Doc Henderson."

Chapter 16

Jonny entered the club from the rear entrance, not wanting to engage in conversation or any distractions. He pushed through the stairwell door then vaulted up the stairs with two things on his mind. Get money from the office safe to insure the doctor's silence, then check on Eddie.

He pulled out the office key and the knob turned under his hand. The door to the office should've been locked. Him and Eddie were the only two with a key. He eased into the room and his eyes adjusted enough to see a shadow crouched by the safe in the corner.

He flipped the wall switch, and the shadow jerked to a standing position, as he squinted against the glaring light. "Looking for something?"

Cheryl's expression confused him. Fear? No, relief.

Her silence prodded him into the room. "You must be pretty good. That safe is state-of-the-art. A nuclear bomb couldn't open it."

She'd played him again, and he fell for it. Goddamn how those pouty lips of hers lied so perfectly.

"It's not what it looks like."

"It looks like you're trying to fuckin' steal from me." Her cock teasing tongue flicked over her bottom lip, but he kept his focus on the open safe behind her.

"I'm sorry."

He couldn't ignore the way the words Paradise Lounge on her white tank top rose and fell against her breasts as she heaved in a deep breath.

"If you were looking for money, you would've been disappointed." He flicked his fingers toward the safe. "All that's in there is petty cash and receipts. The good stuff is in a much safer place."

Only him and Eddie knew about the safe they'd installed under the floor boards of the closet. The flash of her eyes told him that maybe money wasn't her motive, so he pushed the envelope a little further.

"But you could've just asked. Would've been a lot easier than sneaking around in the dark."

He should've been pissed. Anybody else, male or female and he would've had them pinned against the desk with their hands behind their backs. But when he looked at her everything went sideways.

She shoved the pen light into her pocket and held out her hands. "I didn't take anything, so can we just forget I was ever here?"

Probably not. Especially since he dreamt of having her under him again. Naked. Her taut nipples rubbing up against his bare chest. The way her pupils darkened when she came, with her nails scrapping down his back. And now he had the image of her bent over his desk with that heart shaped ass begging him to grab on and—

"Yeah, sure." This woman had turned him into an idiot.

Surprise flickered across her face, but her shoulders remained tense, and then it all came together. She wasn't doing this for her.

He stared at her until her eyes softened to the point of tears. Then she crumbled like she hated herself. He wanted to fuck it all and haul her to him. No questions asked, just the two of them, gone.

~ ~ ~

"Did this have something to do with your conversation with Frank last night?" Jonny asked.

Cheryl fought for control. A way to school her features and not give away Frank's plan. Not act like a freaking amateur on her first job. It should've been easy. In and out. What was he even doing here? She'd seen him leave earlier in his drop-dead gorgeous tux, but he'd only been gone an hour. Who gets all dressed up for an hour?

"No, it had to do with me needing money," she murmured. "And falling back on what I am."

He inched closer.

"A thief?" he whispered.

Logical question, but his voice held none of the accusation or indignation one would expect from someone being robbed.

The fact that she hadn't gotten what she came for was irrelevant. She'd broken into his office and tampered with his safe. She probably should've mentioned that the lock on his office door was shit easy to bust, but the state-of-the-art safe impressed her. Maybe that's why he wasn't concerned about the door.

Even from across the room she ached for him. The erratic way her blood raced hot through her veins, and her desire to be closer to him overpowered all logic and sense. Sick and twisted just like the plan itself.

He closed the distance between them, and she sidestepped bumping her hip on the corner of his desk. The momentary detour placed him directly in front of her. Again, the spicy scent of his cologne surrounded her. Making her weak from the inside out. And for that split second, she wanted to fall into his arms and have him hold her again. Confess everything and just escape. The two of them, gone.

He stroked the underside of her jaw. "Someday you're going to tell me all your secrets."

His expression threw her off balance. Not anger or pity, but . . . Disappointment?

They'd already had sex. Hot, wild, sheet gripping sex and yet she shuddered under his gaze. The sting of hot tears and a choking in her throat cut off her words.

He lifted her chin and brushed her lips with a kiss softer than she deserved.

"But right now I got bigger problems."

He stepped away from her, and she immediately missed him in her space. Across the office, he opened up a closet, crouched down, and shifted some things on the floor. Tumblers fell into place and a metal latch released. When he stood a few minutes later, he clutched a stack of banded bills. Impressive.

Was it possible Frank didn't know about that safe? She guessed someone so ruthless would know everyone's secrets. And now she'd have to explain her failure to a man who definitely didn't take no for an answer.

"Eddie's been beaten up." He held up the money. "This should take care of the doctor." Then shoved the money into his tuxedo pocket.

"What happened?" She followed him out of the office, and up the flight of stairs.

"I don't know." He threw over his shoulder. "You better stay in my room tonight."

When they entered the apartment her cell phone vibrated. The caller ID showed the now familiar number. She hung back as Jonny entered the living room and fired questions at Max.

"Hello."

"You were unsuccessful tonight, right?" Frank rasped through the phone.

She glanced over her shoulder expecting to see him standing behind her.

"Right."

"He caught you in the act?"

"Right, again." Totally fucking creepy.

"Perfect."

"Excuse me?"

"There's nothing valuable in that safe." Frank sighed with contentment. "But if I know Jonny he'll want to come to your rescue now more than ever."

"But . . .?"

"He likes to fix women, and you're about as broken as they come." Frank paused. "And now I assume he's focused on Eddie?"

"You know about Eddie getting beat up?"

He barked out a harsh laugh. "I had to keep him out of that office somehow."

The words caught in her throat and she gripped the doorframe to steady herself.

"That was just a test, and you passed." Frank drew in a deep breath. "The next time will be for real."

The phone disconnected, but she kept it at her ear unable to fully process what just went down. He'd sent her to Jonny's office knowing she'd get caught *and* had Eddie beat up. If she ever doubted Frank's power, she was a believer now.

Chapter 17

Jonny entered the apartment over the club and found Max pacing the living room, and Bambi hunched on the couch crying while clutching a bottle of vodka. Cheryl's phone rang, and she hung back as he approached Max.

"What the hell happened?" Jonny loosened his tie, shucked off his tuxedo jacket, and threw it over a chair.

Max stopped pacing and blew out a long breath. "He was leaving the club and . . ."

"They kept hitting him and hitting him . . ." Bambi pushed herself off the couch, tugged at the hem of her micro mini skirt, and crossed the room. The vodka she'd consumed had her clinging to Jonny's arm for support.

He looked over her shoulder, and Max continued, "They ambushed him in the . . ."

"I was with him." Bambi sobbed. "It was so scary."

"Will you shut the hell up!" Max yelled.

"Don't tell me to shut up," Bambi slurred.

"Both of you, knock it off." Jonny snatched the bottle from her hand. "How much of this did she have?"

"She was freaking out. I had to give her something to calm her down."

"You didn't have to give her the whole damn bottle."

Jonny motioned Bambi toward the couch. "Go sit down and be quiet." He handed the bottle off to Max and massaged his forehead. "Now tell me what happened."

"They ambushed him in the parking lot. Fucked him up bad." He pointed toward the bedroom. "Doc just got here."

Dr. Steven Henderson, the youngest cardiac surgeon at New York Medical Center. A rock star in the medical field, with an addiction to poker. Jonny let him sit in on their private games and Steven took care of the occasional medical emergency discreetly.

Jonny stalked to the bedroom, not liking the sound of fear in Max's voice. He entered just as the doctor cut away Eddie's T-shirt. The harsh ceiling light magnified the red welts on his ribcage.

He stood on the other side of the bed, nodded to the doctor, then looked at Eddie. His right eye and jawline were swollen and bruised, and his tight fists clenched the bedsheets.

"How're you doing?"

"Those fuckers are gonna pay." Eddie's rage shot through his pain.

Steven's gaze darted between him and Eddie, then he moved the stethoscope along Eddie's ribcage.

"Try to relax." Jonny patted Eddie's shoulder.

Steven pulled the stethoscope away from his ears and anchored it around his neck. "It would be best if you waited outside."

"Forget it, I'm staying."

The doc wasn't pleased, but no way was he leaving.

"I know you're in pain," Steven said, "but try to tell me what you're feeling."

"I can't breathe . . . feel like I got a truck sitting on my chest." Eddie wheezed through blood-crusted lips.

"Can you tell me how this happened?"

"They busted me up with a bat."

"A baseball bat?" Steven asked.

"Yeah," Eddie rasped.

"Who?" Jonny asked between clenched teeth.

"Hired muscle." Eddie stiffened as another spasm shot through him. "Frank's guys."

Jonny slammed his fist against the wall. "Fuckin' bastards."

Steven jumped, then stared at him.

"What're you looking at me?" Jonny snapped, frustration coiling through him. "He's in pain. Do something."

Steven quickly opened his medical bag and laid out the necessary instruments. He slipped the stethoscope into his ears and ran it along Eddie's chest again.

Jonny shifted a few times, then popped the top button of his shirt. "What's wrong with him?"

He couldn't tell if Steven was ignoring him or intent on listening to Eddie's chest. After another minute, he moved closer. "I said, what's wrong with him?"

Steven removed the stethoscope. "He appears to be suffering from pneumothorax caused by severe trauma to the chest area."

"You're gonna have to speak English, Doc."

"I believe that one of his ribs has punctured the lung. The air escaping from the lung is causing the pain, but without an x-ray . . ." Steven frowned. "He should be in a hospital."

The docs calm demeanor grated on his nerves. "Can you fix it?"

"I'll have to insert a needle into his chest cavity to relieve the pressure and expel the air. It should equalize the lung pressure, so he can breathe easier."

Cutting a hole and sticking a needle into somebody's chest sounded drastic.

"There could be an infection or other complications under these circumstances," Steven said.

"I know you're trying to cover your ass, but I don't give a shit about circumstances. All I want to know is, can you patch him up, and is he gonna be all right?"

"He's young and in decent shape, so I would say his chances are good."

"Then do it," Jonny growled.

He stayed glued to Steven's side. He probably hated being watched so closely, but too bad. The whole procedure lasted about twenty minutes, but Eddie's breathing smoothed out, and he appeared to be resting easier. Then he injected Eddie with a shot for the pain, cleaned up his cuts, repacked his bag, and snapped it shut. "I'll come by tomorrow to check on him."

He suspected Steven's profession taught him to play it close and tight. Luckily, he didn't have the same gift at the poker table. Jonny peeled off some of the banded money from the safe and handed it to him.

"You do that."

After Steven left, Jonny lowered the lights and stood by his friend's bedside. Eddie could be reckless, doing crazy shit, a different girl in his bed every night, but he'd been there for him more times than he could remember, and Eddie was the only one he'd want covering his back.

"Don't worry. Frank's not gonna get away with this one."

Every raspy breath Eddie sucked in reminded him of Frank's hold on them.

"How's he doing?" Max asked the minute Jonny entered the living room.

Jonny slammed a tumbler onto the granite bar top and grabbed a bottle of Jack Daniels off the glass shelf behind him. He splashed some into the glass and glanced around the room. "Where's Cheryl?"

"How the hell do I know." Max scowled on the other side of the bar. "Is Eddie gonna be all right?"

Jonny slugged back the whiskey, placed his palms on the cool stone, and hung his head between his arms. The whiskey hit his empty stomach, then seeped into his veins. A flash of Cheryl's hopeless expression mingled with Eddie's raspy breathing.

"Is he conscience?" Max ventured.

"I think he's gonna be okay," Jonny said as much to himself as Max.

"This is fucked up." Max poured some of the whiskey into his own glass.

Jonny reached for the bottle. Eddie's blood stained the cuff of his white shirt. He twisted the faucet at the bar sink and held his hands under the hot water until it scalded him.

"Frank did this." He wiped his hands on the towel, and poured another shot for him and Max. "He wants a fight, fine. I've got resources I haven't even touched yet."

"Like?" Max slid onto one of the bar stools and swirled the amber liquid around his glass.

"Like my friends in Miami." Jonny downed the liquor. "Carlos hates sharing the profits from the South Beach club with Frank as much as we do."

Three years ago, Frank acquired a run-down strip club in South Beach as payment for a gambling debt. Jonny and Eddie helped the manager, Carlos Vega, transform the place from a drug-infested hangout to an upscale hotspot on Ocean Drive. Over the years Jonny formed a close friendship with Carlos based on mutual respect and shared heritage.

Max leaned his forearms on the bar. "You want to involve those crazy ass Cubans?"

"Hey, watch your mouth, All American Boy." Jonny leaned in. "Or did you forget I'm half Cuban?"

"Sorry." Max threw up his hands. "I meant I don't think we should be getting others involved in our business."

"You got a better idea?" Jonny waved the glass in his direction. "Carlos and his guys would back us in a minute if it meant breaking away from Frank."

"And what about his nephew, Alejandro?" Max mumbled into his glass. "Drugs, getting arrested, doing stupid shit."

"Big fuckin' deal. He sounds like half the people we know." Jonny narrowed his eyes. "You got something else to say?"

"Frank ain't foolin' around, Jonny." Max placed his glass on the bar.

"Fuck Frank," Jonny shouted.

"He can hurt you." Max removed his jacket, exposing the fear and anxiety seeping through his shirt. "He can hurt all of us."

"Eddie's in there all busted up, can't breathe, and your answer is to roll over?"

"At least he is breathing," Max shouted. "You keep this shit up, and they'll be fishing all of us outta the East River."

Jonny's heart skipped a beat. Max never lost it, but now his eyes were darting from side to side, his usual somber expression on edge and animated.

Silence hung between them. The ticking of the wall clock over the bar clicked off the seconds.

Max ran his hand over the smooth granite. "I didn't mean nothing."

"Forget it. It's been a fucked-up night." He came around the bar and held Max's gaze for an extra second. "You can go if you want. I'll stay with him."

"Nah, I'll stay. In case you need anything."

Jonny went back to the bedroom, dropped into the overstuffed chair and propped his feet up on the end of Eddie's bed.

"Geez, you look as bad as I feel," Eddie rasped.

Jonny slid his feet off the bed and leaned forward in the chair. "How're you doin'?"

"Hurts like a bitch." Eddie dragged in a breath.

"I guess Frank doesn't like our disrespect." His voice vibrated with sarcasm.

"Frank better watch his ass, 'cause when I find him . . ." Eddie winced in pain.

"Take it easy." Jonny gulped more of the whiskey. "Try to get some sleep."

"You gonna sit up in that chair all night?"

"Well, I ain't getting in there with you. So shut up and go to sleep."

Jonny leaned into the chair, and a few minutes later Eddie's shallow, steady breathing filled the room.

Chapter 18

"Fuck."

Jonny blinked a few times to adjust to the dim room.

"Goddamn," Eddie grumbled.

"What the hell are you doing?" Jonny bolted out of the chair to find the bedside lamp in pieces on the floor and Eddie clutching his side with one hand while holding onto the bedpost for support with the other.

"I tried to get up," Eddie croaked. "I gotta take a leak."

"Why didn't you call me?"

"You were sleeping." Eddie shifted his weight to the end table. "I didn't wanna bother you."

"So you smashed the lamp on the floor instead?" He braced his arm under Eddie's shoulder.

"Never did like that lamp."

"What's going on?" Max stood in the doorway, his shirt tails out, rubbing his eyes.

"Help me get him to the bathroom, before he wrecks the whole damn place."

Max screwed up his face.

"Don't worry asshole. I'm not gonna ask you to hold my dick."

"Very funny." Max supported Eddie's other side.

"Geez, that's an image I didn't need," Jonny said.

"Shit, don't make me laugh." Eddie wheezed. "It hurts too damn much."

When they reached the bathroom, Eddie leaned on the doorjamb. "I think I can take it from here."

"If you can't, I'll call up one of your harem women." Max nudged Jonny as they waited outside. "Or maybe Bambi could give you a hand."

"Even with a busted rib and a punctured lung, I'd be able to get more than you," Eddie called through the door.

"Keep dreaming," Max called back.

When they got Eddie back to bed, Jonny stacked the pillows behind him to make it more comfortable for him to sit up.

"Damn," Eddie slowly lifted his legs onto the bed.

"You want a shot of Jack?" Max offered.

"Bring in the bottle." Jonny suspected he'd need that and a lot more tonight.

Max returned with the bottle, handed a shot to Eddie, then refilled Jonny's glass before setting it down on the table.

Eddie downed the shot, eased into the pillows, and sighed. "That should make friends with the pain meds and take the edge off."

"You want us to go?" Jonny asked.

"Nah, talk a while." Eddie shifted on the bed. "How was the dinner?"

Jonny sunk into the bedside chair and searched his brain for a way to put the night into words.

"What happened?" Eddie asked.

Jonny drained the rest of his drink and refilled his glass. "Frank pushed; I pushed back. It was a total fuck up. He set me up good."

He left out Cheryl breaking into their office. No sense giving Eddie more to worry about especially since he didn't even know how he felt about it.

Max perched his bulk on the edge of the straight-backed chair on the other side of the bed. "I told Jonny I think we should back off for a while, maybe . . ."

"And I told you." Jonny narrowed his eyes. "We're not backing off."

Eddie and Max exchanged looks, and he sensed a problem.

"Since when did you ever back down from a fight?" Jonny challenged Eddie.

"I'm sayin' we gotta be careful." Eddie pushed himself higher on the bed.

"Careful? What kind of bullshit is that?"

"I got a fuckin' hole in my chest, and I feel like I'm sucking air outta a goddamn straw," Eddie wheezed. "So yeah, careful." He touched his side and groaned.

Jonny sighed. "All right." He didn't want Eddie all worked up but being careful was not the answer.

Max's cell buzzed. He checked the ID, then canceled the call. Two seconds later it buzzed again, and Jonny joked, "Domestic problems."

"Something like that." Max stood, swiped at the phone, and left the room.

A few minutes later Max came back still staring at his phone.

"Hey, lover boy, what's the matter, bad breakup?" Eddie joked.

Max shoved the phone into his pocket. "Crazy bitch."

"I would think an ass like hers would make you forgive anything." Jonny laughed.

"Shit, this one must've worked you over," Eddie teased.

"Most of the women he hooks up with are like hurricanes," Jonny said. "They start off blowing and sucking, then, in the end, they just take your house."

"Ahh, fuck man." Eddie held his side. "I told you not to make me laugh."

"Yeah, and since when have you been with Bambi?"

"Since I saw her giving you head in your office," Eddie smirked.

"You said she was a slut who screwed everybody." Jonny laughed.

"Exactly, how could I pass that up?" Eddie attempted a laugh, then groaned in pain. "Wasn't long ago you were hitting the same spot. Now you're thinking sideways."

"I know what I'm doing." Jonny ran his finger around the rim of his glass.

"Just make sure what you're doing is for the right reason." Eddie stifled a yawn.

~ ~ ~

An hour later, Jonny pushed himself out of the chair. The twitching of his legs made it impossible to sit any longer. He left Eddie with Max, stepped into the hall, and his gaze fell on the other closed bedroom door.

He should've kept walking down the hall, through the living room and right out of the apartment, but instead, he stopped and stared at the closed door. Cheryl answered after the first knock. Eyes hooded as if she'd failed at fighting off sleep.

She opened the door wide enough for him to slip in. "How's Eddie?"

He did a quick appraisal. Bed still made, TV off. She must've been sitting in the chair staring at the wall all this time.

"He's gonna be fine."

"Good," she whispered, then another awkward silence followed.

"I'm heading back to the penthouse."

She nodded, then her eyes met his. "I really am sorry about—"

"I don't know what the fuck is wrong with me." He ran his fingers through his hair. "I should stay far away from you, but I can't."

She mashed her lips together, and all he could think about was how they felt against his neck. "You've tried to con me, steal from me and I know you're lying to me about something, but hell if I understand it. I can't get enough of you."

"I feel the same thing."

Somehow her hand had gotten into his chest and squeezed his heart. He had no fuckin' clue what he was doing. He just knew that he wanted to be the person that made her safe. He wanted to crush her to him and protect her. He snatched up her hand and pulled her behind him. Her steps were cautious and careful like the slightest misstep would make him abandon her.

Silence filled the SUV and continued up the private elevator and into the foyer of his penthouse. Her suppressed panic crowded the room, and radiated onto him, filling his chest with a fear that made him dread her story.

He walked her to the sofa and sat next to her. "I want you to tell me what's really going on with you."

"Nothing."

"I can help you, if you let me."

"I don't need help."

He pulled at the collar of his starched shirt. He couldn't force an answer out of her. "Are you hungry?"

"No."

"'Cause I can order up some food from the all-night place on the corner."

"No really, I'm fine," she assured him.

"They got all kinds of stuff. Pizza, pasta, maybe some—"

"Frank killed Nicky."

Chapter 19

"What?"

"I was so scared." She rubbed her palms on her thighs. "I couldn't believe he did it."

She bit her lip. Blurting out that secret put them both at risk.

"Nicky was hitting me, so I stabbed him and ran. I felt guilty and when I went back I saw Frank slit his throat."

"With the same knife you used?"

She stared at her hands, and he nudged her chin up with his forefinger. She'd already said too much and involved Jonny just as Frank had predicted.

"And now Frank's trying to pin it on you."

She shivered and Jonny slipped his arm around her shoulders and eased her against the sofa cushions. A few hours ago he'd caught her in his private office trying to steal from him, and yet he still wanted to help her.

"I had no idea you and Eddie worked for him or I never would've come here."

"You were the victim." He caressed her arm.

"He made me break into your office, but the whole thing was a set up to test me. I feel so stupid."

"He used you for his own messed-up reasons."

"I've wrecked everything." Guilt burned her throat.

He pressed his finger to her lips. "Shush."

She shivered again, and he cradled her to him. "And he had Eddie beat up too," she mumbled against his chest.

"I know." He stroked the curve of her jaw, then stood taking her with him. "You're safe now."

He paused when they entered his bedroom, his expression mirrored her confusion.

She pressed against his muscular chest remembering every inch of it until she could feel the heat radiating off him. "We always end up like this. You making me feel safe."

He nibbled that special spot below her ear, then peeled her shirt up, tossed it to the floor, and pushed at the waist of her skirt until it fell from her hips. Lifting her, he settled her onto the bed cupping her breast. When he sucked the soft flesh into his mouth, she sighed her approval. Then his teeth tugged on her nipple mixing sweet pain with pleasure. He licked and nipped at her until she squirmed under him. Needing more but never wanting him to stop this delicious torture.

"I hope you're ready, baby." He yanked off his shirt. "'Cause I'm pretty sure one time isn't gonna be enough."

"I'm ready for whatever you've got."

He pulled away from her breast and placed his hands on each side of her head. His biceps bulged as he hovered over her. She moaned deep in her throat when he grabbed her lips with his teasing and sucking deeper and deeper. Her fingers groped between them, and she fumbled with the button and zipper of his pants. He lifted his hips and she pushed away the material, his hard length pressing against her stomach. A moan vibrated from deep inside his chest, and she clutched at his hips guiding him to her. He nudged her thighs wider, and when she wrapped them around his hips, he slid inside her tight, wet walls.

"Fuck, baby. Ain't nothing better," he rasped against her neck.

He drove deep, and she cried out hanging on to him like a drowning woman in a tempestuous storm.

"Don't worry, I've got you, and I'm never letting go."

Slipping his hand between them, Jonny pressed her nub between his thumb and forefinger and she rocked her hips, her pulse thumping in her ears. Weightless and floating, all the strain and stress of the last few days drifted away on a beautiful cloud of blissed out pleasure.

"Oh God, Jonny," she whimpered as the waves hit.

"So beautiful, so fuckin' beautiful."

Jonny ripped at the sheets under her head. "Feel me taking you?" he snarled, with another thrust of his hips, then another, until he swelled and stretched her in the most perfect way. "Nobody else can make you feel that." With a breathless gasp and one last thrust, he collapsed at her side.

"That was . . ." she panted.

"It sure was." He tugged her closer. Stared into her eyes. "Baby, we're just getting started."

~ ~ ~

The dampness of the alley coated her skin. "You stupid bitch, you're not going anywhere," Nicky threatened. The smack of his hand against her cheek. The glint of the knife in the halogen lights. The lifeless, limp body sprawled before her. Only it wasn't Nicky's face staring back at her, it was Jonny's.

Cheryl bolted upright in the bed. Her heart pounded against her chest, her gaze darted around the room searching for something familiar. Jonny must've closed the drapes during the night because little shards of daylight peeked through the heavy fabric.

After their perfect night, she hated that this hellish part of her life invaded their time. She'd hoped after telling the truth, the nightmares would cease, but her mind had other ideas. A single bead of sweat crept down her bare back as she forced herself to calm down.

Him waking next to a woman who couldn't breathe without gasping was not what she had in mind for the morning after. Of course, the more she fought it, the harder her heart thumped.

She zeroed in on the sheet draped over his muscular back and shoulders as she fought to control her breathing.

"Hey." He raised his head a few inches off the pillow. "You all right?" His voice was rough from sleep and sex, his thick, dark hair a contrast against the crisp white pillowcase.

"Yeah, fine." Her response sounded tinny and fake, and she hoped his sleepy mind would miss her anxious edge.

He propped himself up and stroked her arm. "What's wrong?" He blinked the sleep from his perceptive eyes.

"Sometimes I have dreams." She looked away, so he wouldn't see the fear. "More like nightmares." She fisted the sheets tighter in her sweaty palms.

"Dreams can't hurt you." Enveloping her in his arms, he held her tight, and she knew he could feel the erratic beat of her heart. "No one can hurt you. I'm here."

She swiped at her tears. She'd spent years caring for her brother, Dylan, and Nicky through all his messes, but Jonny was the first one to calm her, soothe her, take away her pain. Her breathing slowed, and her heart, although still racy, stopped skipping every other beat.

He stacked the pillows behind them, then leaned back with her in his arms. "You get these a lot?"

"What, nightmares?" She feared he would somehow figure out the horrible end of this particular nightmare.

"No, panic attacks." He continued to stroke her arms as he held her.

How had he guessed her secret, and what now? Should she admit or deny it?

"Can't catch your breath?" He stopped stroking her arm and looked into her eyes. "Feel like you're coming apart."

He handed her a bottle of water off the bedside table. "Here, drink this."

The cool water soothed her dry throat, as she eased against the pillows.

"I got a thing about small places," he admitted. "Elevators, cramped, tight places."

"Claustrophobia?"

"And I'm not a big fan of the dark either."

"You— Afraid of the dark?"

"Yeah." He kissed his way down her neck and the cleft of her breasts. "I thought I'd never hold you again."

He checked the bedside clock. "It's only eight o'clock. Much too early to get up."

She cuddled into his firm, protective embrace.

"My scars are physical, but the ones you carry around up here are just as bad. He grazed her forehead with soft kisses. "When your brain gets a chance to relax, the nightmares will go away. You're with me now. No more worries."

His words made sense, and she prayed he was right. Her mind was so overloaded and stressed, it needed some time to heal. "Hold me tighter," she whispered against his chest.

A few hours later she awoke to a buzzing, then cool air hit her back as Jonny rolled away from her. Still half asleep, he fumbled with his phone on the nightstand. He mumbled a few words, then disconnected the phone.

"Is everything all right?" she asked.

"Eddie's doing better. Max is taking him back here to his penthouse." Jonny tossed the phone on the bed. "I'm going into the kitchen to get us something to eat."

She enjoyed the rearview as he pulled on a pair of sweat pants and moved toward the door.

She threw back the downy soft sheet, amazed how he kept them so white and fresh. Maybe he replaced them monthly. She chuckled at the extravagance, but he obviously spent on linens what most people made in a week.

Her bare feet sunk into the plush, dove gray carpet, and the cool air conditioning kissed her bare skin. Her clothes were in a crumpled, heap where he'd discarded them the night before. The bright sunlight streaking through the windows reflected against the chrome of the bar that sat in the far corner of the bedroom. Light and dark shades of gray mixed with accents of lilac.

She marveled at the smoked glass cabinet dominating the opposite wall. It stood just above her waist, and she assumed it was a media center of sorts. The tinted glass made it impossible to see in, so she moved closer, and pushed one of the buttons on the side. The cabinet hummed, and the largest flat screen TV she'd ever seen emerged from within, then roared to life.

"Ohhh, shit." She punched at the buttons, and the TV shut off and descended back into the cabinet. She sighed with relief and moved toward the bathroom, making a mental note not to push any more unknown buttons.

Spying the fluffy white robe, she removed it from a hook. It hung to her mid-calf, and even after cinching the tie and rolling up the sleeves a few times, it still swallowed her up. She flipped the collar up and inhaled the scent of his spicy, woodsy cologne and soap.

Aside from a few bottles of cologne and some decorative pieces, also in lilac and gray, there was no clutter or mess on the granite counter tops. The glass enclosed shower had no water spots and appeared unused. His obvious neatness intimidated her since she leaned more toward messy. Okay, she was a slob. Clothes thrown all over, make-up and hair products fighting each other for counter space, with a few wet towels thrown on the floor.

Leaving the bathroom, she peeked into his closet. Stepping over the threshold, a light switched on, and she gawked at the racks and racks of suits, dress shirts, casual shirts, and pants and jeans. After a few hesitant steps into what could pass as a boutique men's clothing store, she ran her hand over the cherry wood shelves that held rows of shoes. She touched the cuffs of cashmere jackets and fine linen shirts and fantasized about having a female version of this closet.

Peeking out from under the clothes, she spied a black and white striped cat. "Hey, pretty girl." She bent, scooped her up, and examined her scars.

Leaving the closet, she was drawn to the bookcase suspended in the corner where the windows met. She jostled the cat to her left side and lifted a book off the shelf. She ran her hand over the smooth leather binding, then cracked the book and sniffed.

"I thought I was the only one who sniffed books."

She snapped the book shut, cheek's warming at being caught in the act.

He moved to her side and caressed the cat's fur. "I see you met Killer."

"Killer?" She laughed.

"She had a rough start, so I gave her the name to boost her confidence." He smiled. "She usually spits at the women I bring home."

A cat with very good taste. This might just work.

"You like to read?" he asked.

"I love to read. Are these limited editions?"

"My decorator insisted it's the way to go."

"Do you have a favorite?" She let the cat jump out of her arms.

He leaned over her to retrieve a book from a higher shelf, and she admired the thin line of fine hairs that disappeared into his low-slung sweatpants.

"*Julius Caesar.*"

"Makes sense." She fanned through the book then closed it. "This leather binding is in such good shape."

"When I can't sleep at night, I read." He replaced the book, then wrapped his arm around her waist. "But I had no trouble sleeping last night."

"Me neither." A heat crept up her spine along with a hi-def image of him hovering over her, muscles bulging, just begging to be nipped.

He pulled her against his bare chest and smiled. "A beautiful, sexy woman who likes to read. I think I hit the jackpot."

"Me too."

Who was this gorgeous man who said all the right words, rescued animals, read the classics, and had knife fights on the docks?

Chapter 20

On the middle of the bed, Cheryl spotted a large tray with a carafe of coffee, a pitcher of cream, plates of fruit, pastries, and bagels, a tub of what appeared to be gourmet cream cheese, and a platter of smoked salmon.

Her stomach growled, and she smiled to cover her embarrassment. "I guess I am hungry."

"I didn't know what you liked, so I put out everything." Jonny hit her with a sheepish smile, like he was uncomfortable being caught doing something nice.

"I like it all, but you didn't have to do . . ."

"Sit, eat. After what you've been through, you need someone to take care of you."

A warm, contented sensation swelled in her chest as she gathered the folds of the robe, tucked her legs under her, and sat on the bed. She plucked some grapes from their vine. Relaxing for the first time in days, she loved the way his biceps flexed when he poured their coffee into heavy ceramic mugs. His sleep-mussed hair fell in ebony swirls over his forehead in a very sexy way.

She reached for four sugar packets, and he laughed.

"A little coffee with your sugar?"

"Do you always have this much breakfast food?"

He tilted his head. "The answer is no. Very few women have seen this penthouse."

"Really?" She wiggled her brow. "Cause I saw a few of those women."

"Sometimes it got a little intense." He threw his palms up in defense.

"I mean, how many women have you been with?" She kept her voice light, then realized she didn't want the answer.

"At one time?" He grinned.

"Soooo, you've been with more than one woman at a time?"

"Hell yeah." He paused, testing her reaction. "But those days are over."

She thrilled at his admission, but still pressed him. "You just happened to have all this food today?"

"After you fell asleep I called my housekeeper, and she stocked the refrigerator."

"Housekeeper, huh? Does she wear a little French maid uniform?"

"Not quite. She's a Polish woman in her sixties who wears orthopedic shoes. She comes in every day, straightens up, and does the wash."

"I see."

"I kinda have a thing for neatness." Again the rueful smile.

"I noticed. You could perform surgery in that bathroom."

"I know. Eddie rags on me, gives me shit about being a clean freak, but he's a total slob. His place consists of a bed, bar, and a pool table, with clothes and wet towels strewn all over. Lives like a freakin' bum."

"Maybe now would be a good time to make a confession." She grinned. "Eddie isn't the only slob."

"Hmm. For you I'll overlook it."

She pointed to the barbwire tattoo on his left bicep. "I wanted to ask you about this the first time we were together, but . . ."

"We didn't have a lot of time for questions and answers."

"Does it mean something?" She traced the ink with her finger.

"Yeah, that I was young, dumb, and drunk. Got it on a dare when I was fifteen."

"And this one?" She pointed to the cross under his heart spanning the length of his ribcage, inked over a thick, jagged scar.

"That one's for my mom."

She examined it closer. The inside of the cross with a shaded heart surrounded by thorns.

He followed her finger. "The scar is compliments of my old man and a bottle of Bud. He'd been gone for three days on one of his meth highs, and my mother had the nerve to ask where he'd been. When I got in the middle, he chugged his beer, smashed the bottle on the kitchen counter, and cut me up."

"That's terrible." She dropped her hand to his arm.

"My father was a bum who spent most of my childhood in and out of jail. He was a miserable excuse for a father, and a lousy criminal too."

"What ever happened? I mean, are they still together?"

"No." He shook his head. "They're both dead."

His frankness startled her, but she took it slow, and stayed silent for a few minutes while he sipped at his black coffee. "I never knew my father, and neither did my brother. My mother wasn't good with details. In fact, my mother wasn't good at being a mother."

"Looks like we both won the fucked-up-family lottery."

Her fingertips grazed the slight crookedness of his nose that transformed his features from pretty to edgy. "I suppose this has a story too?"

He paused, debating his answer, and she feared more bad news.

"Some guy was picking on my little sister—"

"You have a sister?" She remembered the pictures in his apartment over the club.

He snatched a small frame off his nightstand and handed it to her. "Her name's Lena."

"She's beautiful." She studied the picture of the same young girl she'd seen in his other apartment. Only here she was standing in front of a sign that read Boston College. "But it's summer, so . . ."

"She's doing one of those study abroad programs in Spain." Jonny ripped apart a bagel, eating the doughy center first.

"Nice." Now she had ten more unanswered questions.

He smiled at the picture. "She's real smart."

"You miss her." She stated the obvious.

"Yeah, but my life is no place for her. And I sure didn't want her ending up with some neighborhood guy, fifteen and pregnant like most of the other girls we knew."

She handed him the picture and again marveled at the paradox and conflict in his decisions. Safe guarding his sister at all costs, yet totally ignoring the dangerous choices in his own life.

"Lena's lucky to have someone looking out for her."

"Tell her that. She accuses me of trying to run her life and being too bossy."

"You, bossy?" She plucked up a croissant, pulled it apart, then munched on the flaky pieces. "I can't see it."

"Ha, ha, very funny. Now it's your turn."

"Go ahead, ask me anything."

"Why don't we start with how you got hooked up with a punk like Nicky?"

She expected this question, and although she wanted to be honest, it would be impossible to make him understand.

"Believe it or not, he wasn't so bad in the beginning." She tilted her head.

"You're right; I don't believe it."

"Eddie and Dylan hated him. They warned me off him more than once," she admitted. "Guess I have a thing for bad boys."

Jonny threw his hands up. "Don't put me in his category."

"At the time, he saved me."

They both grabbed for the last chocolate donut. "Go ahead." Jonny pushed it toward her.

"So polite." She snatched it up, halved it, and held it out to him. "I'm familiar with the need for chocolate."

He held up his half. "Another one of my vices."

"Anyway, my mother was moving in with yet another druggie boyfriend, and Nicky gave me a place to stay, and—"

"Forced you to steal and run cons for him while he wasted your money on bad bets and blow." He cocked his head like he'd answered the bonus round of *Jeopardy.*

"Nicky had his faults, but I wasn't innocent either." She fiddled with the collar of the robe. "I'd been stealing since I was a kid. First food so Dylan and I could eat regular, but then I advanced to wallets, watches, anything I could get my hands on." She sighed. "That's how I met him. I was trying to lift his wallet."

"You had to survive somehow."

"It started that way, but then the thrill was better than the profit."

He paused a few minutes, and she concentrated on the crumbs from the chocolate donut to avoid seeing his reaction.

"Your days of stealing are over." He raised her chin with his forefinger. "As long as you're with me, you'll never want for anything, and as for the thrill part . . ."

He pushed the tray to the side, wound his arm around her shoulders, and tucked her head against his bare chest. The faint scent of his cologne calmed her. He eased his back against the headboard and pulled a condom out of the bedside table.

"Climb on." He nudged her hips. "Ride me."

She shrugged off the robe and threw her leg over his hips, loving him under her. She slid the condom on him, and rocked forward, drenching him until he slid home. Her hands went from his shoulders to the headboard as she rode him harder.

He captured her breast, and when he sucked her into his mouth, she moaned. “Make it good, Jonny,” she gasped as he stretched her.

He pulled his mouth from her breast and gazed at her with hooded eyes. “Unless the goddamn world comes to an end this very minute, there’s no way this could be bad.”

She moved harder, faster. Each stroke bringing her closer, hitting her spot. The friction and tension building took her to a place beyond conscious sensations.

“I love watching you work me.” His grin was lazy and sated. “Taking me in, squeezing me hard.”

She let go of the headboard and pressed her hands against his chest. Her every movement bringing her closer, bringing them closer.

“That’s right, baby. Fuck me.”

His words made her buck faster, clenching around him with each pull. His hand slipped around her neck, and he pulled her down, his breath hot against her ear. “I want you to come all over me. Drown my dick and melt for me, baby.”

Then he captured her mouth in a wet, sloppy kiss of tongues and nips and bites until she screamed around his lips in the best orgasm ever. He jerked hard a few times beneath her, and she knew he felt it too. Sweat-slicked and spent, he brushed the hair from her face and kissed her forehead.

She shifted to move off him, and he stilled her with his hand.

“Don’t. Stay right there.”

She raised her head from his chest and smiled. Their bodies still connected, his heart beating hard under her cheek, his hand gliding down her back. And again she felt content and tranquil, feelings she’d given up on for herself.

Hours later after more mind-blowing orgasms, they were still snuggled up in bed, legs and arms entwined, his hand in her hair.

"There's something about you that makes me want to be better." He nuzzled into her hair.

"You're already the best to me."

"Nah, it's different." He scrunched some pillows behind them, and she leaned on his chest, their faces inches apart. "When other women would ask me about my scar, I used to say I got it in a knife fight or some other tough-guy bullshit. I never told anybody . . ."

"Shhh." She pressed her finger to his lips. "You don't ever have to pretend with me."

His cell phone buzzed on the nightstand. He groaned, shifted away from her, and swiped at it. "Yeah?"

"Get down to the new club. We got trouble."

Max yelled so loud she could hear him through the phone.

Chapter 21

Twenty minutes later Jonny stood on the sidewalk and sucked in the humid evening air. The setting summer sun cast a deep shadow over the double glass doors etched with Beyond Paradise. He flicked at some anxious sweat popping up on his forehead and pushed through the doors, not knowing what to expect.

Max pounced, his cheeks flushed, and his pressed shirt rumpled and sweaty despite the air conditioning.

"Where the fuck you been?" Max gripped his arm and leaned in. His hushed voice rumbled with frustration.

"So, you decided to come join the party," Captain Farrell's voice reverberated through the vast empty space.

Jonny strode forward with Max at his heels until the large club shrank to include him, Farrell, and the two uniformed cops standing off to the side. The contempt Farrell harbored bounced around the room.

"Nice place." He ran his hand over the brass railing on the edge of the bar.

Jonny kept a wary distance. Farrell's cocky attitude reflected all his years of resentment. All the years Jonny treated Farrell like shit. All the years Jonny was untouchable under Frank's protection.

"Great spot. Sure to make a ton of money."

Farrell nodded, and one of the cops picked up a barstool and smashed it against the granite bar until it shattered into pieces. Max made a move, but Jonny held him back.

"I've been waiting a long time for this, Vallone," he

gloated. “And now Frank has given me the okay to take your punk ass down.”

There it was. The answer loud and clear. Frank’s personal fuck-you. What Eddie feared all along. The legal variances and inspections Simon Davis wrangled didn’t mean shit up against a dirty cop and a hardcore thug.

“Still nothing to say?” Farrell taunted.

Farrell stomped behind the bar, picked up a few glasses, and let them slip from his fingers. “Geez, that was clumsy of me.”

“That’s harassment,” Max yelled.

Blood shot through Jonny’s veins at an alarming rate. His heart thumped so hard he feared a heart attack, but he kept his expression blank.

Smiling, Farrell nabbed the neck of a tequila bottle and pitched it into the massive mirror over the bar. Jonny flinched. All the pride he’d experienced two days ago when they’d hung it smashed to the floor. Large shards of the custom etched mirror crashed into the bottles on the shelves beneath it, leaving the floor awash with liquor and jagged glass.

Max groaned beside him, and anger burned in Jonny’s gut. His jaw clenched until his teeth ached, but he refused to give Farrell the reaction he wanted.

“Now that’s harassment, boys.” He strolled around the bar and motioned to the two uniforms. “I think it's time we drove our point home.”

One cop pushed Max out of the way while the other grabbed Jonny.

“You’re crazy, Farrell,” Jonny spat.

The cop to Jonny’s left cracked his knuckles. “This is going to be fun.”

“Frank sends his regards.” Farrell strolled closer. “It looks like you fucked with him once too often, big shot.”

One cop held Jonny's arms behind him while the other wound up and landed the first few punches into his gut. His muscles tightened on reflex, but he refused to flinch. He glared at the cop and wheezed, "Is that the best you got, cocksucker?"

He'd taken plenty of beatings—as a kid by his father, and on the streets. In his neighborhood, thirty was considered old age, and he'd already beat those odds.

Pain exploded at the first blow to his face. He swallowed the bitter taste of his blood as his head whipped from side to side. When he wavered, he visualized Cheryl. Their fists were her warm hands. Their curses were her words of love.

They released him, and he fell to the floor. He held himself up on his hands and knees refusing to collapse in front of them. The thud of shoes against the floor made him focus his swollen eyes on Farrell's city-issued wingtips.

"What's the matter, Vallone? Where's all your wise guy comments?" Farrell hoisted him up by the collar.

Pain jolted through him, but he bit back his anguish.

"Fuck you," Jonny mumbled through swollen, blood-smeared lips.

Farrell leaned in. "Frank says you keep pushing and he'll tell all your secrets." His harsh breath against Jonny's ear.

The pure hate in Farrell's face didn't scare him. It made him mad. He'd worked so hard to get out, yet Farrell and Frank loved to drag him down.

"Get him outta here." Farrell shoved him toward Max, who helped him out the door.

"Pretty fucked up." They reached the Escalade and climbed in. Max dragged deep on his cigarette. "I told you Frank was pissed. What're you gonna do now? What's Eddie gonna say?"

Jonny slowly rotated his head to the left. "Could you please shut up?" He held his gaze for an extra second to make his point. “And put out that fuckin’ cigarette, the smoke is killing me.”

Max furrowed his brow, pitched the cigarette out the window, and remained silent for the rest of the ride to the penthouse.

~ ~ ~

Jonny leaned against the chrome railing in the elevator as it whisked him to the penthouse floor. The slight movement made him nauseous, so he pressed his forehead against the cool mirrored wall, averting his eyes. He felt bad enough, he didn’t need to see it.

When he shuffled off the elevator, he stared at his penthouse door. Seeing Cheryl and taking a hot shower would have to wait. On impulse he’d called Eddie, who insisted on talking to him first.

“Shit.” Eddie grimaced. “What the fuck did they do to you?”

Jonny glanced into the mirror behind the bar as Eddie filled a Ziploc bag with ice from the freezer.

“Don’t look like your nose is broke.” Eddie handed him the ice, then lifted a bottle of Scotch and two glasses out of the cabinet.

“Nah, Farrell’s a punk. Had to have two other cops with him to do his shit.” He brushed his fingertips over his cheekbone. An irrepressible anger churned inside him when he glimpsed the bruising already turning a sickly shade of purple and green, and the redness of his swollen jaw visible under the dark stubble.

“And don’t worry about Cheryl. You’re not the first guy she’s seen get busted up.”

Jonny winced. He’d ragged on her about Nicky, and now he’d dropped her in the same shit.

“You sure you should be up and around?” He motioned

to Eddie's shirtless mid-section wrapped in gauze from his ribcage to the waist of his low-slung jeans.

"Doc said the lung is fine. It's the busted rib that's ripping me up." Eddie sighed. "I couldn't stand lying in that room over the club anymore. Max was driving me crazy."

"How?"

"Fuckin' questions. What we're gonna do about Frank? What's gonna happen next?" Eddie dragged his hand through his hair. "He's so damn jumpy."

"He grilled me with the same shit on the way back here." He shifted the ice to the other side of his jaw. "You think he's using again?"

Five years ago, Max had a big coke problem and ended up unconscious in a back alley thanks to a deranged dealer even bigger and more strung out than him. After that, he got clean. Or so Jonny thought.

"Nah. He's just rattled." Eddie hunched over, favoring his side. "I gotta sit down." He motioned to the leather sofa.

"And what was with that phone call he got?" Jonny eased onto the soft leather sectional. "Somethings off."

"It's that crazy redhead he's screwing." Eddie shifted his position. "Big guy like him, yet show him a pair of tits and he turns into a pussy."

"She must have him all twisted up." He adjusted the ice bag.

"Women can do that sometimes." Eddie stared to make his point.

"Only Cheryl ain't a whore who spreads her legs for every guy with a dick."

"That's not what I meant." Eddie sighed.

Jonny looked away. "I thought Farrell was gonna lock me up." Jonny gulped at the Scotch as a bolt of heat shot up the base of his neck. "I couldn't go in the box again. I get—sick."

Eddie ran his finger around the rim of his glass. "Maybe we should lay low for a while."

"Frank's out of control and he has to be stopped." Jonny paused. "He killed Nicky."

"What?"

"Cheryl stabbed him, but Frank finished him off and then blackmailed her."

"That is fucked up."

"That's why we gotta move on this. Davis likes our ideas. He says we can make an easy thirty percent profit. That's huge."

"I don't know." Eddie rubbed the back of his neck.

"Davis also has gigs in Vegas and Miami. I'm thinking maybe I'll hook him up with Carlos in the South Beach club, too."

"We got enough to worry about up here without thinking about Miami."

"Frank's bleeding him too, and Carlos is sick of it. Never hurts to have an ally. With Davis and his people behind us, plus Carlos and his crew in Miami, we're that much stronger."

"Have you talked to Carlos?" Eddie asked.

"I made some phone calls." Jonny waited a beat. "I'm going to Miami day after tomorrow."

"What?" Eddie frowned. "I don't think leaving now is a good idea."

"It's something I gotta do in person." Jonny paused. "I'm taking Cheryl too. I don't wanna leave her here with all that's going down."

"I don't like it."

"Davis asked me last week how we get so many people to come to the club, and I told him it's because we came up the hard way, and we know what people want before they do. Now, living how we live, up here in the penthouses but still keeping it real, people love it. You can't teach that."

"So how do you see it?" Eddie lifted an eyebrow. "Frank rolls over, we go legit, and everybody lives happily ever after?"

"This is our time, man."

"It's too risky now, and Max sure isn't gonna like it."

"Since when do you give a fuck what Max likes?" Jonny threw up his hands and regretted the sudden movement.

"Sometimes his questions make sense, especially since you're . . ."

"I'm what?" He dared Eddie to say it.

"You and me got trust." Eddie waved his hand between them. "But lately you're a little preoccupied."

"You talking about Cheryl?"

"Her and I go way back but it's been a while."

"What are you saying?"

"She's had a tough life and then hooking up with Nicky. That would turn anybody. Maybe she's changed."

"You saying I shouldn't trust her. That maybe she's working with Frank?"

"You asked for the forecast. Don't get mad at the weatherman 'cause he says it's gonna rain."

Chapter 22

It was almost nine p.m. by the time Jonny left Eddie's apartment. He forgot how bad he looked until he caught the expression of shock on Cheryl's face. He barely closed the door before she enveloped him in a hug.

"I was so worried about you." Her fingers traveled to his jawline.

"It was just a screw-up."

"Pretty big screw-up." Her hand trembled and the sadness in her eyes killed him.

"Everything's fine."

"Who did this to your beautiful face?" She grazed his cheekbone, careful not to exert pressure on his bruised skin.

"Forget about it." He kept his voice light, hoping to avoid the inevitable questions.

He wasn't accustomed to anyone fussing over him, and although he enjoyed her attention, being laid-open and vulnerable was not his style.

"Forget about it?" She ran her hand over his forearm. "Please tell me what happened."

For a split second, he considered arranging his feelings into words, but it passed, and he reverted to what worked for most of his twenty-nine years. Covering his ass and shoving his emotions down until they no longer existed.

"Let me take a shower and get cleaned up."

"But . . ." She trailed behind him. "Can I at least get you something to eat?" She followed him into the bedroom. "Anything?"

"No, I'm good."

Escaping into the bathroom off the bedroom, he tore off his shirt and pants, balled them up, and threw them into the trash. The best dry cleaner in the world couldn't get rid of the stink of cops and blood.

He adjusted the nozzles in the shower to full pressure, waited until steam filled the glass enclosure, then stepped under the hot water. The pulsing spray soothed his raw skin, but not his mind. He turned toward the spray. The sting of the water against his cuts and bruises reminded him of what was at stake. He realized Eddie and Max had doubts, but they couldn't back down now. When the beating water became too intense, he shut off the faucets and stepped out of the shower. He dried himself, threw on a clean pair of sweatpants, and combed his wet hair into place.

He leaned into the mirror over the sink and examined the damages. His last black eye had come from his father. He shoved the memory down and decided shaving would be too painful. Seeing enough, he dragged in a slow, deep breath, then opened the bathroom door.

"I suppose you think by running into the shower I'm going to stop asking you questions?" She perched on the edge of the bed.

"I was kinda hoping."

"C'mon, tell me something."

"Farrell's had it in for me for a while, and Frank's flexin', trying to show us who's boss." He eased himself next to her on the bed.

"I'd say he's doing a pretty good job. Eddie's got broken ribs." She stroked his cheek. "And you got your face smashed in."

He reached for her, but she jumped off the bed. "Hey, c'mere."

She braced her hands on her hips and stood firm. "Now tell me what's going on."

His ambition thrust himself and others into danger, but he refused to gamble with Cheryl's safety. She'd had enough bad guys in her life, and putting her at risk slammed him with fear. He contemplated an all-out lie, but Eddie was right. She had too much street in her and would definitely smell bullshit.

"Frank doesn't want me opening the club in midtown."

"Why?"

He weighed his answer because if their relationship was real, it had to be about trust.

"Because we're breaking away, not cutting him in for any of the profits." Jonny inched himself off the bed and faced her. "He thinks he owns us, thinks he can tell us what to do." The anger bubbled up in his chest.

"And he thinks this because . . ."

"Because—he took us off the corner. Gave us a shot."

"But I'm guessing you did things that weren't exactly legal?"

"Sure, coming up the way I did, I was looking for any way out," he admitted. "And I'm not gonna lie. In the beginning, I loved the power and the way people treat you when they think you have that power. Wearing the clothes, driving the cars, it's addicting."

"But something changed."

"Yeah." He walked to the windows, keeping his back to her.

"Okay, I told you about all the stuff Nicky and I did."

He wanted to be honest with her, but he feared his truths might scare her, might drive her away.

"Come on, Jonny. Can it be any worse than the things I told you?"

He sucked in a deep breath, and the pressure pushed against his bruised ribs. He braced his palms against the cool window pane and hung his head between his arms.

She stayed silent, forcing him to continue. “My father was an abusive son of a bitch, and one day he went too far.” He dragged in another deep breath and exhaled. “He beat my mother so bad . . .”

She came up behind him, then her arms wrapped around his waist. “He killed her?” she whispered, making it impossible to tell if she was repulsed or shocked.

He drew in a quivering breath. “Left her for dead on our kitchen floor.” Saying the words out loud made his throat raw and dry.

“Oh, baby, I’m so sorry.” She held him tighter and laid her cheek against his back.

“The cops didn’t care about people like us, so I went to Frank, and he gave me a gun.” He relived the day in his memory. “I tracked that bastard down.”

“But you couldn’t do it.”

“No, Frank did it. He’d gone along to back me up and finished the job.”

“Frank’s been holding it over you all this time?”

He kept his back to her. “I never wanted to do anything more in my life, but I couldn’t pull the trigger.”

“Because you’re not a killer.” She tugged at his waist until he faced her.

“No, that’s not it.” He wanted to get the words right. “It’s because he was my father and I was supposed to love him. And he was supposed to love me.”

“We were betrayed by the people who were supposed to care for us.”

Her words made sense. You can’t hurt someone who’s lost everything, and you can’t scare a person who has nothing to lose. Only now he did have something he cared about, and the fear of losing her twisted him up.

She stroked his cheek. “And although it’s made us horribly vulnerable, it’s also made us incredibly tough.”

The tough part he could handle. It was the vulnerable part that scared the shit out of him. His life was being blown to hell, everything boiling up and spilling over in what he feared would be a messy ending. But here she was in his arms, giving it up to him, accepting his past, accepting him.

"How'd I get so lucky." He nuzzled the curve below her jaw and mumbled against her skin.

Chapter 23

Jonny's revelation rocked her, and the pain in his voice made Cheryl tighten her grip around his waist and hold on tight. Being strong for so long had taken its toll on him, and she wanted to be the person that relieved that pain.

Her fingertips trailed down to the fine hairs that disappeared beneath his sweatpants. His muscles retracted and reacted to her touch, and when she arched her back and pressed against him, he cupped her ass and nudged her to him.

"I don't know what you did to me." He mumbled against her sensitive flesh of her breast. "But this thing simmering between us is real."

"I know but . . ." She peeked up at him through her lashes and prayed he would understand. "I have a hard time trusting."

"I get it, but from now on no more secrets. Even if it's bad, real bad, I wanna know."

He walked her backward until her legs hit the bed. He nudged her down and pierced her with those dark eyes. "Understand?"

She nodded then raised to her knees. Her hands tugged down his pants and the strong roped muscles of his thighs clenched when his dick twitched under her soft caress.

"How about I take care of you for a change?"

A groan rumbled from the back of his throat. "You're killing me, baby."

"No, I'm going to make it all better."

She brushed her lips against his abs, inching closer to the prize. She kept her movements careful and deliberate, licking her way down and around his thick shaft. She played there a few minutes before taking him whole, sucking him hard and deep. She pumped him with her mouth, and when she cupped his balls, he drew in a sharp breath. She pulled off slightly and made a show of her tongue taking him from bottom to tip.

His head hit the headboard with a thud, his eyes hazy slits, his face a sexy mix of desire and absolute submission. With him sprawled out beneath her, she braced her hands against his rock-hard thighs and sucked him in a little deeper each time. He swelled in her mouth, and his breathing quicken to raspy gasps.

He gently pushed at her shoulder. "I'm gonna blow, baby."

The warning encouraged her. She craved all of him. And when he quenched her thirst, she drank him in. Happy to give him pleasure after all he'd done for her.

He caught her under the arms and hauled her over his taut abs. She placed gentle butterfly kisses over his swollen jaw, then nestled into his shoulder and drank in the scent of their sex.

"How would you like to go down to Miami with me?"

"Miami?"

"We have another club in South Beach, and there're some people I want to see down there. People that can help me break away from Frank."

"I still have more questions about you getting beat up."

"Laying on the beach all day." His mouth moved lower, past her collarbone, as he pulled at the hem of her shirt. "You and me in my beachfront condo?"

"Sounds nice but . . ."

"Ever been to South Beach?"

"The farthest south I've ever been is Seaside Heights."

One of Mama's boyfriends took her and Dylan to the Jersey Shore when they were kids. They hit the bars while she and Dylan got sunburned, and around midnight, they got thrown out of the motel because they were fighting so loud.

"To answer your question, no. I've never been to South Beach."

"It's nothing like 'Sleazeside."

She laughed at the old joke.

"You'll love it." He moaned when the doorbell rang.

"Who could it be?" Panic overwhelmed her with all the possibilities.

"Whoever is on the other side of that door is majorly fucked." He stood in all his naked perfection, then leaned down, bracing his hands on either side of her head. "Don't move."

Jonny yanked his sweatpants over his hips as the doorbell rang again.

She blew out a heavy sigh, waited until he left the room, pulled on her clothes, then cracked the bedroom door to listen. Way too much was going on in their lives, and if Jonny was in trouble, she wanted to help if she could.

~ ~ ~

Jonny stalked to the door and scowled into the peephole.

He flipped the lock and opened the door. "What's up?"

"I got somebody I want you to meet." Max dipped his chin toward a wiry guy hovering by the elevators, covered in gang tats and decked out in a wife-beater hanging over low baggy jeans. "He's Spanish. You'll like him."

"Cheryl's here."

"Forget about her for a minute."

Jonny cocked his head unsure of Max's game.

Max waved his hand, and the thug bounced over, rolling with attitude.

"Jonny, this is Angel." Max shifted his hand between the two of them.

"Hey, man." Angel pounded Jonny on the back, followed it with a street hug, stepped away, and said in Spanish, "Max says you got some heavy-duty shit going down."

"Nothing I can't handle, *mejo.*" Jonny shot a sideways glance at Max.

"Looks like somebody busted up that Hollywood face," Angel said, again in Spanish.

"Not your concern," Jonny answered in Spanish. "Now cut the homeboy shit and speak English."

Angel shifted his gaze to Max, then to Jonny. "Sure boss, sure."

"You could use a little extra protection." Max moved them into the foyer. The stench of stale cigarette smoke and weed surrounded Angel.

"Nice place, man." Angel strolled around like he was casing the joint. "You must be all about the paper. Fuckin' rolling in it."

"Angel's got the fire power and the backup we need." Max sounded like he was revealing some big secret.

"Yeah, yeah. I got it all." Angel lifted his T-shirt, revealing a .38 stuck into the waistband of his jeans. "Motherfuckers don't mess with me or my crew."

"I figure he can shadow you," Max added. "Keep you safe in case Frank tries to do anything else."

"Better to have a gun and not need it, then need a gun and not have it." Angel's grin revealed a gold front tooth. "I fuckin' take care of you. You feelin' me, bro?"

"Can I talk to you for a minute?" Jonny's eyes bore into Max.

"Jonny?" Cheryl entered the living room, stared at Angel then Jonny.

"I told you to stay in the bedroom." He heard the edge in his voice.

"Damn, that one fine looking bitch." Angel swaggered forward.

"That's it." Jonny stepped in Angel's path and shoved him toward the door.

"Wait outside," Max yelled at Angel.

"Sorry," Jonny said to Cheryl. "Give Max and me a minute."

She furrowed her brow, then retreated to the bedroom. Jonny didn't even want to think about the questions she'd have now.

"What the fuck are you thinking?" Jonny spat after she left the room.

"I'm looking out for you," Max defended.

"I'm trying to get out of this life, and you bring a guy to my apartment who looks like he belongs in a fuckin' rap video?"

"With everything going on—"

"That what? I'd want some thug hanging around, bringing his shit down on me." Jonny threw his hands up and flinched. "Or around Cheryl?"

"If you'd forget about her for a minute, you'd see I'm right."

"Does Eddie know about this?"

"Kinda. I told him you needed more protection, and he agreed."

"I don't think this is what he had in mind." Jonny heaved out a frustrated sigh. "Anyway, I'm going to Miami tomorrow."

"Miami?"

"I'm gonna meet with Carlos, firm up our connections down there. We're leaving tomorrow night."

"You and Eddie?" Max asked.

"Me and Cheryl."

"Right, and how are you gonna concentrate on business with her there?"

Jonny closed the gap between them until they were only inches apart. "I gave you a pass before, but you better knock this shit off." He splayed his hands. "Bringing some gangbanger here? Telling him my business? I think you're spending too much time with those strippers. They're starting to fuck with your brain. Now get outta here and try to keep things together until I get back."

Max stormed off and flung the door so hard it bounced on its hinges. Jonny stood behind the door, squinted through the crack, and listened.

"What the fuck, man?" Angel said, as he bopped by the elevators. "How's it gonna play out now?"

"Shut up," Max growled. "I'll think of something else." Max jostled Angel onto the elevator and stabbed at the buttons until the door whooshed close.

Chapter 24

"How's everything going?" Jonny gripped the phone in his hand, hoping the late morning view of swaying palm trees from his balcony on Ocean Drive would calm him.

He hadn't slept on the late-night flight to Miami, and after settling Cheryl into the bedroom at his condo, he'd spent most of the night sitting on the balcony. He stared into the vast, dark sky, his mind doing a constant loop over the events of the last few days. Now at noon, his bruised ribs and the lack of sleep left him edgy.

"Quiet for now," Eddie said. Then the rustle of sheets, a woman's giggle, and Eddie's guttural rasp. "Oh yeah, baby."

"You talking to me?" Jonny added sarcasm to his frustration.

"No, no—"

"Who the fuck is there with you?"

"Bambi, she's helping me recuperate."

"Aren't you supposed to be resting, not straining yourself." More movement and muffled voices.

"Believe me, that part works just fine," Eddie mumbled into the phone.

"It sure does, baby." Bambi's squeak toy voice shrieked through the phone, followed by kissy noises.

"Will you please take your dick outta her mouth and focus on what I'm saying."

"Take a break, baby." More shifting. "I gotta talk to Jonny."

"Hi, Jonny," Bambi squealed in the background.

Jonny gripped the phone tighter. “You gotta keep your head in the game.”

“Yeah, yeah,” Eddie barked.

“Why are you acting like a punk?”

“Maybe because I’m up here in New York looking over my shoulder every time I go out for a pack of smokes. This morning a guy stood too close to me at Duane Reade, and I almost decked him. Then I got Max bitchin’ and moanin’ and telling me Frank’s gonna take us all down.”

“Did you ask him about the guy he brought to my apartment?”

“He said he was trying to look out for you.”

“Did he mention the guy was a fuckin’ gangbanger from Bed-Stuy?”

“He’s worried, Jonny.” Eddie paused. “We all are.”

“You wanna jump, say so now. If not, man up and grow a pair.”

A few seconds of silence, then, “We’re not jumping.”

“Things are hot now, I get it, but I know we’ll have Carlos’s support.”

“I hope his support in Miami helps us in New York.” Eddie always the voice of reason. It was fuckin’ annoying.

“It will,” Jonny said with more confidence than he felt.

Eddie drew in a breath. “And don’t forget to look over your shoulder once in a while, too,” Eddie warned. “Just because you’re in Miami doesn’t mean you’re safe.”

Fifteen minutes later Jonny still gazed down on Ocean Drive. The warm, flower-scented air drifted over the balcony as tourists geared up for a weekend in South Beach. Stretching his arms over his head, his gaze traveled to the sparkling blue water on the horizon. Sitting on the plane did nothing for the ache in his ribs.

He yawned and moved inside to the bedroom where Cheryl was tucked into his bed. The light shadowing her smooth, golden skin, and the sexy line of her leg showcased against the cream-colored sheets. She needed this sound sleep after the shit she'd been through. She deserved a life without worry, where she could depend on him to do right by her.

Moving away from her perfect silhouette, he showered and dressed. Sunlight spilled in through the floor-to-ceiling windows in the living room and danced against the sleek stainless steel of his kitchen appliances. He rummaged through the cabinets and found that Anita, his housekeeper in Miami, provided all his favorite snacks, plus a box of Honey Nut Cheerios. He hadn't been here in months, but he could depend on her to keep the kitchen stocked, and the condo pristine. He craved cleanliness and guessed a shrink would say his roach-infested childhood was the reason.

Pulling out a bowl and spoon, he splashed milk over the Cheerios and munched on the little circles as he mentally rehearsed the conversation he would have with Carlos. Draining the last of the cereal-sweetened milk from the bowl, he rinsed it, stacked it in the dishwasher, and left the condo.

He preferred to walk the few blocks to the Paradise II. The salt air helped clear his thoughts, and the people who crowded the sidewalk and overflowed into the wide boulevard energized him. A funky mix of models, movie stars, and cross-dressers strolled alongside flamboyant gays, trannies, and old Palm Beach money. Ocean Drive combined Fifth Avenue elite with Coney Island sleaze. The cream-colored beaches and swaying palms competed with the neon-blaring hotel and club signs. A crazy combination of nature and glitz, but he loved it.

When he arrived at the club, he surveyed the outside. The building merged the Art Deco design of the forties with the flashy Miami Vice of the eighties, and promised the rich, and wish-they-were-rich, the opportunity to mingle with celebrities of all varieties. By day they played in the clear blue waters and tanned on the wide sandy beaches. By night, they were ready for whatever exotic, erotic diversions the club offered.

He pushed through the doors, and although it was early afternoon, the bartenders and waitstaff were already setting up the bars and VIP tables on the first and second floors. At only ten thousand square feet, Paradise II had a more intimate feel than the New York club.

Across the room, he spotted Carlos dressed in tapered black pants that were probably Gucci and a crisp white button down. Euro-Miami cool. His black, close-cropped hair, deeply tanned skin, and trim build made him appear much younger than his forty years. Jonny respected the man and enjoyed their shared bond of heritage and friendship over the years.

"So good to see you, Jonny," Carlos said in Spanish.

They embraced, clapping each other on the back.

"Same to you, my friend," Jonny returned in Spanish.

Carlos extended his arm and led him to the back of the club, and into the private elevator. They ascended in the glass-enclosed elevator, and the club grew smaller beneath them until the doors reopened into Carlos's fourth-floor office. White furnishings, white marble floor, a polished brass bar, and a wall-to-wall view of the ocean. Very South Beach.

"The place looks great." Jonny gravitated toward the floor-to-ceiling windows showcasing the wide beach and glistening water. He geared himself up, knowing Carlos would waste no time getting to the point.

"Hard work pays off." Carlos moved behind the bar and extended a shot glass of tequila from his private stock. "Now, tell me what's on your mind."

He appreciated Carlos' directness. "Things in New York have been sensitive."

"You've come up against some resistance?" He pointed to Jonny's bruised face.

Although the swelling went down, his eye was still shadowed a dusky blueish, green. Jonny raised his hand to his cheek. "It's important you understand this won't be easy."

"Nothing worth having ever is." Carlos spread his hands in front of him. "I put the club's success first always, but Frank gives nothing back. Only takes."

"It's the same in New York. That's why I'm breaking out with my own club."

Carlos digested the information. "Eddie too?"

Jonny nodded but didn't mention Eddie's latest injuries or his apprehension. "Yeah, he feels the same way."

"Independence from Frank is worth it." Clear determination shone in the older man's eyes, and he knew Carlos remembered his family's struggles and all they'd worked for to become Americans. Him getting jobs on the New York docks for many of Carlos's family and friends had strengthened that bond.

"I hoped you'd agree."

"You have our support." Carlos extended his hand. "My people down here have been waiting for this day."

Jonny extended his hand, and the two men shook.

"I arranged for *South Beach Magazine* to do an interview with you and Juan Martinez, the city manager, tomorrow. Explore the parallels between your assets to the Cuban business community, creating jobs and honoring heritage."

"Nice."

"We held Juan's campaign party here last month and matched his donations. Since he's the new city manager, I would say he's very grateful."

"Politicians." Jonny curled his lip. "They're all the same."

"True, but I know what the people want, and I also know whose word means something in this town."

"Publicity is good. The more people who know what we're doing, the better. That way if things get shady, they can't hide."

"Tonight, I've invited Jared Klein from the Delano to meet you here. They're opening another club in Vegas, so he wants to hear your opinion of Simon Davis."

"You got a lot together in a short time."

"I believe in this, Jonny." Carlos clapped his shoulder. "I believe in you." Carlos stepped to the bar to refill their glasses. "To making things happen." Carlos raised his glass, and they downed the shot. "Graciela is downstairs. Should I call her?"

"Not this trip."

"What?"

In the past, he and Carlos would hang with three or maybe four obliging females and not go home until the sun rose.

"I'm with someone."

Carlos's eyes widened. "You've never brought a woman to Miami. You said there were too many . . ."

"All that's changed."

"All right, you bring your lady tonight, and we'll celebrate this new beginning."

Carlos walked him to the door and lowered his voice. "Stay safe, *amigo.*" Carlos embraced him, and he couldn't help hearing a cryptic message in his simple words. Carlos's warning gnawed at him all the way back to his condo.

Chapter 25

Cheryl ran her hand over the soft sheets and the empty spot alongside her. She shared Jonny's bed for only a few nights, but she'd become addicted to his heat pressed up against her and his spicy, musky scent.

Her sleepy mind reviewed the last twenty-four hours. The late-night flight to Miami, and car service to Jonny's beachfront condo in South Beach. A million stars in the night sky, and the calming sound of the waves crashing in the distance.

Jonny played it off, but the tension in his actions was real and tangible. He'd come to bed and tossed and turned, finally leaving to sit on the balcony. After all he'd done for her, she wanted to help him in any way possible. The black eyes and bruises on him and Eddie spoke volumes, and you didn't have to be street savvy to know Frank was coming down hard.

Then there was the guy Max brought to the penthouse two days ago. Jonny said he was an old friend, which was total bullshit. Their conversation sounded anything but friendly, and clearly, this trip was about way more than sun and fun on the beach.

She stretched and enjoyed the cool air wafting over her from the ceiling fan. Slivers of light seeped through the white wooden shutters shielding the windows. Sleek furniture in grays and whites decorated the room, similar to his Manhattan penthouse, but much lighter, more beachy. The digital clock on the bedside table read one in the afternoon, and she realized this was the first sound sleep she'd had in forever.

He'd texted her saying he'd be back in an hour, so she stood and opened the shutters. The dazzling sunshine made her squint. She unlatched the sliding door and stepped onto the balcony that wrapped around the corner condo. Leaning against the railing, she soaked in the warm sun and gentle breeze. The spectacular sight of the waves breaking on the beach across the street made her fantasize about her and Jonny laying on the beach all day, far away from the worries and pressures of New York. The buzzing of her phone broke the spell, then her back stiffened at the number on the caller ID.

"Hello?"

"Good afternoon." Frank's rough, edgy, voice rasped through the phone.

Her heart quickened, but she stayed silent.

"I understand you and Jonny are in Miami." There was a slight pause. "South Beach to be exact."

She dashed inside, snapped the shutters closed, then peered through one of the slats, half expecting him to be standing on the street below. When she realized how ridiculous her reaction was, she willed herself to calm down and focus.

"Yes," she admitted, since he knew as much about her whereabouts as she did. Maybe more.

"Catch some sun. Relax a little."

This inane conversation unnerved her more than if he'd come right out and threatened her.

"What do you want"

"You're a tough bitch, huh?" He cleared his throat. "I like that in a woman. Lets me know you can get the job done."

"I did what you wanted with the safe." She struggled to

keep her edge. The last thing you showed a guy like Frank was fear.

"Shut up and listen." His voice iced over. "Unless you want to end up in jail for murder."

"I'm done letting you blackmail me." She'd already decided to go to the cops when they returned to New York. She'd had enough lying.

"Really?" Frank drawled. "Even if it means keeping that brother of yours alive?"

Now, she was afraid. Now, he had her full attention.

"Leave my family out of this." Her threat sounded weak even to her ears.

"Family?" He spit out an evil laugh. "A mother who spreads her legs for a hit of meth and a brother who can't stay out of jail. Sounds more like the freak show at a circus."

Her insides crumbled at the truth. He'd finally found her weak link. Family.

"I'm listening." Her hand tightened on the phone.

"In about twenty minutes a package is going to be dropped off for you. You're going to take that package and hide it from Jonny, then plant it on him when I tell you to."

"What's in the—"

"Enough coke to get him locked up. Florida jails aren't very safe, and I have some friends who owe me— No sense in getting into all the gory details."

"But . . ."

"I've dropped hints, but he's not getting it."

She assumed his hints included using Jonny and Eddie's face as a punching bag.

"Unfortunately, Jonny has too much heart. Punk couldn't even kill his deadbeat father. I had to step up and do the job."

Wow, the psycho was proud of killing someone in cold blood.

"So now it's up to you, and if you don't do what I say, your brother's dead."

Her head spun, and she slumped to the bed. "Please . . ."

"The Russian your brother jacks' cars for is a crazy motherfucker." Frank clucked his tongue. "And all kinds of accidents can happen in a garage."

Dylan told her he was working in a body shop. Fixing cars, not stealing them.

"But why me?" She was desperate to reason with him. "I'm sure you have people here in Miami . . ."

"But you have so much more to lose, which makes you very useful."

"How do I know you still won't hurt Dylan even if I do this?" She couldn't let herself use the word *kill.*

"You don't. But what's the alternative?"

She gasped for air and braced herself against the soft mattress.

"And don't go telling Jonny about this phone call, because if anything goes wrong, that brother you care so much about is done."

She startled when the door chimed sending a new swarm of locusts to her stomach. She peered through the peephole and saw a nondescript man in his early forties.

"I have a package for Cheryl Benson," he said through the door.

She exhaled and undid the lock. The man handed her a manila envelope, then turned toward the elevators without another word.

She closed and locked the door, then pulled at the adhesive closure. Inside the envelope was a clear plastic bag filled with fine white powder. She'd never indulged, but she knew from her time with Nicky that this was a substantial amount of cocaine with a high price tag and a long arrest time.

She dropped the baggie back in the envelope, then frantically searched for a hiding place. Finally settling for the inside pouch of the suitcase Jonny had given her for the trip. She sat down on the unmade bed then laid back, staring at the blades of the ceiling fan. They still spilled cool air over her, but now everything felt chilled and different. The spooky sense of being watched invaded her space.

Frank's low, harsh threats echoed in her ears, and the guilt of even thinking about betraying Jonny made her sick. She had to think. There had to be a way around this, but soon her head hurt from the endless loop of dead ends. Frank Barnett had a reputation that rattled even the toughest thugs. A dangerous man unafraid of consequences and crazy enough to make his threats a reality.

Again, she was forced to use her conning skills, but the hardest part would be acting normal when Jonny returned.

~ ~ ~

As Jonny promised, they toured South Beach in the afternoon. How ironic he appeared more relaxed, while her every nerve vibrated with tension. He dedicated the day to treating her like a tourist. They scoped out the glitzy souvenir shops on Washington Avenue, and he indulged her with Jimmy Choos and Louboutins in Bal Harbour. Every woman's dream shopping spree, but it only fueled her guilt.

She wanted to enjoy the light blue sky and sparkling, turquoise water at the beachfront cabana at Nikki Beach, but her insides twisted with fear. The beverage manager, a friend of Jonny's, already sent over a complimentary bottle of champagne, and she gulped one then two glasses. She played it off as thirst from the heat hoping it would calm her jangled nerves.

He smoothed the coconut-scented oil over her lower back, letting his hand slip into the bottom of her bikini.

"Better than Sleazeside?" he joked.

"Much better. I see why you like to come down here." She motioned to the beach. "This place is outrageous."

"Even better with you." He leaned in for a kiss, and she sensed they weren't alone.

"Hello, Jonny."

They propped themselves up on the daybed, and Cheryl scrutinized their sudden guest. A shapely, brunette with big dark eyes and long, raven hair. Her exaggerated Sofia Vergara Spanish accent made her pronounce his name "Joanie."

"Cheryl, this is Graciela." Jonny swung his legs around to a sitting position.

Graciela extended her tan, manicured hand toward Cheryl but kept her eyes glued to Jonny.

"I had to hear from other people you were in South Beach."

In seconds, her string-bikinied bottom settled dangerously close to Jonny.

"I just finished a shoot with a major photographer here on the beach." Her sexy voice was in overdrive. "It will be in all the important magazines."

"That's great." Jonny repositioned himself, but she slithered closer until he teetered on the edge of the lounger.

"We should get together later." She leaned even closer and said in a stage whisper, "I've heard some interesting things about you."

"It's been great catching up." Jonny quickly stood. "But as you can see, I'm with someone."

"Yes, of course." She stood with him and thrust out her ridiculous 36DDs. "You make sure you take care of yourself."

Was she paranoid, or did Graciela's last sentence have a double meaning?

"Who the hell was *that* rude bitch?" she asked the minute Graciela left.

"An old friend."

"I knew you were going to say that." She rolled her eyes. "Do you know anyone who doesn't have fake boobs?"

"In New York, yes. In South Beach, no. It's kind of a ritual down here. Get your hair done, get your nails done, get your boobs done."

He searched for their cabana hostess. "Why don't I get us some drinks?"

"We still have champagne."

"I need something stronger."

"You like to use food to change the subject. That and sex."

"I go with what works." He leaned in for a quick kiss. "I'll get us some Caipirinhas. You'll love them."

He walked toward the bar, and she expelled a long-held sigh. Conning someone you didn't care about was one thing, deceiving the man you were falling in love with sucked.

Her phone buzzed, and she grabbed it from the beach bag and flinched.

"Enjoying the sun?" Frank asked.

She jackknifed off the lounger and scanned the beach.

"Before you get to the club tonight, plant it on him."

A shiver jetted up her spine. Somehow, someway, he had eyes on them.

Chapter 26

Jonny made a swift retreat to the outdoor bar before Cheryl could protest or ask any more questions he didn't want to answer. He placed his drink order and enjoyed the warm sun on his chest. The huge rectangular bar serviced the pool and the beach, with most of the crowd gathered by the poolside DJ.

"I need to talk to you."

Graciela was at his elbow, and he couldn't help his sigh of exasperation.

"How many times do I have to tell you, I'm not interested. And would you please drop the phony accent? It grates on my nerves."

"Fine, be a fuckwad, but you should check that ego, lover boy, 'cause this isn't about you and me," she said in her best Brooklynese.

"All right, what?" He played along hoping to speed things up.

Graciela glanced over her shoulder, then leaned into him. "There's a lot of talk you're pissing off the wrong people."

"Story of my life."

"No, I mean you're the topic of everyone's conversation."

"Who's everyone?"

"People who matter." Graciela paused for effect. "People who say you're on the run and hiding out because things are hot in New York."

"Stop talking in code." The bartender placed his drink in front of him and he downed it then motioned for another.

Graciela loved to be the center of attention as she dished the latest juicy story.

"You've pissed off Frank Barnett, and Carlos has his own problems."

The bartender placed another drink in front of him and he raised it to his lips. "Like?" His heart beat at an irregular pace, but he struggled to concentrate.

"Like somebody running drugs through the club. Selling the shit right out in the open."

He squinted at her over the glass. "And Carlos knows about this?"

"He does if he knows what business his nephew Alejandro is in."

Carlos knew his position on drugs in the club, how guns and bloody bodies were bad for business, but Carlos had a soft spot for family.

She bit at her bottom lip. "I'd be real careful if I were you."

His hand grazed the still-tender skin under his eye as he struggled to suck in the humid air.

"Doesn't mean you and I can't get together later. Maybe go to Mansion." She let her finger trail down his bare chest and flirt with the waistband of his trunks. "You know, the place with those big stalls in the ladies' room where you used to slam me against the wall and tell me I was the best fuck—"

"Stop talking shit." He turned to block any view Cheryl might have, then yanked her hand away.

"Fine, just stay healthy."

Jonny dragged in a deep breath and picked up their drinks. He wouldn't share this with Cheryl but trying to act normal after that strange conversation would be difficult. He hadn't detected any issues with Carlos earlier, but tonight at the club he would examine him closer. Maybe he'd missed some sign, or maybe Graciela was spinning her usual drama queen shit.

Paranoia clutched at his gut and snaked through his nerve endings as he weaved his way to their cabana. The same couples he'd passed on the way to the bar now seemed to be staring at him, while the warm sun and tropical breeze became hot and steamy.

"What happened to the people who were next to us?" He handed Cheryl her drink.

"I don't know. They left."

He checked the cabana on the other side of them, finding it empty too.

"Jonny?" She sat up on the lounger.

"Yeah?" He spun around and spilled some of the ice onto the lounger.

"Everything okay?"

He flicked the ice cubes onto the sand, sat down, and forced a smile, hoping it appeared more natural than it felt.

"Are you going to tell me how you met Graciela, the Spanish model?"

"Her accent's as fake as the rest of her. She's from Bensonhurst. She came down here about ten years ago, shaved five years off her age, and got herself shot up with silicone."

"Unbelievable. Is she even a model?"

"Sure. If you consider posing for a magazine that sells sex toys and being photographed by an ex-porn star named Dick Dragon."

"I guess South Beach is the place to reinvent yourself." Cheryl laughed, but she seemed off, or maybe he was projecting his own tension.

"Are you all right?" He drained the rest of his drink.

"Funny, I was going to ask you the same thing."

She searched his expression, and he swooped in for a kiss. He opened his mouth over hers, and the warm taste of the sweet Brazilian rum made him deepen the kiss. He wanted so much for her, for them.

He broke the kiss off and let his lips rest on hers. “As long as you’re with me, everything’s fine.”

He wanted to salvage the rest of their beach day, but he couldn’t enjoy the breaking waves or the bright blue sky anymore. He dissected every word of his conversation with Carlos earlier, but he couldn’t remember anything odd. He also replayed his encounter with Graciela. They’d had a few hook ups in the past which meant nothing to either of them, so she had no reason to lie to him. Nothing made sense. Exhausted and frustrated, he suggested they go back to the condo and was surprised when Cheryl appeared relieved.

Chapter 27

When they entered the condo, Cheryl escaped to the bedroom and into the shower and Jonny mumbled something about fixing himself a drink. If her screwed up stomach could handle it, she would've gotten totally wasted just to forget the last few hours.

Jonny seemed off too, but maybe it was her imagination. Trying to act normal while her brain screamed in protest was exhausting. Frank's cryptic call on the beach, totally freaked her out and nearly brought on a full-blown panic attack.

She stepped into the warm water of the spa shower and let the water beat down on her, but it did nothing for her nerves. After a few minutes, she shut it off, stepped out, and pulled a towel off the rack. When she felt hands at her waist, she yelped.

"Hey, I didn't mean to scare you." Jonny nuzzled the back of her neck. "I was gonna join you in the shower." He splayed his hands over her hips and held her tight. She could feel him hard and hot against her bare ass. "All bent over just waiting for me."

She spun around, her heart still beating double time. "I know I've said this before, but you've made me so happy." Her voice hitched, and she covered it with a cough.

He smoothed his hand over her damp hair. "What's the matter?"

"Nothing," she answered much too quickly.

"You sure?"

"Remember you told me about your friend that could get us fake ID's and passports?"

"Yeah?"

"So why don't we do it?"

"What are you talking about?"

"Become different people, fly to another country. We could even take my brother. I'd love to get him away from Brooklyn." Her voice shook with desperation, but she couldn't control it.

"Baby, I can't leave now."

"It could be a new start for all of us."

"I got too much going on." He moved her closer. "But you don't have to worry anymore. I told you, nobody's ever gonna hurt you again."

She leaned into him and pressed her cheek against his chest. She drank in the smell of salt air and summer heat on his skin and clamped her eyes shut to hold back the tears. She planned on betraying him, and yet he still protected her.

"I know," she whispered. "It was just an idea."

"Let me get everything together." His lips grazed her neck, and the rough stubble on his jawline pricked her skin. "I'll have so much fuckin' money you can buy out all those designer stores, and we can go anyplace you want."

She blinked a few times to hold back a fresh set of tears and let her hands roam over the smooth skin of his rock-hard muscles. It hurt so much knowing something so perfect couldn't exist for her. Her chest ached, but how dumb was that? Hearts didn't really break, did they?

His mouth covered hers, and his tongue plunged deep, searching. Like he sensed her desperation or was maybe trying to rid demons of his own. His breathing grew ragged, and she sensed a hunger in him, a neediness, or a desire to be needed. It darkened his eyes and tightened the muscles of his neck. It created an urgency in his touch like his life depended on them making love and making love now.

"I'm burning up for you." He grabbed her ass and ground against her. "I need to be in you. Now."

He yanked open a drawer next to the sink, pulled out a condom, ripped it open with his teeth, and sheathed himself. He whirled her around, and she leaned in to brace the counter. He clung to her hips and drew her to him, hard. A reckless need tingled through her as a heat settled between her legs seconds before he thrust into her. He pulled her hips tighter, nudged her legs further apart, and when his fingers found her clit, she squirmed and twitched against him.

"Fuck . . ." He groaned, leaning one hand on the counter for support as his hips pounded harder and his fingers moved faster. "Fuckin' perfect."

Skin slapped against skin, and she hoped the counter was bolted to the wall. She bucked back again, and the pressure built as his fabulous fingers worked her until she was helpless to do anything but give into the lust and the love, and what would be their last time together.

"Who's making you feel good, baby?" He thrust into her hard and stopped.

"Mmmm." Words and full sentences were not an option.

"Answer me," he demanded.

"Damn it." She wiggled her ass against him. "Don't stop."

"Then answer me," he repeated. "Who do you belong to?"

If he didn't move soon, she would go crazy.

"You," she panted. "Only you."

Her words unleashed a magic spell. She shouted his name and repeated the murmured litany seconds before she flew apart. No big build up, just a hot, wild, hard come that left her shaking and clenching.

His back stiffened as his wet heat shot into her. He collapsed against her, bracing his hands against the counter, his warm breath against her neck. He lay there for a few minutes, their bodies slick and panting. She pushed against the counter, and he slowly lifted with her, his free hand snaking around her waist, pulling her around.

With a shaky hand, he traced his finger over her jaw and down her neck.

“You giving me this . . . letting me be real with you.”

She knew by ‘this’ he meant her.

“I wouldn’t want you any other way.” She stroked his still-swollen jaw.

“Whatever happens, I’ll always put you first, keep you safe.”

She desperately wanted to return the favor, but how could she choose between blood and love?

He guided her back to the bedroom where they collapsed on the bed. He stretched out in his oversized bed in his beautiful South Beach condo with the sheet draped over his hips. His tanned arm flung behind his head tightened the smooth skin of his ripped abs and narrow waist. A tattoo on his bicep that meant nothing, and another on his ribcage that meant everything.

He threw his attitude around in a hard, rough way, pretending to be tough, yet his sensitivity and insight floored her. His soul clashed with contradiction, while his eyes were filled with love. She longed to tell him how she loved him and never meant to hurt him, never meant to blow his life apart.

He flung his arm out. “Get in here nice and tight.”

She snuggled into his chest, and he wrapped his arms around her as if protecting her from the shadowy shreds of life that opened them up and made them vulnerable.

“Always, baby,” she murmured against his chest.

She could have spent the rest of the night in his arms, pretending there were no consequences or repercussions for decisions she had to make, but Jonny had other plans. He wanted to take her to the club and show her off to his friends, but they’d never make it.

Chapter 28

Cheryl shifted in the leather seat, adjusted the bustier Jonny bought her the day before, and palmed the bag of coke. At just before midnight, the limo crept through the parade of cars and motorcycles clogging Washington Avenue along with the steady stream of people spilling out onto the street slowing them down to a crawl. Every agonizing minute stretched out before her.

She leaned in and kissed him softly on the cheek. "You know how much you mean to me?"

"As much as you mean to me." He deepened the kiss, and her throat tightened with emotion as the limo slowed and eased to the curb.

Flashy club clothes replaced skimpy bathing suits, amping up the vibe on Ocean Drive. She swiveled around on the sidewalk, overwhelmed by the men in outrageous black leather outfits and women dressed in colors so bright they competed with the vibrant neon signs. The swirling scent of tropical flowers and sweet perfume curled her nervous stomach as she waited for the inevitable.

"You look great, boss," the valet greeted. "We miss you down here."

It intrigued her how everyone from the uniformed valet to the big, hulking bouncers at the door vied for Jonny's attention. He greeted them warmly by name, and she could tell they respected him.

Pounding music escaped from inside the club every time the door opened. The beefy doorman stepped forward and let a smile invade his dour expression. He opened his mouth to say something but was cut off by the sound of screeching tires at the curb and two uniforms bolting out of a patrol car marked Miami Beach/Dade County Police.

"Juan Miguel Vallone?" The taller one shouted in Jonny's direction as the shorter, fatter one pushed through the crowd.

The constant stream of people on the street halted, and even the noisy crowd corralled behind the velvet ropes quieted.

A few second later she realized they were talking to Jonny.

The enormous doorman stepped to Jonny's side, and the taller cop jerked his head. "Tell your goon to back off."

Jonny nodded, and the doorman stepped off and clasped his hands behind his back in some relaxed military-street posture.

"We have reason to believe you're in possession of illegal drugs." The taller one yanked Jonny around, shoved him to the outside wall of the club, and patted down the front of his shirt.

Jonny stayed cool and composed as he looked over his shoulder. "You're making a mistake, boys. Drugs ain't my thing."

"Keep quiet." The cop skimmed the pockets of Jonny's pants and his inseams.

"Go easy." Jonny shifted. "Don't wanna disappoint my girl later."

The officer stood and addressed the other cop. "Nothing."

"Nothing?" The shorter cop asked. "Impossible."

He stepped forward and repeated the entire procedure, only rougher.

"What's the matter, you both want a feel?" Jonny drawled.

The two cops exchanged a look. "Just watch yourself, wise guy."

They returned to the squad car, said something to each other, then sped away.

"Fuckin' cops." The bouncer advanced to Jonny's side. "You okay, boss?"

"Yeah." Jonny held his mouth tight as a storm loomed behind his eyes.

"Hey?" She moved to his other side. The plastic bag burned against her breast bone when in reality it was undetectable to anyone but her.

"I'm fine," His tone meaning the exact opposite.

She'd made her decision about two minutes after they'd gotten into the limo. Two minutes after Jonny slid in next to her and cradled her in his arms. Two minutes after he told her she was the first woman he'd ever trusted, and that trust was the most important thing to him. She'd saved Jonny, but by now those cops were texting Frank about the botched job, and a shit storm was sure to follow.

She palmed her phone and sent an urgent message to Dylan while Jonny joked with the bouncers about which cops were bigger assholes, the NYPD or Miami-Dade. She advised Dylan to go to the "safety zone," code for Dylan's parole officer. She'd sheltered him before when things fell apart with their mom, and she couldn't chance Dylan staying alone. Hopefully, he wouldn't blow off her warning, and she could keep him safe until something could be figured out.

The bouncer barked orders into his headset, then ushered them into Paradise II. Anxious club-goers craned their necks to get a better view, but the drama was over, for them anyway. She swallowed hard imagining Jonny's reaction to her latest secret. Trust and loyalty were high on his hit list, and betrayal would be a deal breaker, the one thing that could wreck them.

The crowd parted as security escorted them toward the stairs leading to the VIP Room. Jonny's firm hand on the small of her back guided her deeper into the club, where the pulse of the music thumped louder, and the crowd of gyrating bodies grew thicker. The DJ suspended in his overhead cage commanded their attention and set the mood. The floor vibrated with energy as people jostled for position at the main bar. Shimmering fabric draped from the ceiling lent the vast room an intimate feel.

Jonny stopped many times to greet people. He knew most by name, and when he didn't, he acted as if he did. It hit her how much was at stake for him, and why this trip was so important. They climbed the spiral staircase, and she skimmed her hand against the iridescent tile water wall spanning both levels of the club from floor to ceiling.

At the top of the staircase, the bouncer pointed past columns of twinkling amber lights to a table in the front corner. "Have a good night, boss."

"Juan Miguel?" she questioned, after the bouncer left.

"My mother's effort at keeping Cuban roots."

"I like it."

"Too ethnic, that's why I changed it, but being only eight, I came up with my own spelling, and it stuck."

She furrowed her brow and pictured him as a little boy.

He clasped her hand in his and led her to a deep green suede banquette that wrapped around a kidney-shaped table already set up with bottles of Patron Platinum and champagne submerged in silver ice buckets. Sheer gauze separated each section of the prime spot, providing full view of the dance floor below them.

A handsome, impeccably dressed man, whom she guessed to be in his early forties, appeared at Jonny's side. He could also rock the cover of GQ with his tight cropped black hair and warm brown eyes.

"So this is the beautiful lady who stole Miami's most eligible bachelor." His rich, seductive accent rippled over the house music.

"Cheryl, this is Carlos. He's my right hand in Miami." Jonny's words sounded sincere, but his eyes remained watchful.

"He gives me way too much credit," Carlos said graciously.

"How's the table service tonight?"

"Full house, boss." Carlos motioned around the VIP Room.

Genuine respect filled Carlos' voice, but Jonny remained stiff and edgy. Probably left over tension from his encounter with the cops.

"Raul and Isabelle are on the dance floor. They asked to join you tonight."

"Fine." Jonny leaned into Carlos. "Can I have a word?" His voice remained soft, but his eyes shone like hard, black pieces of onyx.

"Of course." Carlos turned to her. "Again, it was a pleasure to meet you, and if you want anything, you need only ask."

Jonny eased her onto the soft suede cushions and brushed her lips with a kiss. "Back in a minute."

He straightened and followed Carlos to the far side of the service bar. She drew in a cleansing breath and scoped out a ladies' room, anxious to get rid of the coke and any evidence of her deception.

Chapter 29

Carlos stopped at the end of the service bar, where they could talk in relative quiet. He motioned for the bartender. "I'll have a bourbon."

"What the fuck is going on?" Jonny demanded.

Carlos spun away from the bar. "What?"

Jonny couldn't figure if Carlos was confused or defensive.

"I nearly got popped outside the club just now." Jonny pinned him with a cold, steady glare.

"Cops?" The bartender placed Carlos' drink in front of him, and he gulped down half of it.

"Patting me down for drugs. You know about this?" Jonny cocked an eyebrow. "Or maybe you set it up?"

"Jonny." Carlos frowned. "How could you say that?"

"The cops seemed disappointed." He paused. "No, surprised, like they expected to find junk on me."

"And you think I had something to do with it?" Carlos set his glass on the bar, and Jonny glimpsed the slight tremor of his hand.

"I saw Graciela today, and she said someone's running drugs through the club."

Carlos tipped his chin. "And you believe her, a coked-up party girl, over me?"

"I'm thinking you didn't tell me because it's Alejandro doing the dealing."

Carlos sucked in a deep breath and blew it out.

"Don't fuckin' lie to me," Jonny warned.

"Yes." Carlos hung his head. "I've tried talking to him." He splayed his hands over the bar. "What can I say? He's my sister's son. He's always been trouble, a disgrace to the family."

"You know the way I feel about this, and family or not, it has to end."

"I understand. I'll try again."

"No, I'll take care of it."

Carlos' eyes went wide.

"I'm just gonna talk to him, that's all."

"But this other thing I don't understand. We own the South Beach cops."

"Unless they're getting heat from somewhere else," Jonny suggested, as he observed Carlos' expression. He'd come to this man as an ally, a friend, and the possibility of deception made his chest hurt.

~ ~ ~

While Jonny was with Carlos, Cheryl located the bathroom, locked herself into the stall, and dumped first the coke then the baggie into the toilet. She'd flushed numerous times to get rid of all traces, so many times the women in line must've suspected some intense stomach issues. If only she could dispose of her guilt as easily.

As Jonny approached the banquette, she admired the self-confidence radiating off him, the way he owned every space he occupied. He motioned to a girl in black bootie shorts and a matching halter top.

"Let's try that champagne."

"Good evening, Mr. Vallone. I'm Monique, and I'll be your hostess tonight." Her wavy, chestnut-colored hair cascaded over her perfect figure.

Normally, Cheryl would've sized the girl up as competition, but her mind was too crowded with how she would begin to explain why the cops had him pinned up against the wall and why she didn't warn him. How after all he'd done for her she deceived him. Again.

Monique extracted the champagne from its ice bath and nudged the cork until it popped. She filled two fluted glasses and handed one to each of them, then faded off to blend into the sheer gauze separating each VIP section.

Jonny draped his arm over her shoulder as the icy liquid numbed her fingertips. He leaned in and lifted his glass. "To the best thing that ever happened to me."

She sipped at the bubbly champagne and gazed at him over the rim of the glass. The setting and moment were perfect, but she couldn't stand it any longer. "Jonny, I have to tell you . . ."

"Shush." He put the tip of his index finger over her lips. "You don't have to say anything. Just you, here, being so true, is all I'll ever need."

The guilt swelled in her chest as she struggled for the words that could blow his trust to pieces.

"Hey, Jonny!"

An attractive couple approached their table, interrupting her thoughts. The man shared Jonny's Mediterranean features and sense of style, while the woman at his side had an exotic mix of flawless ivory skin, almond shaped brown eyes, and a waterfall of straight, ebony hair. Her lithe figure was draped in a one-shoulder Valentino dress Cheryl admired in the Bal Harbour shops earlier.

The couple convinced her that South Beach exceeded its quota for good-looking people. They greeted Jonny affectionately in Spanish.

"Only English tonight," Jonny said. "Isabelle, Raul, this is Cheryl."

"Carlos told us you were here with a gorgeous woman." Raul slid into the opposite side of the booth.

"You must be special to lock this one down." Isabelle pointed to Jonny. "Many have tried, none succeeded." She leaned into Cheryl. "I'll fill you in on all the gory details later."

"Don't believe a thing she says." Jonny winked at her.

After more good-natured ribbing, Cheryl and Isabelle settled into casual conversation about shopping in South Beach.

"I'm so glad he took you to Bal Harbour. It has the best stores." Isabelle's soft, lilting accent fit her personality.

Raul leaned into Jonny with a serious expression. "I understand you saw Graciela today."

"News travels fast."

"Did you see the new fall line at Chanel?" Isabelle asked.

Cheryl tried to concentrate on both conversations. "No, I missed that."

"You must have Jonny take you. They have some fabulous purses."

"Bad news always does," Raul said.

"Bad news?" Jonny's voice was casual around his tightened jaw.

"And of course their shoes are the best." Isabelle sipped her champagne.

"Probably nothing to worry about," Raul offered. "Just Graciela with her usual shit and party girl drama."

"Why don't you tell me what you heard and . . ."

"Jonny, so glad you're in Miami," a voice boomed as another man approached the table. Jonny locked eyes with Raul for another second, then greeted the man standing to his left.

"Jared, good to see you." The two men shook hands, as Jonny switched gears.

"Cheryl, this is Jared Klein. He manages the Delano."

"Nice to meet the woman I've heard so much about," Jared said.

She marveled at the grapevine in Miami. Jonny having a serious girlfriend aroused everyone's scrutiny. Jared sat at the end of the table between the two men, his milk-white complexion and red hair in direct contrast to Jonny and Raul.

Jonny broke the seal on the bottle of Patron and poured each of them a shot.

"A toast." Isabelle held her glass up, and they all followed. "Here's to Cheryl, the only woman who could tame our Jonny."

They shot the smoky liquor and chased it with lime slices.

"Now, if the beautiful ladies will excuse us for a minute, I have some business questions for Jonny." Jared turned toward the men. "Tell me all about Simon Davis. Is he worth the investment?"

The men talked business, and they did more shots. The champagne and tequila swimming through her bloodstream made her feel weightless, lifting her anxiety and guilt, giving her an excuse for putting off the inevitable and enjoying this magical night. Jonny played the perfect host, but he passed on the last few shots, and his gaze continued to skitter past them to the first floor.

She leaned into his ear. "What are you looking for?"

"Nothing." He forced a smile. "Are you having fun?"

"Yes, your friends are great." She loved his exclusive attention, like no one else existed. Making her his priority squashed her gnawing insecurities, but amped up the guilt to a dizzying level.

He pressed his lips against her ear. "I'm so proud you're mine."

His words sent her back to their bedroom and the way he'd made her claim him. The memory brought a familiar tingling between her legs, and when she caressed his thigh under the table, he flashed her a wicked grin. But two minutes later when his gaze shifted again, her instincts ramped up, then ebbed away on a wave of tequila.

"I'll be right back." He brushed a kiss to her cheek, then bolted from the booth and bounded down the stairs to the main floor.

"He's preoccupied when he's here." Isabelle rested her hand on her arm. "Hard to take his mind off the job."

She'd seen the same tension mixed with a heavy dose of anger on Jonny's face at the beach this afternoon, and again tonight when he talked with Carlos. Maybe he had secrets too, but the question floated away on a champagne cloud as Isabelle refilled her glass and recited the latest fashion news.

~ ~ ~

When Jonny hit the first floor, he let the people move and surge around him, so he could observe first and then act. Alejandro stood by the line of unisex restrooms, shielded by the sheer size of the water wall. As people moved past him, they either purchased his product or moved on. The cocky way he held himself made it clear they expected and accepted his presence.

His black hair slicked into a sleek ponytail at the nape of his neck accentuated his hollowed features, while the designer club clothes clung to his skeletal frame. He definitely used as much as he sold. He had to give the kid credit though. He'd figured out how to run a business within a business. Seeing enough, he moved in behind him.

"Alejandro?" Jonny shouted over the music.

Alejandro jumped, whipped around, and twitched. "Jonny? What the fuck are you doing here?"

"I run the place, remember?"

"Sure, I just didn't expect to see you," Alejandro shot back as he closed his right hand into a tight fist.

"You seem a little jumpy," he deadpanned, then moved him off to the side, away from the line.

"Nah, everything's great." Alejandro kept smiling. "Couldn't be better."

Jonny grabbed his fist and pried it open. They stared down at five small glassine bags of white powder. “You got balls, I’ll give you that much.”

“C’mon.” Alejandro puffed up full of attitude. “You wouldn’t stop a guy from making a few bucks.”

“Not this way, and not in my club.”

“Maybe you’d like it better if I cut you in for some of the take.” Alejandro’s arrogance floored him.

“You dumb shit.” Jonny yanked him under the stairwell. “Your family didn’t come all the way from Cuba for you to be a dope dealer.”

Alejandro spun out of his hold. “My mother works her ass off in a hotel, and my uncle works for you, but I’m making real money.” He pounded his chest with his fist. “They call me the Prince of South Beach.”

“You’re gonna be the dead Prince of South Beach if you get in any deeper with this shit.” Jonny stepped forward, crowding his space.

“Who are you kidding?” Alejandro waved his hands around. “I’ve heard the stories about you and how you came up.”

“You don’t know shit.”

“Busting heads on the Brooklyn docks. Jacking cars and making collections for Frank Barnett. You did it the old-school way. I’m just putting a new spin on it.” Alejandro’s lips twisted into a sneer. “You’ve probably done worse than me.”

The kid had him there. The arrogant punk was right. He had done worse. Admitting it to himself didn’t make it any easier, but it sure did give him a great excuse for slamming him against the wall.

“You need some help, boss?” One of the bouncers appeared beside him.

In seconds, two other human blocks of cement were at his side. When the boss shoved people around on the main floor, others noticed.

Jonny leaned into Alejandro. “Just keep that shit outta my club.”

“You can’t protect what’s not yours.” Alejandro zeroed in on Jonny. “Word is, you can’t protect shit anymore.”

“What?” Jonny got in his face.

“So maybe you should be worrying about your own ass.”

“Shut the fuck up, punk,” one of the bouncers growled as he dragged Alejandro toward the back door.

Jonny stayed under the stairwell and sucked in some deep breaths. Was Alejandro’s warning wise guy bullshit or the real thing?

Chapter 30

A half-hour later, Jonny maneuvered Cheryl through the lobby of his building. After his encounter with Alejandro, he'd collected her from the VIP and said his goodbyes. He made it appear like he couldn't wait to get his sexy woman home to bed, but that was only part of it. Jonny's growing paranoia since coming to Miami, and his encounter with Alejandro, put him on edge and examining even the most casual of remarks.

She swayed in his arms. "I had the best time tonight."

She attempted to wrap her arms around his neck, which caused her dress to hike up dangerously high. The doorman stared and winked until he realized Jonny's scowl was meant for him. After tripping a few times, she kicked off her shoes, and now he carried them in one hand while trying to guide her onto the elevator with the other. For a drunk little thing, she was very wiry.

"I don't know what's the matter with me," she slurred.

"You're blasted, baby." Jonny laughed. "Drunk off your ass."

"I am not." She giggled. "Well, maybe a little."

The elevator doors whooshed closed, and the slight movement made her lose her balance.

"Easy now." He righted her, but she whirled around and flung her arms around his neck.

"I don't understand it. Isabelle drank as much as I did, and she was fine."

"Isabelle's Brazilian. She can drink me under the table."

She shoved him against the mirrored elevator wall, pressed her lips against his, and sighed. "You are sooo hot. You were the hottest guy in the club."

"You think so, huh?" She made him forget Alejandro, the club, and all the shit squirming around inside him.

"Absolutely."

She tugged at the buttons of his linen shirt and then moved down to his belt. As drunk as she was, she unfastened the leather straps in two quick moves. Hanging on to the loosened buckle, she sank to her knees, and his dick twitched. The scraping sound of his zipper snapped him back to reality.

"Whoa." He stilled her hands and tugged her up along with his zipper.

She dropped one of her hands to his crotch. "You are sooo big. Huge, immense, gigantic. And so hot, too." She paused. "Did I already say that?"

"Yeah, you did." He snatched her hand away again. "C'mon, baby. Not here." With his luck, the doors would open, and the gay couple who shared the other condo on his floor would be standing there.

"You had sex on your desk all the time in New York."

"This is different. You're different." Her sucking him off in the elevator seemed sleazy.

"I was trying to be nice." She stuck out her bottom lip in a childlike pout, and he loved it.

"I got a big private bedroom waiting for us. You can be nice to me there."

Bending down, he swooped her into his arms. She squealed and pretended to fight him, but then buried her head in his neck. Her warm tongue, nipping and nibbling, made him stagger off the elevator while he rummaged in his pocket for the key.

He eased her down, closed the door behind them, and held her for a second so she could steady herself. Throwing him a teasing smile, she swayed toward the bedroom. He followed her, caught her from behind, and whirled her around pressing his lips against her neck. A shiver slid up her spine when he yanked at the thin straps of her dress.

"Be careful. You'll rip it."

"Fuck the dress." He moaned into her mouth. "I'll buy you another."

With the straps off her shoulders, the soft material skimmed over her hips and pooled around her heels. She stood before him naked except for the white lacy thong accentuating her tan and those sexy fuck-me stilettos.

"Exactly how I wanted to see those shoes when we bought them."

She attempted to push them off, but he stopped her. "Leave them on."

He shrugged off his shirt, coaxed her onto the bed, slid his hands down each leg, then settled her designer-clad feet around his waist. She rubbed the sculptured spikes against his bare back, and he groaned.

"Fuck me, baby, that's sweet."

She did it again, and he groaned louder.

A heat boiled in his chest while his dick pushed and pulsed against the zipper of his pants. Fuckin' thing had a mind of its own, and it wanted out and into her wet, hot body.

"I need that hard dick of yours in me now." She rocked against him and sank her hands into his hair. "Rubbing up against me and making me come."

"I want you too, but this is more than sex. Do you get what I'm trying to say?"

Letting go of him, she sprawled herself across his king-size bed, her blond hair wild and disheveled against the sheets, her arms outstretched and welcoming. A sexy mix of innocence and raw need made her every man's wettest dream.

"Sure." She drew him closer. "Now will you please shut up and get busy here?"

"I feel different when I'm with you and . . ."

"I get it." She wiggled her hips against him.

Great. He couldn't believe it. For once in his life, he'd put it out there, bared his soul, and all she wanted was his dick. She wasn't even listening to him. This had to be some kind of screwed up payback for all the women he'd fucked and forgotten, as Eddie so eloquently put it.

When she snaked her hand into his pants, his mind shut down. Blood rushed through his ears, while his heart pounded. He toed off his shoes and vowed to have this conversation with her tomorrow when she wasn't rubbing against him in a way that made his eyes cross.

She squirmed under him, arching her back, her slick heat against his thigh. He nipped at the front of her throat, then soothed it with his tongue. When she dragged away his pants and boxers, he kicked them to the floor. The flat palm of his hand pressed under her thong, and she shimmied her hips enough for him to work them down her legs.

"I'm glad you didn't rip those." She cupped his chin. "They're my favorites."

He crooked his finger. "Mine too." Then flung them to the floor.

He slid higher, still working her, plunging his fingers into her, his thumb twisting and hitting her spot until she arched up, lips parted in a strangled cry. She kissed him hard and their tongues tangled with the taste of smoky tequila. He moaned into her mouth, then trailed wet kisses down her stomach, and when he got to her thighs he smiled.

"Please, Jonny," she pleaded.

He replaced his fingers with the tip of his tongue. Her hips bucked, and he spread her thighs wider hooking one leg over his shoulder, the heel of her stiletto digging into his back. He growled against her sensitive flesh and she pressed harder. His tongue found her swollen clit and he sucked it in while he squeezed her ass. When her breathing turned sharp and short, he changed direction and latched onto the soft skin of her inner thigh.

"Don't stop," she moaned.

"My greedy girl wants more?"

"Yes."

He sucked the delicate skin of her thigh hard enough to leave a mark. To remind her that she was his. She wiggled and moaned again as he broke free, admired his work, then laved the tender skin with his tongue.

"Marking your territory?" Her breathy voice teased while a fuck-me smile curled her lips.

"Yeah. You. Are. Mine."

He pressed his lips against her mouth, hard and possessive. He took his fill, then pulled back. "You like the way you taste on my lips?"

"Oh, yeah." She moaned as he hovered over her and captured her hands above her head. Sinking inside her, he let her soft, sweet body set him free. She moved with him and let him go hard, pushing it to the edge until her teeth grazed his shoulder and bit down. When her spasms hit and she clenched around his dick, he couldn't stop the smile of satisfaction from knowing he'd brought her to that place.

"You're so tight, so wet, so fuckin' beautiful," he whispered into her hair.

Each thrust punctuated his desire. She stripped him bare and tripped off a primal sensation deep within him. Intense and unforgiving, he drove harder. Needing all of her. Giving her what she wanted and taking what he needed. He bottomed out and his balls filled to the point of sweet pain. He swiveled his hips, and the tension built for a brief eternity before he broke apart and shattered into pieces. Their bodies slick and breathless, still entwined and sated. Boneless and unable to move, he collapsed at her side. All his emotions of the last few weeks bubbled up and collided together.

"I love you, baby," he murmured against her ear.

He heard the words like someone else said them. Then the realization hit. He'd said them. He waited, his heart pounding, his skin damp, his breathing choppy. Nothing.

Maybe his admission freaked her out. Was she trying to figure out a way to let him down easy? What would she say? I love the sex, but not you? He couldn't stand it any longer. He needed a response. Something. Propping himself on his elbow, he stared down at her. Her legs were still wound around his thighs, her hair tousled, and her eyes closed in a deep sleep. After all that, she hadn't even heard him.

He brushed her hair off her forehead and smiled at the woman he loved. Tomorrow, when she was sober, he would make sure she knew how much. He would tell her he loved her, ask her to move in with him and be a part of his life.

Chapter 31

The next morning Jonny woke before Cheryl. The sight of her all cuddled up in his bed calmed him, and with any luck, from now on he would get to enjoy this sight every morning.

He'd hoped the ocean view from his balcony would help him sort his feelings into words, but everything sounded lame and stupid. Either too forced and stiff or too corny and dumb. He'd already drunk his way through one pot of coffee, which left him tense and jittery, and when dark rain clouds gathered, he went inside.

Cheryl surfaced at noon, paler than the white robe she'd wrapped around her.

"Why did you let me drink all that tequila last night?" She massaged her temples as she eased herself into the kitchen chair.

"There was no stopping you. You and Isabelle kept pounding them down." He handed her two Advil. "Take these and then you need to eat."

She crinkled her nose at the bagel and cream cheese he'd fixed for her, complete with napkin and a steaming cup of coffee.

"This was sweet of you, but I don't think I can eat."

"Try. It'll make you feel better." He nudged a bowl of sugar packets toward her. "If it's not enough, we could raid a sugar factory."

She grinned at his teasing and tore the bagel apart. "I think I might have done or said some things last night . . ."

"You did."

She tugged her hand through her tousled hair and moaned. "How bad?"

"After I pried you off the top of the bar . . ."

Her eyes grew wide.

"And insisted you put your clothes on . . ."

Her choking gasps made him take pity on her.

"I'm kidding. Although I will agree I was the hottest guy there, and I have the biggest . . ."

She threw up her hands and pleaded. "Please, stop."

"I was gonna say brain." He laughed with her.

Large pellets of water slapped against the glass and ricocheted off the skylights. Cheryl jumped when a loud clap of thunder rattled through the room.

"Not good for the head," she moaned.

He continued to rehearse the words in his head, but nothing sounded right.

"Why do you keep staring at me?" She furrowed her brow.

He opened his mouth, and his heart skipped. If he didn't say something, he would explode from sheer nerves.

"Cheryl, I want . . ." No, bad beginning. "Cheryl, do you think . . ." What the fuck was the matter with him? *Just say it, asshole.* "Cheryl, will you . . ."

His cell phone buzzed. Happy for the distraction, he fished it out of his pocket. "What's up?"

"How's it going down there?" Eddie asked.

"Making some good connections. Everybody's onboard." Jonny kept the incident with the cops to himself. No sense in making Eddie more nervous. "How's everything else up there?"

"Quiet. Nothing from Frank."

"How about Max?" Jonny leaned against the arm of the couch. "He calm down any?"

"Haven't heard from him yet today. Probably laid up with that redhead."

"When I get home, we find out where his loyalties run." They'd come too far for any slip-ups now. "Jumpy is one thing, flipping sides is something else."

"I'll keep an eye on him." Eddie paused. "We all good?"

"You gotta ask?" Eddie might piss him off with all his worrying, but he always gave it to him straight.

"All right. See you tomorrow."

He shoved the phone into his pocket and stared at the rain water slide down the windows in long, unending streams. The waiting and the planning paid off. The incident with the cops probably had to do with Alejandro's shit, and now he had that straightened out too.

He'd wait till tonight to tell Cheryl how he felt in a nice, quiet booth at Scarpetta's overlooking the beach.

~ ~ ~

"Everything all right?" Cheryl asked.

"Yeah. Just thinking about the future."

A future she would love to be included in if she could find the guts to tell him about her latest secret.

"Sometimes I feel guilty," she said.

"About what?"

Where did she start? Involving him in her screwed-up life, or not telling him about a scheme to wreck him?

"About involving you and Eddie in my problems." She cursed herself for the generic answer. Her brain screamed words like *chicken-shit* and *coward,* but there was no good way to spin it.

"Why don't you go in and fill up the Jacuzzi with nice warm water?" he suggested. "It'll help your headache."

Her headache worsened, but guilt cursed her more than alcohol. Now she struggled to answer him in a way he expected.

"Only if you join me." She leaned up and kissed him.

Her brain screamed at her to blurt it out, but the words sounded so feeble and weak. *Frank called, gave me drugs to plant on you, threatened your life, and I kept it from you.*

So many things she'd done wrong, but staying quiet when Jonny professed his love last night tore her up. She'd played it off like she'd passed out, but she heard his raspy voice so soft, so gentle. His warm breath close to her ear. She'd wanted to hold onto him and never let go. To say the same words back to him a hundred times over, but knowing how much her trust meant to him she couldn't, wouldn't start their relationship with a lie between them.

"Mmmm." He snuck his hand inside the fold of her robe. "Soaping you up and drying you off?"

She stepped away from him and cinched her robe tighter. "Give me a few minutes before you come in. I want everything to be perfect." She moved toward the bedroom leaving promise in her wake while her insides trembled with dread.

"You naked in my hot tub is about as damn perfect as you can get," Jonny called after her as she closed the bedroom door.

She hugged the robe around her and pulled out her phone. After her betrayal, she'd expected another threatening call from Frank, but nothing. She shivered again as the rain pelted against the window. Frank's silence unnerved her more than his threats. She wanted to be honest and unburden herself, but she'd waited all her life to be loved, and now she feared putting it all in jeopardy.

Their first time together, she knew—maybe not that she loved him, but that he was different, and he made her feel different. He'd told her she made him want to be better, but he made her want to expect better, not settle and accept the unacceptable. He made her believe she could have goodness in her life, and if she forgot, he would remind her.

The little zing in her heart when he said her name. The glimmer in his eyes when he teased her, and the security when he held her. How could she gamble with losing something so precious, so vital to her existence?

Chapter 32

Jonny switched on some lights, hating the way the storm turned the day into night when a knock on the door interrupted him.

He squinted through the peephole, gripped the doorknob, and paused. Another knock, stronger than the first rattled the door. He flipped the locks and hauled the door open.

"What the hell are you doing here?" Jonny fixed on Max's unreadable expression, then on his rain-soaked jacket. A jacket much too heavy for the Florida heat.

He led him into the living room. Max's footfalls echoed behind him on the marble floor, then stopped. Jonny spun around and froze. The .45 Max leveled at him said it all.

"It shouldn't have come to this."

"What the fuck?"

"Frank warned you so many times." Max's massive frame sagged, his voice a conflicted mix of anger and frustration.

"So this is it, huh?" Jonny edged away, his hand skimming the top of the couch. "We grew up together." The painful edge of betrayal cut through his words. "We even went to juvie together."

"You wouldn't stop pushing."

"The night Eddie got jumped, your phone call when we were hanging out in his room." Suddenly it all made sense. "It was Frank, huh?"

"Yeah, it was Frank," Max shouted. "I was in the fuckin' middle. What was I supposed to do?"

Frank having Max do the job really hit home. The psychotic bastard knew how to find the weakest link.

"All your goddamn questions." An untamable anger boiled up in Jonny and replaced the hurt.

"I tried to make you see what the fuck you were doing." Max waved the gun around.

"And your friend Angel," Jonny snapped. "How did he play into it?"

"He was supposed to shadow you and make sure you had an accident."

"So how much is my life worth?"

"It's not about money. It's about power," Max barked. "How do you think *I* felt, being your lackey? "If I do this, Frank said he'd . . ."

Jonny shook his head. "You stupid motherfucker, he's not gonna give you shit."

Max paused, weighing his words.

"Just like Brutus and Caesar." Jonny side-stepped around the couch.

"What?" Max clutched the gun in a white-knuckled fist.

"Caesar got too ambitious, and Cassius didn't like Caesar's new popularity, so he sent Brutus, Caesar's trusted friend, to kill him."

"Stop talking shit." Max jerked at the collar of his shirt.

"Brutus felt justified. Is that how you feel, Max? Justified?" He needed to keep Max talking so he could get closer.

"Quit moving around," Max warned, raising the gun higher.

The storm raged louder, and Max flinched when thunder rumbled, and gales of wind slapped rain against the windows.

Jonny's biggest fear centered on Cheryl coming into the room. What's the matter, Max? Not as easy as you thought it would be?"

Unarmed in a gun fight, Jonny would lose. His street fighting days taught him distraction and deception worked best. Fool them into thinking you were easing up, then take your shot.

"Jonny?"

Max spun around to the sound of Cheryl's voice, but kept the gun trained on him.

Cheryl, entering the room in one of the skimpy negligees he'd bought her, was not the diversion he'd hoped for. He cut her a look that said, *Get the hell outta here.*

She flicked her hand at Max. "What's he doing here waving a gun around?"

"Everything was fine until she came along," Max growled. "Fucking your brains out, filling your head with shit."

Jonny needed to force his fear down and use this horrible twist to their advantage.

"C'mon, can you blame me?" Jonny threw his palms up and advanced two steps. "I mean, is she not the most fuckable piece of ass you've ever seen?"

Cheryl loosened the satin ribbons of the bustier crisscrossed under her breasts, and without missing a beat she played Max with nerves of steel beneath her teasing grin. All her years of running cons might just keep them alive.

Max stared and licked his lips. The muscles in his back tightened, and the gun wavered.

"Picture those tits and that ass in a bikini." Jonny kept the right amount of sleaze in his voice, while his insides churned. "Did I ever tell you how much she likes threesomes?"

"That's because she's a fuckin' slut ready to sell you out. Max sneered. "Didn't tell you about that, did she?"

Jonny stiffened. "What the hell are you talking about?"

"Frank called her right after you got down here. Offered her a sweet deal."

Jonny moved his gaze to Cheryl. "Did Frank call you?"

The guilt etched across her face floored him.

"Yes, but . . ."

"Shut up, you fuckin' whore," Max yelled.

"Jonny, let me explain," Cheryl pleaded.

"Frank called you?" Being held at gunpoint meant nothing now. "*You* set me up?"

"Nooo," she wailed.

"What do you think of your little whore now?" Max waved the gun in her direction.

Jonny's mind blanked, a fist squeezing his heart.

Once again she'd played him, and he fell for it. Nothing mattered anymore. Another bolt of lightning flashed through the apartment, followed by a room-shaking clap of thunder. The lights flickered for a second, and Jonny sprung from the side. He grabbed Max's wrist, yanked hard, and drove his foot against the outside of his knee. A pop and a grunt of pain as Max hunched over and staggered back two steps.

Another boom of thunder rattled through the room, but Jonny barely heard it. His focus shrunk to include Max and the gun. When Max relaxed his hand, and let the gun point to the floor, Jonny lunged. He realized his mistake a split second too late. Distraction and deception. He'd never forget the smirk on Max's face.

A loud crack, Cheryl's scream, heavy shoes on the stone floor, then a burning heaviness spread through Jonny's midsection. The buzzing in his head made him stumble and slump onto the couch. His heart pounded hard, then slowed. Sweaty and cold at the same time. He wanted to say something, but the dark red stain on his shirt entranced him. He pressed his hand against it, and his fingers were covered with the warm stickiness of his own blood.

Cheryl kneeled in front of him. "Jonny, stay with me!"

So many thoughts flew through his brain, but he couldn't form the words.

"Hang on," she pleaded.

He searched her face for anything that would take away a pain much worse than the one in his gut. But when her guard dropped for a fast second, the hard truth shone through, and now his brain zeroed in on one thing. She'd sold him out. His vision blurred like one of those cheesy movies with the dream sequences. Yeah, that's it. This was a dream. A big, bad fuckin' dream.

Chapter 33

"It's fuckin' crazy out there." Eddie jerked his thumb to the entrance of Miami General where reporters jockeyed for position, all trying the get the latest juicy story on the high-profile shooting.

"I know." Cheryl's gaze darted behind Eddie, grateful for the hospital policy of restricting reporters.

"How's he doing?" Eddie embraced her, and she held onto him, desperate for support and comfort. They'd called and texted furiously before Eddie boarded the red-eye from New York.

"He made it through surgery, and they've moved him to ICU, but the doctor said it could go either way." Saying the words drained her, but she gathered herself together and relayed the doctor's words. "The bullet ruptured an artery in his abdomen. He lost a lot of blood, and the next twenty-four hours are critical."

"Fuck." Eddie stepped away from her, flexed his fists a few times, and swiped the visitor's sign off the information desk.

The two elderly ladies manning the desk gasped in shock, and the gray-haired security guard hurried over, fixing a stern glare on Eddie. "Is there a problem here?" he asked, puffing out his chest while trying to suck in the fifty pounds that proceeded him.

Eddie threw up his hands in apology. "I'm sorry, man." He bent to retrieve the sign.

"He got some bad news." Cheryl stepped between them.

"We don't allow those kinds of outbursts here, son." The guard backed off when Eddie straightened to his six-foot-three height of solid muscle.

Eddie righted the sign, but the two women were still staring, so he dug in his pocket, peeled off a fifty, and placed it on their desk. "Have lunch on me tomorrow, ladies."

Cheryl tugged at Eddie's forearm and led him down the hall into a private sitting area away from prying eyes. She motioned to one of the chairs. "Now sit and calm down."

He stood by the chair but didn't sit. "I'm fine. Just tell me again what happened."

The storm raging outside, Max holding a gun on Jonny, it seemed like a weird joke until she'd seen Max's dead, cold expression.

After that, the minutes alternated between speeding by and slow motion. But nothing prepared her for the up-close, ear-splitting sound of gunfire, or the sight of Jonny slumped on the couch clutching his stomach, his hands covered in blood. Max stood there at first, not moving, looking as terrified as her. Then he half limped, half ran out of the condo. She'd frantically called 9-1-1, then waited for an eternity.

Eddie ran his hands through his hair. "I told him I had it under control. I should've seen this coming."

"Don't blame yourself. I just can't believe he didn't shoot me too." She stroked Eddie's hand.

"He's not a professional. He probably freaked." Eddie paused. "It's not like in the movies."

"The story's all over the internet. It's crazy."

"How about the cops?"

"They were here already. Typical cop questions, but for once I could answer honestly."

"I guess there's something to be said for being the victim." His wry comment didn't hide his anxiety.

The waiting and mindless, vacant hours were torture. She paced, and Eddie smoked his way through a pack of

Marlboro's. When it became obvious Jonny wasn't regaining consciousness any time in the near future, Eddie suggested they go to the hospital cafeteria. She didn't think she could even look at food, but at least walking to the cafeteria gave them something to do.

At one in the morning, the hospital cafeteria had a steady stream of doctors and nurses trying to revive themselves with coffee and carbs, along with clusters of families holding each other together for support. They found a table off to the side and sat. Eddie folded his bulky frame into the molded plastic chair, rested his arms on the table, and held his Styrofoam coffee cup in a way that made the tats on his forearms stand out.

"He's strong." The glaring fluorescent lights etched shadows of fear across Eddie's day-old stubble. "He's gonna get through this."

"I know," she said without conviction.

She stared at the cracks in the Formica tabletop.

"You sure you don't want something?" He motioned to his coffee. "You should eat."

"I'm fine." The sight of food made her stomach churn.

Eddie played with the plastic stirrer. "Jonny was always the smart one making it all work." His large hands wrapped around the steaming cup. "All I ever wanted was to get paid and get laid."

"It was the same way here in Miami," Cheryl told him. "Everybody wanted to be around him."

"He could've been one of them big executives." Eddie smiled wryly. "Me, I liked giving the beatdowns, but Jonny's heart was never in it." Eddie made a fist, then unclenched it and smoothed his hand over the tabletop. "Back in the day, he got me straight, kept me from going off the rails."

"He liked to act like a tough guy, but inside . . ." Her voice choked, and she swallowed hard. Guilt gnawed at her stomach.

Eddie sucked in a breath. "Frank's a fuckin' psycho." He slammed his fist down, and the cheap table wobbled under the force. Heads jerked in their direction until Eddie's glare made them turn away.

"Calm down." She patted his hand, as hot tears ran down her cheeks.

"Ahhh, shit." Eddie stood, scraped his chair to her side of the table, and held her. "I'm supposed to be making you feel better, not worse."

"It's not you." Her chest tightened. "Jonny thinks I set him up."

"What?"

She relayed the whole story, starting with Frank's phone call at the condo and ending with the cops frisking Jonny outside the club.

"Fuckin' bastard," Eddie hissed.

"Max told Jonny right before he shot him, and now Jonny thinks I . . . What if something happens and I never get to tell him the truth? What if . . ." Another flood of tears erupted, and her chest heaved with long-held sobs. She burrowed her face against Eddie's shoulder and released all the tension of the last few days and the fear of the last few hours. When the sobs quieted to little choky gasps, Eddie lifted her chin with his forefinger.

"Jonny's a tough fucker, and he's not gonna give up."

She prayed Eddie was right because losing Jonny was unthinkable, but losing him before he knew the truth was unbearable.

~ ~ ~

It all seemed so surreal, but Cheryl wanted to believe Eddie's words. Jonny was tough. He would make it. He had to. The doctors said his loss of blood caused his coma, and it would take time for him to heal. Now, five days later, reality hit, hard. The shades half drawn to keep out the hot, bright

Miami sun. The room's cool, controlled air conditioning. Machines and monitors humming and buzzing. Wires and tubes snaking their way in and out of his arms.

ICU nurses were stationed on the other side of the glass wall, observing his every move. His flawless complexion was sallow and waxy, and his skin clammy and too fragile to touch. Each breath was weak and shallow. What she wouldn't give to hear that low-down rasp teasing her just one more time. She blinked hard, thinking she didn't have anything left in her to cry, yet every day she sat here, and the tears fell.

"I'm here, baby, and I'll never leave you." She leaned closer. "And when you get better, we'll go somewhere where no one can hurt us."

His eyelids fluttered for a second, and his back became rigid. The alarms on the monitors shrieked. The ICU nurse swept into the room, followed by a doctor and another nurse with a crash cart. They pushed her to the side, powerless, scared, and shaking with fear.

Chapter 34

Night Club Owner with Alleged Mob Ties Dies

That's how the headline would read. What else could explain the complete darkness? Jonny twisted his head to the side, but nothing. No shadows, no reflections. He was lying down, but where? Oh shit. Maybe he was already in the coffin. He unclenched his fist and felt warmth—human warmth—skin against skin. He reached farther, and it responded.

"Jonny?"

The darkness said his name. What was this place? Then a flash of light. He clamped his eyes shut. It was too bright. It hurt.

"Are you awake?" the voice asked.

He knew the voice. He opened his eyes again, slower this time, letting them adjust to the harsh light. His vision was blurry, like an unfocused camera.

"Can you hear me?"

He could hear her fine.

"It's me, Cheryl."

Right, Cheryl.

"Can you see me?"

Sure, he could see her. Why was she asking him so many dumb questions?

"Please, say something."

Her voice was shaky and choppy, then her eyes flooded with tears. Damn, he didn't want to make her cry. He had to concentrate and drag himself out of this foggy Neverland.

“Don’t cry.” Those two words required tremendous effort.

“I can’t believe you’re awake.”

Her voice sounded happy, but hell, she cried harder. She leaned in and hugged him, and she smelled so good. He wanted to hold onto her too, but his arms were weighted down. He glanced around the room, then down at himself. Tubes snaking around his arms, machines hooked up to his chest, and every breath tight like his chest was wrapped in Velcro. What the fuck was going on?

“Try to relax.” She squeezed his hand. “You’re in the hospital. You’ve had surgery, but you’re going to be fine.”

“Surgery?” He croaked out the one word, his throat raw and dry.

Cheryl called for one of the nurses, and he became the center of attention as they shined lights in his eyes and asked him stupid questions like his name, his birthday, and the year. He stared past them into Cheryl’s eyes, and it all came rushing back. Max holding a gun on him, Max telling him she had betrayed him.

Pain seared through his chest and a steady beeping grew louder and faster. A nurse moved to his side, pushed a syringe into the IV tube and the light faded away.

~ ~ ~

Forty-eight hours ago Jonny couldn’t hold his head up, and now he sat in bed, scraping the very last piece of lime Jell-O out of its plastic container. It even impressed the doctor who moved him into CCU this morning.

Now, Cheryl mentally rehearsed her confession, tossing around the right adjectives and verbs to make what she did seem less awful, less painful. She’d even written some of it down, so he would completely understand the position she was in and hopefully forgive her.

"Are you comfortable?" She fidgeted with the blanket, as her mind froze and her throat dried. The elephant in the room was sitting right on her chest.

"No, I'm starving." He held up the empty plastic container. "This shit sucks, and I don't care what they say, Jell-O is not solid food."

"I'll go speak to the nurse."

"No, sit down." He patted the bed.

She averted her gaze busying herself with smoothing the blanket and tucking in the edges. His dark eyes tracked her, and when she met his gaze she sucked in a deep breath, and the words tumbled out.

"Frank called me the first day we were down here. I was supposed to plant coke on you, or he would hurt Dylan. That's why the cops came to the club." She drew in a deep breath. "But I couldn't do it." She exhaled as the ten-ton elephant waddled out of the room. "I could never do that to you."

His lack of response amped her up all over again.

"You don't remember Max telling you, huh?"

"I remember."

"You do?"

"Yeah."

"And?" She braced herself for the worst.

"And nothing."

"But I . . ."

"I'm not gonna deny what Max said blew me apart, but I saw you taking care of me, worrying about me. The nurses said you were camped out here the whole time I was in ICU, so I knew there had to be more to it. "

"Why didn't you say anything?"

"Because I knew you'd tell me when you were ready." He laced their fingers together. "I told you, I trust you."

And that explained it all. He trusted her, and she had to trust him enough to be straight with him. She'd spent so much of her life deceiving people, she'd forgotten about truth and honesty. To most people those virtues came naturally but learning to trust others, and even herself would be her biggest challenge.

"I wanted to tell you so many times, but I was scared you'd turn me out."

Jonny struggled to sit higher in the bed, fighting against the IV in his left hand and the heart monitor strapped to his chest.

"Baby, that wouldn't be possible." He reached for her. "Because without you the pain would strip the blood from my veins faster than any bullet."

Her lip trembled as she leaned into him, careful to avoid the IV, but needing to feel the warmth of his body. She'd worried about telling him, when she should've believed in him, believed in their relationship.

"Doesn't mean I wasn't pissed as shit at you for walking into that room with Max waving a gun around."

"In a perfect world, you wouldn't have gotten shot, so it wasn't a complete success."

"Forget me, Max could've shot . . ."

"But he didn't, and just maybe I helped you?" She glared at him.

"You helped me for sure, but . . ."

"And you'd be having this same conversation if Eddie tried to save your ass?"

"That's different."

"Except for him not rocking that negligee, I don't see the difference."

"Eddie and I have each other's backs and . . ."

"What was I supposed to do? Hide in the bedroom and hope for the best?" She jerked her hand away. "I tried to help, and you're mad."

"Hey, c'mere." He grasped her wrist. "You're wrong about Eddie. It is different."

"'Cause he's a guy?"

"No, 'cause I love you," he shouted in frustration.

"You love me?" She leaned into him, and he hauled her onto the bed.

"Yeah, I do." He threaded his hand through her hair and drew her in for a kiss.

Chapter 35

Not the way Jonny had planned on telling her. No romantic dinner at sunset. Just the two of them in this crappy room that smelled like Lysol, with lights bright enough to perform surgery, and yet she didn't seem to mind.

"I love you too," Cheryl murmured against his lips. "I was so worried I'd lose you and never get the chance to make things right."

"When we get back to New York I want you to move in with me."

Again, her silence rattled him until he saw the fresh tears in her eyes. "Please tell me those are happy tears."

"Oh, yeah." She hugged him to her. "Definitely happy tears."

"And from now on, we got no secrets from each other."

"It's like fate wanted us together." She snuggled closer to him. "The crazy way we met. You collecting for Frank and me being at the Oasis."

He tugged her closer and squeezed her ass. "I tried to forget you after that night, but I couldn't."

"And the last thing I needed was more drama, but here we are—together."

He held her tighter and covered her mouth with his. Her hair fell forward, and the flowery scent of her shampoo made him forget where they were. The bed dipped as she settled next to him. The warmth of her skin against his palm was almost enough. Almost.

The beeping of his heart monitor increased, and he whispered against her lips. "See what you do to me?"

"What the hell are you trying to do now?" Eddie sauntered into the room. "Give him a heart attack?" He pointed to the IV. "Sure, I'm out there busting my balls, and you're in here getting juiced up."

Cheryl hopped off the bed, and Jonny made a face. "Your timing sucks."

Eddie laughed with them as Cheryl straightened her clothing.

"Will you go check on that food for me?" Jonny flashed his sweetest smile.

"I can take a hint." She studied them both before her gaze settled on Eddie. "Just don't get him worked up."

"Never happen," Eddie assured her with a wink.

"I'll ask if you can have something besides Jell-O."

"A nice twelve-ounce sirloin would be great," Jonny called after her. "With onion rings and fries?"

The minute Cheryl left he dropped the smile. "Frank used her brother and fucked with her mind." He'd kept his anger in check with Cheryl, but now it blazed through him.

"She told me. And when that didn't work, he sent Max." Eddie's jaw twitched. "Fuckin' Max."

"I nearly lost my shit when he pulled that gun," Jonny muttered.

"He never made it to the airport. Popped up as gator food in some swamp at the edge of the Everglades two days ago."

"Frank doesn't like mistakes, and Max was disposable." Jonny drew in a ragged breath filled with anger. "He sucked him in with promises of power, but you know how that goes."

"And he fell for it. Greedy cocksucker."

"Power changes people." The two men locked eyes. The simple statement explained it all.

"You were in pretty bad shape." Eddie lifted his chin. "Scared the fuck outta me."

Eddie's way of saying he cared.

"But Cheryl had your back," Eddie added.

A memory of her a few feet from the barrel of Max's gun shot a flicker of fear through him.

"You heard what she did?" Jonny asked.

"She's ride or die. You ain't gonna change her."

That truth hung in the air between them.

"I don't want her left alone." Jonny tugged at the bedsheet. "And make sure her brother's safe too."

"Don't worry, I already got him at the apartment over the club, and she don't go anywhere without me." Eddie swiped at his phone a few times, then frowned. Then his phone beeped with alerts and he swiped a few more times.

"What's up?"

"I wasn't gonna show you this till tomorrow." Eddie handed him his phone.

South Beach Hot Shot in Hot Spot

Things heat up at Paradise II, where two victims were shot gangland style and disposed of behind a dumpster. Is it coincidence that Brooklyn's Jonny Vallone was also shot? Or is a New York City mob war heating up in South Beach?

He fisted the sheets until the IV pulsed against his hand. "Who?"

Eddie swallowed hard. "Carlos and Graciela."

"Fuck!" A dizzying rush of adrenaline shot through Jonny's veins.

"Word is, Max was gunning for Carlos because he wouldn't help Frank take you down, and Graciela was in the wrong place at the wrong time."

"Shit." Carlos and Graciela lying dead in some dirty alley left him numb inside.

He threw back the sheet and swung his legs over the bed then struggled against the wires and tubes holding him prisoner. The steady tick of the machines became erratic, until one of the floor nurses marched into the room, all business.

"What do you think you're doing, Mr. Vallone?" she demanded as she moved alongside the bed.

"I'm getting outta here." Jonny jerked forward. "There's things I gotta do."

"If they include ripping out your stitches and falling flat on your face, then you're in luck." She fixed her hands on her ample hips and stared him down.

The IV dragged against his hand. His feet hit the floor, and a clammy sweat slithered through him like he was either gonna pass out or puke. He didn't know what upset him more. Eddie's revelation, or feeling too weak to do anything about it.

"Calm down." Eddie gripped his shoulder.

The nurse helped Jonny move his legs onto the bed, adjusted the IV, then glared at Eddie. "He needs his rest."

"Just another few minutes," Eddie mumbled. She even intimidated him.

"Fine, but remember it's his first day out of ICU." She pinned them with a threatening glare.

"We should sic her on Frank," Eddie said.

"Oh, don't worry, Frank's gonna pay." He wanted to slam something and toss every fuckin' machine in the room out the window.

"I got a few ideas."

"Me too." Jonny snorted in disgust. "And all of them end with a bullet in Frank's head."

Eddie bared his teeth in a feral scowl. "He's not worth twenty to life in the joint."

"I don't give a fuck." He banged his fist against the bedrail, then gritted his teeth against the pain.

Eddie glanced over his shoulder and leaned in closer. "We'd be the first ones the cops would grab."

"Fuck that." His fist clenched, and the IV pulsed against his hand again.

"Don't talk crazy."

Eddie didn't feel his rage. He hadn't had a gun pointed at the only person he'd ever loved. He'd placate him for now. Tell Eddie what he wanted to hear, then make sure Frank got good and dead.

"It's these fuckin' pain meds." Jonny sighed. "They screw with my head."

"Cheryl didn't want me to tell you about Carlos and Graciela yet, but I figured you should know." Eddie moved closer to the bed. "And don't go telling her I got you worked up, or she'll be ragging on my ass all day tomorrow."

"Right"

~ ~ ~

Later, after Eddie and Cheryl left, Jonny's mind churned and twisted. When the night nurse arrived with his sleeping pill, he faked taking it, then crushed the capsule with his fingers when she left. He didn't want to sleep. He had too much to plan. Fuck careful. He fantasized about the ways he would take Frank out. From fast and deadly to slow and painful, anything to make him suffer.

Then Cheryl dominated his thoughts. She was fearless and reckless. Even Eddie agreed. And now that they'd admitted their love, she would stop at nothing to help him. If he truly loved her, he had to protect her from his violent life. Stop acting like a selfish punk and set her free.

Chapter 36

For the last seven days, Cheryl and Eddie walked the corridors of Miami General. They were on a first name basis with the nurses, security guards, and even the cafeteria staff. The *Miami Herald* made Jonny their most popular patient. The doctor finally released him, and tomorrow they would be on a plane to New York.

Eddie surprised her by not stopping at the nurse's station to do his usual flirting, but Cheryl chalked it up to the pressures of returning to New York. Jonny and Eddie had business to deal with, but she never questioned Jonny's loyalty to her. Most of her life she'd ached for the simplest emotions from people, emotions most people took for granted. But he filled a void and wrapped her in the security of his love, and although it didn't come easy, she trusted him to put her first.

She stood by his bedside as he sipped the Starbucks coffee that became their daily routine. A few feet away Eddie stared out the window, apparently intrigued by the view of the parking lot.

"I have something for you." Jonny studied her for a moment, then set the coffee aside. He opened the metal drawer of the hospital night table, extracted an envelope, and handed it to her.

She ripped it open, pulled out the printed e-ticket, and glanced at the dates. "Weren't we leaving tomorrow?"

"*I* am." He shifted his gaze to the bedsheets for what felt like an eternity. "But I want you to leave today."

"Why?" She moved closer to the bed.

"So you can get settled in Brooklyn Heights." He drew his lips to a firm line.

"Brooklyn Heights?"

Her heart thumped hard against her ribs, and the blood pounding in her ears made it impossible to concentrate.

"Luxury building. Big enough for you and your brother. Great view of Manhattan."

She looked to Eddie, but he continued to stare out the window. Had she fallen into some kind of bizarre vortex and spit into another universe?

"What are you talking about?"

"I also started a bank account in your name. There's enough there for the first six months." He focused on his hands. "After, if you need more . . ."

"I don't understand." She grabbed the bedrail for support. "You said you wanted me to move in with you."

"Not anymore."

His voice sounded so matter-of-fact like he was reciting his phone number or reading the daily receipts from the club.

"Please tell me what's going on." Her hands trembled against the cold metal bars. "You're scaring me."

Again, he diverted his attention to the bed covers. "It's too dangerous for you to be with me."

"I don't care about that," she said stubbornly.

"But I do." He swore under his breath.

"Please think about what you're saying," she pleaded.

"All I do is think." He slammed his hand against the bedrail, and she jumped.

"Did you know about this?" Her gaze darted to Eddie, demanding a response. His blank stare and stiff nod sent a cold chill up her spine.

"Ahhh, of course, you did." She blinked a few times and struggled to make sense of this nightmare and her own raging fears. "So you've discussed this with everybody but me."

"It has to be this way."

"Right, because the hell with what I want." Her voice quivered with heartbreak. "Or what I need."

"Don't you get it?" Jonny shouted. "Max could've shot you, too."

At last some emotion. An indication he hadn't been drugged or gone crazy.

"This is your answer? Hand me a plane ticket, tell me you're throwing me out of your life, and I'm supposed to roll over and take it?"

"I'm not throwing you out." The vacant expression returned. "You're gonna have a brand-new place and plenty of money."

She stared at him, astonished he thought this would placate her. Did he have any idea of the depth of her love? How leaving him would demolish her and strip her bare?

"But I only want you." Her voice broke on that truth.

Humiliating silence followed, and when he refused to look at her, she lashed out.

"I don't want your condo, and I don't need your money." She struggled to scrape up her last ounce of pride. "I've taken care of myself in the past, and I'll do it again."

"Don't be stupid, Cheryl." His voice was rough and unyielding. "Take what I'm giving you."

Then the truth hit her square between the eyes. Jonny Vallone didn't give up when he wanted something. He'd told her pretty lies in his bed when it was convenient, 'cause it got him off, but when it became too difficult, he bailed.

"You're right. I am stupid. Stupid to think you were different. Stupid to think we had a future." She staggered backward, needing distance from him. "I guess all that shit about loving me was the usual thing you say to a woman after screwing her brains out?"

"Don't make this any harder than it has to be."

It couldn't get any harder. The hope of someone truly loving her disintegrated and broke apart. The misery of having a glimpse of happiness only to have it snatched away.

"Don't worry, Jonny." Her voice sounded flat to her ears. "I'll make it real easy for you." She held up the plane ticket. "I'll take this and go to New York, but you can keep your condo and your money. Give it to the next girl who wanders into the minefield you call a life."

Seconds before the tears blurred her vision, Jonny jerked his chin toward Eddie.

"He doesn't need to follow me." She backed her way toward the door. "I'm not your problem anymore."

"Go with her." Jonny's voice sounded distant and detached.

"Hypocrite." She stopped and fixed him with a deadly glare. "Acting like you care."

"I'll always care," he mumbled it so low she wouldn't have heard it if her every nerve wasn't tingling like a high voltage wire laying in a puddle of muddy water.

She bolted for the door and stumbled down the wide, white corridors in a daze. Her whole world had shriveled up and crashed against her brain.

Chapter 37

One week back in New York, but it wasn't enough. The sad shakiness in Cheryl's voice haunted Jonny. Alone in bed at night in the dark, it screamed above the silence. Her sorrow and absolute dejection haunted him. It reminded him of every other bum who drifted into her life, messed with her, then bailed.

What he wouldn't do for an IV filled with morphine now. His pain meds were downgraded to Tylenol, but they couldn't squash the guilt or the ache from turning her away. Emotions he couldn't afford, feelings that made him vulnerable and weak at a time when he needed anger and hate. His obsession with revenge and keeping Cheryl safe made him push her away. Putting a bullet in Frank's brain left him no choice but to do this, and do it right.

Shadows covered the end of the dark pier, making it the perfect place to park. The foggy mist that drifted off the water made him flip up the collar of his jacket. From here he could walk alongside the abandoned warehouses using the darkness for cover. He sure as hell didn't need lights. He'd roamed these alleyways since he was a kid, memorizing every squeaky board and broken brick.

Frank's compulsion for schedules made him vulnerable. Like the way he drove himself to his weekly poker game every Thursday night, then returned to his office at midnight to lock up his winnings, arrogant that his power made him untouchable.

A noise to his left drew his gaze deeper into the shadows. He squinted against the blackness as he closed his fist around the .45 in the waistband of his pants. A dark form materialized under the glow of the halogen security lights.

"What the hell? You gotta get outta here."

"Oh, no." Cheryl planted her hands on her hips. "You're not pushing me away this time."

"You shouldn't be here," he rasped through the mist.

"I'm not some delicate flower that needs taking care of."

Right, just a stubborn woman who wouldn't listen to reason and once again put herself in danger.

She stepped into the light. "Let me help you and prove that we're equals."

He stared at her dressed in black from head to toe. Even her beautiful blond hair was tucked into a black skull cap. Cat woman.

"Going in guns blazing, or a more subtle approach?" She motioned to the gun he gripped. "I suggest subtle."

"I suggest you get the hell outta here and let me finish the job."

"Not going to happen." She shook her head in stubborn determination.

"You know how I'm gonna do this, right?"

"Well, I hope you're going to shoot the bastard 'cause I'm really anxious to get this done and declare our freedom."

Freedom, yeah.

Headlights reflected against the water. "He's right on schedule."

"I'll go in first. He knows I double-crossed him but I'm sure I can distract him," Cheryl said.

"Distract him, how?"

She cocked her head in a "how do you think" look.

Jonny pressed them against the bricks in one of the alcoves as Frank's BMW i8 rumbled over the cobblestones.

"That cocksucker was hitting on you?" Jonny narrowed his eyes.

"Every chance he got."

"Did he put his hands on you?"

She shrugged. "Nothing I couldn't handle."

"Another good reason to end him."

"We're wasting time," she said.

"You got five minutes to get him where I want him."

"That's four more than I need."

He looked deep into her eyes. "You don't have to do this."

"Trying to set me up for murder, threatening my brother, threatening you? Yeah, I do."

Frank's car slowed, then stopped in front of the metal stairs leading to the back of the warehouse. The driver's side door opened, illuminating the interior, indicating Frank was alone, as expected. Then he slammed the car door and climbed the metal steps to the warehouse.

"It's showtime." She flashed him a smile and turned.

He grabbed her arm and pulled her to him. "Be careful." Then he cupped her head and leaned in for a kiss in a rough, wild attempt to tame her. Impossible.

She squirmed out of his hold.

"Always." She stalked off along the building shielded by the shadows.

He missed her stubborn attitude. He hadn't even told Eddie he was coming here so how had she'd known? He'd made himself clear in the hospital room, but here she was again brave to the point of reckless. The darkness swallowed her up as he counted off the time in his head.

He pushed off the wall, and the weight of the .45 pressed against his abs. He dipped his chin against the damp wind gusting off the river. His pace quickened, and the incision in his chest burned. By the time he reached the warehouse stairs, he gripped the metal railing for support. He stood for a few long minutes and listened to the wheezing of his lungs when a gunshot rang out. Then another.

Sprinting up the stairs, he ignored the searing pain that ripped through his chest. He gulped in a few deep breaths, but it didn't help, so he slid the .45 from his waistband and bolted toward the office. He stopped short outside the door and listened. A terrifying silence made him squeeze the gun tighter. He counted to three, nudged the half-open door with his gun, then slowly shouldered through to the office, and froze.

"What the fuck?" Jonny shouted.

Alejandro jumped at the sound of his voice.

Jonny inched further into the office, the smell of gun powder hung in the air, with Cheryl plastered against the wall.

Jonny scanned the room. "Where's Frank?"

Cheryl pushed off the wall and pointed behind the massive wooden desk. "I was working my magic, and this guy"—she jerked her thumb at Alejandro— "pushes me aside, says something in Spanish, then blasts him between the eyes."

Jonny closed the gap between them and grabbed onto her, hugged her tight and then held her at arm's length. "Are you okay?"

"I'm fine, but my freakin' ears are ringing."

A consuming exhaustion crept through his bones. What if Cheryl had startled Alejandro and he shot her or got in his way. There were a million fuck ups and ways he could've lost her.

Jonny shook off the fear and edged around the desk to stand alongside Alejandro. They stared at Frank's lifeless body.

"I've avenged my family. Now my uncle can rest in peace." Alejandro nodded to Jonny's gun. "Looks like we're more alike than you think."

Jonny squeezed the butt of his gun and pointed it at Frank.

"Go ahead," Alejandro encouraged. "It made me feel better."

Silence filled the room. For too long Jonny let the hate and anger choke him, while Frank pulled the leash shorter and shorter until it snapped. With one harsh breath, he lowered the gun and let his hand hang limp at his side. Jonny dragged his gaze away from Frank's body, laid his gun on the desk, and met Cheryl in the middle of the room. "When I heard that gunshot—"

"I'm fine, really."

She stroked his cheek, but he couldn't shut out the picture of another woman he loved lying dead on the floor.

He leaned against the desk, suddenly exhausted.

Alejandro's voice filled the silence. "Carlos and Graciela wouldn't have been in that alley if it wasn't for me."

Jonny drew in a deep breath, unsure if he wanted to hear about their last moments.

Alejandro's eyes were dark with torment. "After you threw me out of the club, Carlos followed me and caught me selling to Graciela." Alejandro flexed his hand as he focused on the gun again. "We fought, and I left. I was halfway up the alley when I heard the shots. I hid in one of the doorways, and Max ran past me."

"Didn't you go back? Try to help them?"

"Of course I did, but they were already dead, so I ran home, got trashed, and when I woke up the next morning, I thought I was tripping . . . until I saw the news."

"Oh, man." Jonny rubbed his hand over his face.

Cheryl came up alongside him and rubbed his back, but his insides heaved with guilt. Carlos and Graciela dead and Cheryl put in danger again. All because of him.

"That's why I needed to make things right," Alejandro said.

Jonny turned to Cheryl. "Are you sure you're okay?"

"I'm fine."

The sound of heavy footsteps in the hall silenced them. The slow, deliberate gait tipped Jonny off.

"Looks like I'm a little late to the party." Eddie strode into the office, glanced at the guns, then peered over the desk.

"I did it just the way you told me," Alejandro said to Eddie.

"You set this up?" Jonny raised an eyebrow.

Eddie moved around the desk. "You didn't think I believed that act in the hospital, did you?" Eddie's brow shot up. "You're a lousy actor, and I knew you wouldn't let this go, so I set it up with Alejandro before we left Miami. Then tonight I saw the gun missing from the safe."

Eddie's gaze flicked to Cheryl. "And I see you don't do as you're told either."

"You knew she was coming down here," Jonny said.

"She's just as fuckin' stubborn as you."

Yeah, even Eddie saw it. Cheryl would never listen to reason or back down, and that's why he'd sent her off in Miami.

Eddie stood behind Alejandro. "He was more than happy to get a little revenge."

"I never pulled a trigger before." Alejandro fished a pack of Marlboros out of his pocket. "I just carried a piece for show." His hands shook so violently he had trouble putting the cigarette to his lips and lighting it.

"There's a big difference between flashing it and using it," Jonny muttered, remembering the day he'd pointed a gun at his father.

Alejandro drew in a deep drag of smoke. "That fucker deserved what he got."

"Our boy finally got his dick wet." Eddie clapped his hand over Alejandro's shoulder.

"The bastard never saw it coming. He tried to pull on me, but I beat him to it." Alejandro nodded to Cheryl. "Your girl being here was a big help."

"It was a worthy cause." Cheryl smirked.

"I told you she had some street in her," Eddie added.

"Too bad Frank didn't get some shots off," Jonny snapped. "Make it really exciting, huh?"

They exchanged glances until Eddie nabbed one of Alejandro's cigarettes and lit up. "Now we gotta concentrate on the cleanup. Or did you think you could come in here, shooting it up like a fuckin' video game?"

"What about the river?" Alejandro suggested around a cloud of smoke.

"Amateur," Eddie mumbled. "The tide's way too low on this side. You dump him in there, and he'll pop up like yesterday's garbage."

Alejandro's slim frame shrank deeper into the chair as Eddie's bulk loomed over him. "Relax kid." Eddie pounded him on the back. "I'm just fuckin' with you. Got it all taken care of."

He squinted through the smoke at Jonny. "I didn't realize you and Carlos got so many Cubans work up here." Eddie crossed the room to Frank's private stash. "Very loyal people," he said over his shoulder. "They were more than happy to lend a hand with the cleanup after I told them what happened to you and Carlos."

He spun around, holding up four shot glasses and a bottle of Jack. "I think it's only fitting we toast Frank with his favorite drink." Eddie filled the glasses.

"To freedom," Eddie toasted.

Cheryl used the same word.

Freedom.

But Jonny didn't feel free. His guts were twisted, and his head felt about to explode.

They raised their glasses and shot the whiskey, but he pushed his aside and stepped away from the desk. "I'm out."

"What's with you?" Eddie asked.

"Nothing," Jonny mumbled.

"Are you okay?" Cheryl came to his side, and when she put her arm around his waist, he pulled away.

Eddie righted the toppled chair and motioned toward Alejandro. "I got him on an early morning flight back to Miami."

"I'll take him to the penthouse," Jonny said.

Eddie shifted a glance between him and Cheryl.

"Jonny?" She reached for him.

"Don't." He stepped away from her then swiped the half-empty bottle of Jack off the desk. He gulped a healthy swig, then waved it at Eddie. "Yeah, I plan on getting good and drunk."

Eddie shrugged. "I'll wait for the cleanup committee."

He knew Cheryl would be safe with Eddie. Safer than being with him right now, 'cause he couldn't control the mess clawing through him. As close as they were, Eddie could never understand his jumbled emotions. He trailed behind Alejandro as they walked in silence down the deserted pier. The sharp stench of brackish water and the smoke from Alejandro's cigarette merged in a smoldering, salty mix.

He remembered the first time he'd come to Frank's office, young, scared, and begging for help. Wanting revenge for his mother's death. That day changed his life. It left a gaping hole where he stored his emotions. He didn't have the ability to love Cheryl the way she deserved. Telling himself he'd let her go to protect her from his life was easier than admitting the truth. It wasn't his life that was too dangerous, it was him, and because of that, he'd left the best thing in his life standing in that same office.

He hit the bottle again, but it wasn't helping. He wiped his mouth with the back of his hand and tried to feel something about Frank's death—satisfaction, redemption. But there was nothing, but an empty numbness. All the anger and rage drained out of him, leaving just blood and flesh stretched over a lifeless core.

When they reached the end of the pier, he dug into his pocket and tossed Alejandro the keys to the Escalade. “You drive.”

“Yeah?”

He lifted the whiskey bottle dangling from his fingertips. “I’ll have this finished off before we hit the bridge.” Anxiety and a touch of judgement filled Alejandro's eyes. The judgement pissed Jonny off. “What?”

“A few weeks ago you were telling me to dial it down.” Alejandro motioned to the bottle. “And now . . .”

“Maybe I was wrong.” He raised the bottle in a toast. “Maybe getting fucked up is the way to deal with shit.”

Chapter 38

Eddie wanted Cheryl to stay at his penthouse, but the possibility of running into Jonny would've unraveled her. Then Eddie insisted that he loan her some money, but she turned that down too. She'd understood his concern, but she needed a clean break.

Now, a week later she was determined to stand on her own no matter what, but it pained her to return to a place that held nothing but bad memories. Two doors away from the room she shared with Nicky at the Oasis and working for Sal. It wasn't her first choice, but under the circumstances, it was all she could afford, and the cheap rent would allow her to save her money. Of course, Sal hadn't forgotten the three months back rent she and Nicky ditched, but she knew how to work Sal's gruff exterior.

"I'll make it up to you," she wheedled. "I'll work extra shifts."

Sal shuffled through the mountain of papers covering his desk.

"I'll clean up around here too," Cheryl bargained, then motioned around the cluttered office.

"No salary, just tips." Sal lit a new cigarette from the tip of the old one.

"Half salary till the back rents paid, and I get to keep my tips." She placed her hands on the battered wooden desk.

"I've always been a sucker for beautiful women." Sal shrugged. "How do you think I got three ex-wives?"

With negotiations done, she settled into her room over

the Oasis. She'd rifled through the one garbage bag Sal saved but never found the tampon box with her money.

She sat on the bed and surveyed her surroundings. Same scarred wooden furniture over a threadbare rug in a small dingy room with an even smaller bathroom and kitchenette area. Although her time with Jonny was short, his luxurious lifestyle had spoiled her and made her see another side of life. But thinking about the past only brought pain, a tangible pain stabbing at her and stealing the air from her lungs with such force she struggled to breathe.

The blank expression in Jonny's eyes when he left Frank's office. Like she didn't exist. She'd wanted to prove her resilience and desire to help him with Frank, but that freaked him out even more.

The room spun when she stood, so she leaned on the dresser for support. For one terrible moment, she feared she might vomit. She drew in a steady, deep breath as the familiar wave of nausea overwhelmed her, followed by a cold sweat. Slow. In and out, try to control it.

She stared into the mirror over the dresser at her pale, washed-out image searching for answers, but only seeing fear. Old fears of becoming a woman with no self-control. A woman ruled by desires who did whatever felt good at the moment without worrying about the consequences. A woman like her mother. But drugs and alcohol weren't her downfall. She'd been stone cold sober, and on the run from Frank when Jonny's strong body and soothing words made their actions primal, instinctive, beautiful and unprotected.

After a nerve-wracking trip to the drug store, she'd sat alone in her bathroom with a blue dot, a blue strip, and clearest of all, the word *pregnant* printed across the plastic applicator. No doubts. She was having Jonny's baby.

The sound of footsteps down the hall set her heart off again. Paranoia over Frank's death settled in her gut and made her suspicious of every sound or person who came within five feet of her. Freedom apparently came with a price. The long, heavy stride came closer, then stopped two seconds before the wooden door vibrated under the persistent knock.

"C'mon Cheryl, I know you're in there."

She sucked in another deep breath, unlocked the three security locks, and opened the door.

Eddie stepped through the door and eyeballed the locks. "Nice." The sarcastic lilt followed him into the apartment.

She closed the door, and they stared at each other. She'd held off this inevitable visit with texts and phone calls, but she still wasn't ready for his questions, and she certainly didn't have the answers he wanted. Plus, she had to act normal and keep the biggest secret of her life.

His muscled frame crowded the tiny room. He did a half turn, which allowed him to view the entire apartment. "This place is a fuckin' dump."

His brutal honesty made him honorable, but very annoying.

"It's not so bad, and Sal gave me a good deal."

"Good deal? He oughta let you stay in this rathole for free."

Eddie nailed her with a long examining gaze like he could see the baby growing inside her. She placed her hands on her still-flat abdomen, then felt foolish.

"Why are you here?" Her voice sounded small and strained.

"I came to check on you."

"For Jonny?" She didn't know what she hoped his response would be.

"No, can't a friend check on a friend?"

"Of course." Disappointment overwhelmed her as she motioned to the only chair in the room, then perched on the edge of the bed.

"Sal working you too hard?" Again, his blue eyes pierced through her. "You look like shit."

"Just a little stomach thing." The lie made her heart beat faster as a hot flash surrounded her neck.

"I'm just sayin' . . ." Eddie surveyed the room again and frowned. "You could've had a condo overlooking the river, cash in the bank, but what do you do?"

"What any self-respecting woman would do. Throw it back in his face."

An uncomfortable silence followed. She wanted so badly to blurt her condition and be comforted, but this was one secret she had to keep. The last thing she wanted was Jonny coming back to her out of obligation, or worse, pity.

"He's been all fucked up since you left."

"I didn't leave, he threw me out, remember?" Her anger bubbled just below the surface. "Then I tried at the warehouse to make him see that he needed me, that I'm tough, and that I can take care of myself."

"That screwed with him even more."

"I'm done." Easy to say the words, hard to believe them. The familiar twinge clutched her heart. The image of Jonny hurting caused her physical pain. "He's not my problem anymore."

"He knows he can't control you, and he knows how strong you are." Eddie scrubbed his hand over his jaw. "The same things he hates are the things he lov—"

"No, don't." She couldn't bear to hear about feelings that no longer had any meaning. If he'd loved her as he said in Miami, he wouldn't have left her.

"You're both stubborn as fuck," Eddie mumbled.

"I've got to get ready for work." She stood, hoping he would take the hint.

The room shifted, and she swallowed hard against the simmering nausea.

Eddie moved to her side. "Are you sure you don't want me to talk to Sal? Let you rest a little."

"I'm fine." It was only a matter of minutes before she would be hurling up her lunch. "You should go."

Eddie grabbed her hand and pressed a wad of bills into her palm. She pulled back, but he closed her fist over the money.

"For fuck's sake, just take it." He moved toward the door. "I'll be back next week. You need something before then, call me."

She mumbled her thanks, embarrassed she needed the money, yet happy to have it for her slowly growing baby fund.

Eddie began to say something else, but she quickly closed the door, threw the locks, and bolted for the bathroom.

Ten minutes later she sat on the bathroom floor with her back against the cool porcelain tub, her elbows resting on her knees, her hands holding her head. Her barfing sessions were violent but quick, yet they left her washed-out and drained.

She struggled to a standing position, splashed cold water on her face, and reminded herself that this would be a temporary condition. Although the baby growing inside her and the reality of raising it alone was permanent. Along with the loneliness of never having her baby's father. The only man she would ever love.

Chapter 39

Eddie appeared at Jonny's side with an expression way too serious for the grand opening of Beyond Paradise.

"Smile, this is our big night." Jonny held up his shot glass of tequila, and the blonde VIP hostess giggled, so he wrapped his arm around her waist and jerked her closer. "Why don't you do a shot with me, ahh . . .?" He paused, forgetting her name, and she giggled again.

"Samantha's working, Jonny." Eddie leaned in and whispered something in the girl's ear.

She scurried off to the bar, and Jonny craned his neck as she weaved around the crowd.

"When'd you hire her?" he asked.

"Last week. You were sitting right next to me."

Jonny tilted his head, pissed at the sarcastic edge to Eddie's voice.

"You were already three shots in," Eddie added.

He threw him a glaring challenge. "Counting my drinks now?"

Eddie blew out a breath and mumbled something too low to be heard over the music.

Samantha walked from the bar and avoided them. "What the hell did you say to her?"

"I told her she had a good chance of making a thousand bucks tonight unless she gets fired for fooling around with one of the owners."

"Since when did you become such a hard ass?"

"Since you stopped." Eddie waited a beat. "Josh Turner wants you to—"

"Josh Turner's an asshole," Jonny said low enough to be covered by the pounding music, but loud enough for Eddie to hear him.

"You might want to keep that to yourself since he's booked five VIP booths and brought half of Hollywood with him."

"He keeps calling me 'pal.' It's fuckin' obnoxious." He waved his empty glass, lost his balance, and swayed against the railing, making the tiny gold lights imbedded in the metal shimmer against the brass.

Eddie clasped his shoulder and spun him around, giving them an aerial view of the club. "We got sixty thousand square feet of people dying to throw us their money. You got Tiesto spinning for seventy-five K in the DJ booth. The bouncers are making it harder than fuck to get in, and yet"—Eddie waved his hand at the two tiers below them— "the place is packed."

"Yeah, yeah, I get it."

"Good, then let the girls do their job, stop acting like a punk, and put on your party face." Eddie pushed off the railing and pointed to his glass. "And slow down with the booze. You're drinking up all the profits."

"Hey, guys, this place is great." Josh Turner ambled over, all swagger and fake charm.

He'd made a name for himself with his pretty-boy looks and a string of second-rate action/adventure flicks he felt entitled him to be obnoxious and condescending. The old joke about looking taller onscreen applied to Turner, and he guessed his muscles, and his receding hairline wasn't the only thing digitally enhanced.

"Glad you're enjoying yourself." Eddie kept his voice cordial.

"My pal here is treating me good." He tugged Jonny around the shoulders in a half-hug, and the smell of gin and sweet cologne made his stomach flip end over end. "Some nice pieces of ass up here, too."

Eddie flashed Jonny a quick glance that said *keep it together*, and Jonny sucked in a sharp breath.

"I bet you got them coming and going," Turner yelled in Jonny's direction.

"What else can we get you, Josh?" Eddie kept his voice lazy and relaxed, but Jonny saw the telltale clench of his jaw. "Another bottle of . . ."

"We're good." Turner leaned into Jonny, all confidential. "Listen, pal, my next movie is about the mob, and you growing up on the streets, maybe you could help me with the lingo and life in the 'hood.'" He paused for a buddy-buddy wink. "Or how it feels to whack somebody."

Jonny narrowed his eyes, and his lips twitched.

Eddie moved to Josh's other side. "Why don't I show you around, give you a behind-the-scenes tour."

"Or . . . why don't you get me and my friends some hookers for the night?" Turner challenged while making a frat boy gesture with his hand.

Eddie laughed without humor, as the heat of the liquor burned through Jonny's veins. Josh shoved his shoulder again. "I bet my pal here could set us up with some real hot babes who like to party."

Jonny jerked away from Josh's arm and shoved him with the flat of his hand. "I'm not your fuckin' pimp, and if you call me 'pal' one more time . . ."

Josh staggered a few steps, not used to violence without a stuntman at his side. His eyes widened in fear, his mouth gaped open, and Jonny doubted the skinny prick had ever been in a real fight.

Jonny advanced and pointed at his own chest. "You wanna fuck with me?"

Josh shrank back further and raised his hands. Not to

fight, but to cover his face. Probably worried about his capped teeth.

"That's what I thought." He sliced his hand through the air. "Fuckin' punk."

"Whoa, c'mon now." Eddie stepped between them and signaled Samantha. "Get Mr. Turner another bottle of Patron Platinum."

Samantha earned her tip by taking Josh's arm and leading him to his table.

"What the hell is the matter with you?" Eddie dragged Jonny out of the VIP, and down the hall to the offices.

Jonny twisted around and shouted down the hall, over Eddie's shoulder. "The guy's an asshole."

"Shut the fuck up already." Eddie tightened the grip on his arm, heaved the office door open, and shoved him inside.

"Did you hear the shit he said to me?" Jonny raged and pulled out of Eddie's grasp.

Eddie pinned him with his hard, ice blue eyes. "Stay in here until I come back." Eddie's voice matched his eyes as he slammed out of the office.

Jonny found himself drunk, pissed off, and standing alone in his office. When the door opened again, he expected Eddie, not one of the starlets from the party strutting in, full of attitude.

"Have you been sent to your room for being a bad boy?"

"Story of my life, babe," Jonny grunted.

"I heard you tell off Josh Turner."

"The guy's an asshole."

"He sure is." She stripped her top off and yanked her skimpy mini skirt down. "I've been watching you all night."

"Un-fucking-believable." Right above her well-manicured Brazilian, the words "Easy Money" were tattooed in gothic letters.

Putting her hands on her hips, she thrust forward and preened. "You like?"

"What are you, some kinda Hollywood hooker?" Her laughter disappointed him. For some reason, he wanted to make her mad.

"You'll have to do better than that. I'm from L.A. I've been insulted by guys with lots more money and power than you." She slithered closer and slid her hand over his zipper.

"Not interested, babe." He brushed her hand away.

"There's one part of you that's very interested."

She bent from the waist, presenting him with the perfect curve of her ass as she fumbled around with her skirt. When she straightened, she held up a little baggie filled with fine white powder. "Let's get this party started."

His raised brow must've made her curious.

"Don't tell me you've never done it?"

"I've done it." The one time he had, it made his eyes twitchy, his skin itchy, and he hadn't slept for two days. After that, he decided it wasn't for him.

"But I bet you've never done it this way." She hopped on the edge of his desk, pinched the bag open, then sprinkled its contents over her perfect, pink nipples.

Hitting some coke and getting balls deep in her would scramble his mind until nothing mattered. Until his desperate emotions and thoughts of Cheryl faded to a hopeless hunger, but when she arched her back and thrust her sugar-coated nipples in his face, he stepped back.

"You should go." He'd had enough meaningless sex in his life.

"What the hell are you doin' now?" Eddie entered the office, slamming the door behind him.

Without missing a beat, the redhead hopped off the desk and proudly displayed every naked inch of her sleek, well-toned body.

Eddie zeroed in on her tat. "Great advertisement, sweetheart, but the party's over."

"Are you sure?" She stuck out her bottom lip in a perfect pout.

"C'mon, let's go." Eddie pointed to the door as she shimmied into her top and skirt. "Out."

"Come visit me in L.A. sometime." She winked and blew them both a kiss.

After Eddie closed the door behind her, he stalked back into the room and swiped his fingers over the desk. "So?" He held up his fingertips covered in white powder. "This is what you're doing now?"

"I didn't do shit, I was sending her off."

"Yeah, right." Eddie snapped.

"Why you acting like a dick?"

"Maybe 'cause I'm tired of saving your drunk ass. First, you start a fight in the VIP with Josh Turner, and now I find you in here shoving coke up your nose while trying to bang his girlfriend." Eddie brushed the coke off his fingers. "Taking care of you is becoming a full-time job."

"She came on to me. And I didn't do any blow." He rubbed his temple. "And if I had fucked her it would've been the first man she'd had in weeks. Her boyfriend's a punk."

"He sure is, but he's one punk we can't afford to piss off."

"Fuck 'em. Fuck 'em all," he slurred and lurched toward the door until Eddie stepped to him.

"You want me?" Eddie pointed to his jaw. "Go ahead, it'd be a lot cheaper than hitting that Hollywood hotshot out there."

"Forget about it." He squinted at Eddie then swayed his way to the bar in the corner of the room.

"Yeah, good idea, like you need more to drink."

"Either I go out there and pop that guy, or I sit in here and drink." He threw his hands up. "Take your pick."

"You better dial it down," Eddie warned.

"So I got a little crazy." Jonny fumbled with a pack of cigarettes laying on the bar until he knocked one out. He flicked the lighter three times before he connected the flame with the tip of the cigarette.

"You're getting 'a little crazy' a lot lately. You're smoking again, getting wasted. You're all fucked up."

"Why are you getting in my business?" He gulped the little bit of tequila he'd managed to get into the glass, then slammed it straight from the bottle.

"Your business is my business. You screw up, and it comes back on me. You're getting sloppy, and I'm not working with you while you're like this."

"You don't know what you're talking about," he snapped.

Eddie faced him, and they stared each other down. The heavy boom of the music from the club rumbled through the plush carpet. Tense silence.

"We finally have everything we wanted, but you're hell-bent on fuckin' it up."

"Right." He waved his hand around the office. "I got a bigger office, more clothes than I can wear, more women than I can fuck, but it don't mean shit."

"Ohh, boo hoo, send yourself some flowers. You sound like a goddamn baby." Eddie frowned.

"Aren't you the supportive son of a bitch."

"There's no gray for you. Everything's either fantasy or fucked up. I swear, I think sometimes you miss the drama. Blowing through everything in your way."

"Wow, now you're a fuckin' shrink." He snatched up the bottle of tequila, listed to the side, righted himself, and staggered around the bar.

"Do yourself a favor and call Cheryl," Eddie pleaded.

"This has nothing to do with her."

"Bullshit! This has everything to do with her."

"That's why you sent her down to the warehouse the other night?"

"I didn't send her. She came to see me, and she overheard

me talking to Alejandro. Then wouldn't get off my ass till I told her." Eddie said. "She's as stubborn as you are."

"She could've gotten her fuckin' head blown off," Jonny yelled.

"I give up." Eddie threw his hands up. "You two deserve each other."

Jonny weaved his way from behind the bar.

Eddie sighed and pointed to the couch. "Lie down and sleep it off. And please think about what I said, 'cause I can't take you anymore."

Jonny sucked in two more deep drags, then crushed the cigarette into the ashtray. He wanted to ignore Eddie's advice, but Cheryl invaded his thoughts and his dreams. At first, he'd suspected the edginess and the ache in his chest were some kind of flu, but when no other symptoms appeared, the hard truth hit him. Losing her made him sick.

He slammed his fist on the bar, then picked up the cut glass tumbler. He weighed it in his hand, then hurled it across the room. It made him feel pretty good, so he sent the bottle in the same direction.

Chapter 40

Cheryl played her conversation with Eddie over and over. Had he exaggerated Jonny's reckless behavior? She would always care and worry about him, but she couldn't let those emotions get in the way of taking care of her baby. She refused to have someone in their lives who wasn't committed one hundred percent, and she was determined to work hard and make a better life for both of them.

"Hey, Cheryl, snap out of it." Jack, the bartender dragged the dirty rag over the beer she spilled. "It's a good thing Sal has a hard-on for you, 'cause you sure have been out of it."

Rolling her eyes at his terminology, she walked to the end of the service bar and pressed her hands against the small of her back. She hoped to relieve some of the pressure from the sky-high heels strangling her feet, as Sal sat reading the *Post.*

"Beyond Paradise opens to rave reviews in the wake of Frank Barnett's disappearance," Sal read aloud to the bartender. "No leads have been uncovered on the alleged mob murder."

Her heart ricocheted against her ribcage, her legs wobbled, and she gripped the bar with both hands to avoid falling off her shoes. Finally, Sal folded the paper and set it on the bar. The top half of the headline above the fold read:

MOB RUMORS DON'T STOP GRAND OPENING

She leaned across the bar and flipped up the paper.

"Mind if I take this?"

Not waiting for an answer, she tucked the paper under her arm and retreated to the ladies' room. With shaky hands, she locked herself into the stall, sat on the edge of the toilet, reread the headline, then flipped to the article inside.

Innuendo and speculation confirmed what she already knew. Frank was dead, and his body was nowhere to be found. Splashy pictures of Frank, the club, and one particular photo jumped out and slapped her in the face. Much larger than the others, it screamed of sex and sleaze. It showed Jonny slouched against the bar in the VIP Room with a voluptuous blonde draped over him. His head cocked to the side, with his trademark cocky grin focused on her overflowing assets. His left hand splayed just below her mini-skirted hip, with his other hand casually thrown over the bar.

As the only color photo on the page, it stood out along with the caption: "*Business as usual for Jonny Vallone.*"

She read the article a second time. What a fool. Not five minutes ago she'd worried about his well-being. Did she honestly think he'd locked himself up in his penthouse mourning the end of their relationship? Of course not, and this photograph proved it. No regrets, no remorse. Like the article said—'*business as usual.*' She stared down at his image again, those haunting dark eyes, his smooth, perfect skin, the smug, arrogant leer that masked his insecurity.

She left the stall, and angled the paper into the trash chute, then drew her hand back and ripped out the page with Jonny's picture. She folded it in fours, shoved it in her pocket, and disposed of the rest of the paper.

The illusion of Jonny rescuing her with the standard "happily ever after" didn't happen in real life, and especially not in her life.

~ ~ ~

The slamming of Jonny's office door jolted him to a sitting position on the couch. A move he immediately regretted. His tongue stuck to the top of his mouth, and his eyes felt like they were drowning in sand.

"What're you doin' here so early?" Jonny mumbled.

"It's four o'clock in the afternoon," Eddie said.

"Shit, I feel like I got a jackhammer in my head." He dragged his hand over his day-old stubble and massaged his stiff neck.

"Doing some redecorating?" Eddie crunched over the broken glass.

"I can't believe I got so fucked up last night." He stifled a yawn and held his head. The floating sensation made his stomach clench. He struggled to a standing position and stretched to get the kinks out of his back.

Eddie threw the *Post* on his desk. "This might raise your spirits."

He leaned over the desk and read the headline. "Unbelievable. Frank's still missing."

"Your Cuban friends dragged his ass out to one of the landfills. Nothing says 'fuck you' like being dumped in Jersey." Eddie pointed to the color picture of Jonny and some blonde. "Where did they dig this one up?"

"Who knows? That photo has to be at least a year old." He rubbed his eyes which made them hurt worse. "Remind me to send them some new ones."

Eddie screwed up his face and stepped around him. "Go home and get washed up. You smell like something scraped off the barroom floor."

"Ahh, c'mon, I'm not that bad." He shoved his hand through his hair.

"Did you think about what I said?" Eddie asked.

"I told you, seeing Cheryl's not an option."

He'd never been faithful. He didn't understand the first thing about a real relationship or how to love her the way she needed, and he refused to hurt her again.

"You know what? Don't do it for you, do it for me," Eddie pleaded.

"I'm sure she's doing fine without me."

"Sure." Eddie turned toward the door. "She's great."

"You've seen her?"

"We were friends way before you came into it," Eddie said over his shoulder, then continued toward the door.

"Wait . . ." He hated himself for asking. "How is she?"

"She looked a little pale," Eddie mumbled.

"Why didn't you tell me this?"

"'Cause you said you didn't wanna hear her fuckin' name. That it was too painful."

"Now, all of a sudden you listen to me?"

Eddie liked to torture him with reality.

"She's working at the Oasis again, and she has a room upstairs."

"What?" His alcohol-induced headache exploded behind his eyes.

"She said she wanted to be self-something." Eddie threw his hands up in defense. "I can't remember."

Jonny ignored the sharp pinpricks that stabbed at the back of his eyes as he stormed around the room, muttering curses in Spanish and English.

"Why don't you quit dickin' around and go talk to her," Eddie said.

"Maybe I will," he said with a defiant attitude he didn't feel.

"And for fuck's sake, stay cool," Eddie tossed over his shoulder before he left.

Jonny rubbed at the base of his neck and caught a glimpse of himself in the ornate mirror hanging behind his desk. Bloodshot, hooded eyes, dark circles, sallow skin with a scruffy growth along his gaunt jawline and an insolent scowl. He stared into his biggest fear—waking up one day and being like his old man. That quick glimpse into his future scared the truth into him.

He had everything he always wanted, and yet—

His mind dared him to finish the thought, but it was no use. He could smell her perfume, feel her hands on him, hear her moans when he made her come. He wanted to hold her, crawl inside her, anything to make this pain go away. He needed her as much as he needed to eat or breathe and there wasn't enough liquor in the State of New York to numb that truth.

Chapter 41

Jonny's hangover subsided to a dull ache behind his eyes, and a raw gnawing in his stomach. Standing outside the Oasis, engulfed in the stench of rotten fish from the pier, didn't help. But something else had his guts churned up worse than all that eighty-proof tequila. Fear.

The broken neon sign dangled sideways over the doorway with only the 'O' and the last 'S' flashing. The splintered wooden door creaked when he pulled on it. He stepped through the dingy doorway, and the stink of spilled beer, piss, and mildew shot straight to his brain. The air had the clammy feel of an air-conditioning system that was broken half the time. A month ago he hadn't even known Cheryl, but now her working here and living upstairs made his stomach twitch.

Scratchy music blared out of a bad sound system and scraped against his nerves. He scanned the room, squinted against the haze of smoke, then patted the little velvet box inside his pants pocket. Knowing Cheryl, she'd fight him, back him down, and throw him plenty of attitude, but he had only one shot to make good, so screwing up was not an option.

Something crunched under the leather sole of his shoe, and he was grateful for the dim lighting. He shuddered to think what lurked in the dark corners, or what horrors were revealed in the daylight. Even Jon Taffer couldn't rescue this bar.

Jonny scanned the crowd. Lowlife guys half-drunk to

falling down sloppy, and women with too much make-up and ratty hair flashing fake tits in tight tops, but no Cheryl.

The crowd parted, and he spotted Sal, the owner, perched at the end of the bar. A huge bear of a man in his mid-forties, he used his hands to punctuate every word of his thick Brooklyn accent. After three ex-wives, his personal relationships consisted of his bookie and the horses at Belmont.

He approached him, and a wary smile tilted Sal's lips as he extended his hand. "Jonny, good to see you." He snapped his fingers for the bartender. "What can I get you?"

"Nothing." He wouldn't drink the water in this place.

Sal grabbed a pack of cigarettes off the bar, knocked one out for himself, then offered them to him. He waved them away. As of this afternoon, fixing things with Cheryl meant no more smoking and binge drinking.

Sal lit up and released two hacking coughs. "This business sucks." He caught his breath. "I got bartenders I can't trust. Bouncers shoving coke up their noses." He hawked up more phlegm and pounded on his chest. "It's killing me."

"I can see that," Jonny agreed.

"I heard about Barnett." Sal leaned in. "Just disappeared, like that other scumbag, Nicky."

"Yeah, a real shame."

Sal was fishing, trying to figure how much of the street gossip was true.

"I want to talk to you about a girl," he shouted above the grainy music, desperate to change the subject. "Cheryl Benson?"

"Sure." Sal's dower expression became animated. "She's here. Works almost every night." Sal leaned in again. "Her and me had some problems, but we worked it out, and now I give her a cut on one of the rooms upstairs."

"You're a real philanthropist, Sal."

"A what?" His puffy cheeks scrunched up in confusion.

"That's a . . . never mind." he craned his neck, searching the crowd.

"I got her working our VIP tables."

"VIP tables?" Jonny whipped around. "They must be the ones without the layer of grease and overflowing ashtrays."

"Don't be a wiseass. This may not be like your uptown club, but . . ."

"Forget it." He waved his hand in surrender. "Point me in the right direction."

Jonny edged his way around the crowded tables, passed a few guys in their Brooks Brothers casual wear, trying to act cool so they could tell their buddies on Monday they'd been to an actual "dive bar" down by the docks.

The VIP area consisted of a raised platform in the back of the room. It held six tables, and his worst nightmare: Cheryl, in a black micro mini barely covering her ass, and a hot pink midriff top exposing about three inches of her toned abs. He stood close to the wall, hidden in the dingy shadows, and watched. Guys were such suckers. Flash some tit, sweet talk them with a few well-aimed compliments, and they were goners.

She leaned in close to a beer-bellied guy with a straggly beard wearing a leather vest like a reject from *Sons of Anarchy.* She was obviously flirting for tips, but when the fat fuck's big, meaty hand squeezed her ass, he lost it. Eddie said to stay cool, but there was no way this was going down. He stormed over to the table in time to hear Cheryl warn. "You know the rules. No touching."

"Fuck the rules," the lowlife slurred. "Me and Cheryl are friends, right, babe?"

"Take your hands off her," Jonny growled as he twisted the guy's wrist into an unnatural position.

"Who the fuck are you?" The drunk struggled to stand, but Jonny ratcheted his arm even higher, until he slid off his chair and onto his knees. "All right, all right."

He released the guy. His buddies helped him off the floor, and they made a quick departure to the door.

Cheryl gawked at him, but before she could respond, he had her firmly by the arm. When he stopped at the rear of the club, she walked out of his grasp.

"What are you doing?" she demanded, eyes wide and wild.

"Taking you outta here," he shouted.

"Like hell you are." Her neck flushed to match the color of her shirt. "Now leave."

"Fine, but you're leaving with me." He reached for her, but she dodged to the side.

"I'm not going anywhere with you." She spread her legs in a firm stance of defiance. "And I don't have to listen to you."

"When did you ever?" he huffed out. "Now let's go."

"No!"

"You're not staying here in that outfit." He eyeballed her with her breasts on display, hammering against the thin top with every angry breath. "You're dressed like a damn hooker."

"A . . ." She made little choking sounds. "A hooker?"

"You heard me." He waved his hand in the air. "What the hell are you thinking dressing like this in front of these bums?"

She huffed a sarcastic laugh. "According to the *Post*, you like that look."

"What are you talking about?"

"I saw the photo of you and the blonde on *Page Six*." She stabbed him in the chest with her index finger, and he flinched. "It didn't take you long to move on."

"For your information, I don't even remember her name." He realized too late how bad that sounded.

"Isn't that typical," she mocked. "Another blowjob in your office?"

"That's not what I meant, smart ass. It was an old publicity shot taken over a year ago."

"Whatever. But you still can't tell me what to do. 'Cause I do what I want, when I want, and I make my own decisions."

"And your decisions suck."

"Once again . . . I. Don't. Care. What. You. Think."

"Hey, Cheryl," the bartender gestured and yelled over the pounding music. "The guys over at table five are getting restless."

She pivoted on her stilettos and lost her balance. He leaned in to steady her, and the small round service tray she held jerked up smacking him in the face.

"Damn!" He jumped back.

"Ohhh, shit."

"Is this guy giving you a hard time?" One of the bouncers loomed behind him.

Jonny blinked and glared at him through watering eyes. "Where were you ten minutes ago when some jerk had his hands all over her ass?"

"Everything's fine," she assured the hulking bouncer, but he still hovered. "We're good."

He threw Jonny a threatening glare and meshed into the crowd.

"Did I do that?" She zoomed in on what felt like a boulder erupting on his cheekbone. The corners of her mouth turned up as she bit back a smile. "I'm sorry."

"It's not funny." He massaged his cheek. "You fuckin' clocked me."

"I'll get some ice at the bar."

"Forget the ice." He sucked in a deep breath. "I'm fine."

She tugged him down the back hall and stopped by the stairs that led to the upstairs apartments.

"Why are you here?" Her voice quivered.

"I wanna talk to you, that's all."

"There's nothing to talk about."

"You seem tired." He touched her arm. "You shouldn't be working here."

"It's not so bad."

"Not so bad? C'mon, Cheryl, these guys just wanna get in your pants." Her evil glare forced him to regroup. "Nothing's right without you."

"It wouldn't have worked anyway." Her voice tightened, and she slumped with defeat.

He might've believed her if he hadn't caught the tremor in her shoulders.

"You're wrong," he whispered, grasping her hand and rubbing his thumb against her palm. "I never felt the way . . . I mean, you made me feel things . . ." He blew out a frustrated sigh. "I'm saying this all wrong, but you're the best thing that ever happened to me, and I was wrong to push you away."

"But you did, twice, and how do I know you won't do it again?" She snatched her hand away and stepped back. The shadowy lighting blurred her expression, but the single tear that spilled down her cheek broke him. "You can't run every time things get hard." Her voice quivered. "I don't want that for myself and I won't do that to my baby."

"Baby?"

The service tray clattered to the floor, and she bolted for the stairs.

He stared after her, and by the time his feet reacted, she already had six stairs between them. Fast for a woman in ridiculously high shoes. He reached the landing in time to hear her slam and lock her apartment door.

He knew it wouldn't open, but he jiggled the knob with one hand anyway while pounding his fist against the door with the other.

"Open up," he shouted.

"No," she yelled back.

He pounded harder and kicked at the bottom of the door. "Cheryl, I'm not playin' here. Now open the damn door."

"No."

"I'm telling you for the last time, open this fuckin' door."

The door opened across the hall. "Hey, buddy, shut-up or I'm calling the cops."

"Mind your own damn business," Jonny snarled over his shoulder. "Ahhh, fuck this." He raised his foot and kicked the cheap door so hard it flew open, splintering at the hinges.

Cheryl stood in the middle of the dingy room, wide-eyed. "You're crazy."

He stepped around the door hanging half off the frame at an odd angle. "I told you to open the door."

"And I told you to go away." She slapped her hands on her hips.

"You had to know that wasn't happening." He closed the gap between them until they were inches apart. "Now tell me the truth. Are you pregnant?"

Chapter 42

Cheryl looked away, but he cupped her chin. "Yes," she murmured, then flinched away from his touch. "And don't ask the usual male question, 'cause it's yours."

"Don't worry. If you're pregnant, it better be mine." He furrowed his brow. "Now tell me everything."

"Everything?"

"Like how long have you known? Have you seen a doctor, and most important of all, why the hell didn't you tell me before this?"

"Six weeks, yes, and I don't know."

"We're not gonna play that game again, are we? After all, this is my kid we're talking about." He walked around her to the center of the room, did a half pivot, and frowned. "I can't believe you're living here."

"It's all I can afford."

He surveyed the windowless room and the battered wooden furniture. Seeing the shabby room through his eyes made her flinch slightly, but it was enough to make him soften his voice.

"That ends now, 'cause I'm supporting you."

"I have a job."

"Are you fuckin' kidding me? There's no way you're wearing this skimpy outfit and shaking your ass for tip money." He motioned around the seedy room. "And I'm not having our kid coming up poor and running the streets. He'd be hanging out on the docks, getting drunk or strung out on drugs, then end up in the joint doing time."

"Geez, that's a sad picture." She flailed her arms in the air. "And what makes you think *she's* going to be a boy?"

The room spun, and she listed to the side. He jumped up, and wrapped his arm around her waist, avoiding her abdomen as he eased her onto the bed. "Calm down."

"I'm fine, it's . . ." She leaned her head against his shoulder. The warmth of his body made her burrow in deeper.

Jonny stroked her back. She shuddered, and his hand froze. "Ahhh, don't cry, baby."

"I'm not," she whispered into his shoulder as tears scorched her cheeks.

"Yeah, you are." He swiped away the droplets with the pad of his thumb, then scrubbed his hand over his jaw. "I mean, how did this happen?"

"The usual way." She smirked through her tears not able to suppress the sarcasm.

His jaw tightened, but she couldn't resist. Served him right for kicking her out of his life.

"But we used something."

"Not the first night you brought me to your penthouse."

"Ohhh, yeah."

"And if you remember, it wasn't once, it was . . ."

"Yeah, I remember."

His eyes glazed over and she knew his memories were as vivid as hers. They'd been so desperate and hot for each other, so needy, they fell into each other's arms. Arms, legs, and everything else. The way his tongue slicked away the pain. His hard body loving her, giving her what she craved. It was the first time in her life she'd truly felt safe.

"Why didn't you tell me about this before now?" She shivered, and he wrapped his arm around her tighter.

"I didn't find out until we were back in New York, and . . ." She choked back more tears.

"I pushed you away."

"Did you ever think of asking me what *I* wanted?" Emotion made her voice thick. "You didn't trust me enough, didn't . . ." A gasping sob caught in her throat.

"Don't say it."

"You broke my heart that day." Her voice hitched again, and an agonizing silence hung over them.

"When I heard that shot go off in Frank's office it was the same as in Miami. You could've gotten shot both times." He cupped her chin. "But it wasn't just because of the danger I put you in." He paused. "I pushed you away because you were so fearless. So sure of what you wanted. So sure of us."

"Fearless?" she echoed. "I'm scared all the time. Scared of being pregnant and alone. Scared of not being good enough for . . ."

"No, it's me that has to do better. Be better." He pressed his lips to her forehead and sucked in a shaky breath. "I want you to marry me."

"What?" She reared back.

"Yeah. Especially now with the baby coming."

"Wait." She placed her palms against his chest and pushed out of his arms. "Is that why you're asking me, because of the baby?"

"No."

"I'm not marrying you because I'm pregnant." She stood from the bed. "Or because you feel guilty."

"I don't believe this. Most women get pregnant to lock a guy down, and here I am willing to take care of everything, and you're saying dumb shit."

"I'm not most women."

"Tell me about it." He huffed out a frustrated breath.

The last thing she wanted or needed was his pity.

"All my life I've been screwin' around with women I don't care about, and I finally get serious and ask one to marry me, and what do I get?" He stalked away from her mumbling, "So you know what? Forget it."

When she moved behind him, his back went rigid, and she heard little choking noises. She jerked him around by the arm. "Are you crying?"

"No." He jabbed at the tears and turned away again.

She never would've believed it. He was crying in a strangled, repressed way that touched her heart more than if he he'd been hysterically sobbing.

She leaned up and kissed the base of his neck. "You really want to marry me?"

"I already told you that." He flinched away. "I've got everything I dreamed about, but it doesn't mean shit. And why do you think that is?"

"Does it have something to do with me?"

"It has everything to do with you." He spread his arms wide. "You're all I think about. You're the one I wanna be with, and you're the only one I want in my bed."

"You're the only one I want to be with too." Her shaky hand stroked his damp cheek.

He nudged her back to the wall as his lips possessed hers. Their tongues twisted and teased until he had his fill, then he moved to her ear. "Now I'm gonna try this one more time." His hands closed around her waist, and he pulled her to him. "Will you marry me?"

He fumbled in his pants pocket, then flipped open a small velvet box and held it out to her.

"Oh, Jonny, it's beautiful." The brilliant diamond sparkled even in the dim lighting. "I guess you *were* going to ask me before you knew about the baby."

"I think I already said that." He slipped the ring on her finger and tossed the box on the bed.

"I've never had something so beautiful." She couldn't stop staring at the elegant ring and what it represented.

She trailed her lips over his jaw and down his neck. The soft butterfly kisses made him shiver, and she enjoyed the power she held.

"My sweet baby." He caged her to the wall and slipped his hand into the back of her skirt, palming her ass. His other hand pulled at the hem of her tank top and yanked it over her head. "These were beautiful before, but now they are damn perfect." He suckled her nipple into his mouth.

They'd definitely become more sensitive with pregnancy because his tongue was sending a spasm of pleasure right down to her toes.

"I'm probably not gonna stop saying stupid shit, but I'll always be honest with you and put you first."

"I know," she whispered as she undid the buttons of his shirt, then pushed it off his shoulders, desperate to feel the warm, smooth skin of his chest.

He pushed his hips to hers until he was melded around her. The rumbling in his chest barely covered the sound of his belt sliding open and his zipper scraping down. "I'm bossy and stubborn, but I love you."

He pushed her skirt down over her hips, and it fell past her thighs to the floor. His palm splayed lower until his fingers found her wet center.

"I love you too." She gasped as he entered her and set off a pulsing rhythm that sent blood pounding through her ears and blurred her vision.

"And there's nowhere I'd rather be than between your legs, feeling your heat and knowing I trip something in you that lights you up."

She sighed, as she wrapped her leg around his waist, searching for relief, yet not wanting it to end.

"Ohhh, yeah." The heat of his breath on her ear matched the heat of his skin. "I wanna show you how good you make me feel. How much I love you."

Then he stilled. Completely shut down. The abrupt change brought her up fast. Like teetering on the edge of a cliff, two seconds from plummeting over the edge.

"What's the matter?" she croaked, her throat dry and hoarse.

"Should we be doing this?" He held her leg around his waist, but his face filled with fear.

"If we don't, I think one or both of us is going to die."

"No, I mean with the baby and all." He stared at her abdomen. "I don't wanna hurt anything. Do anything to . . ."

She burst out laughing, a combination of her pent-up emotions and his serious expression of horror and concern.

"Don't laugh at me." He frowned like a five-year-old being bullied in the school yard. "I'm fuckin' serious."

"You are so adorable." She cradled his cheek. "We're fine. Nothing's going to happen to the baby."

He furrowed his brow. "You sure? 'Cause I don't wanna . . ."

"I'm positive." She assured him as her lips fought off a grin. Her big, tough, bad boy had no idea how a woman's insides worked. But his concern was sweet. "We're fine."

She threaded her fingers behind his neck and pulled him in for a kiss. "Now, where were we?"

He tightened her leg around him, and she felt him, hard as steel, a whisper away from where she wanted him. She ground into him harder because if she didn't have him soon, she would implode.

He arched his back and rocked inside her. The relief was short-lived because he filled her with such want it made her helpless to do anything but surrender to her needs. He angled himself, hit her spot, and thrust harder. No teasing, no mercy. With her leg hitched up, every inch of him stretched her until all that mattered was the smack of their bodies.

"No more leaving." Her warning gasp grazed his ear.

"Never." His hand slapped her ass.

Every tense, hard muscle thrust faster, telling her he could never leave. Not if he wanted to live because, like her, there was no life without the other.

His lips touched hers fierce and claiming, swirling together, stealing her air, then easing back to nip at her swollen lips, and her eyes drooped close.

"Look at me, baby." His hand slapped on the wall. "I want eyes on me when you come." The mounting pleasure wound tight within her as his hips lost control. He kept his hand pressed against the wall. "Fuckin' perfect. Yeah."

His strangled growl undid her.

One more thrust and the coil within her unwound and spiraled from her core to her toes. The bolt of pleasure had her clenching around him, leaving her too weak to scream. Too weak to breathe. Too weak to do anything but grab onto his shoulders for support and hope she didn't crash to the floor.

He panted, their skin slick as he slowly lowered her leg. His one arm wound around her waist, while his other hand braced the wall.

"So? Is that a yes?"

Two heartbeats were all it took for her to make the biggest and best decision of her life.

"You're bossy and arrogant, saying stupid shit, but I love you." She smiled at him. "And yes, I can't wait to be Mrs. Jonny Vallone."